The Element of Fog

The Element of Fog

Boudhayan Sen

JUGGERNAUT BOOKS
C-I-128, First Floor, Sangam Vihar, Near Holi Chowk,
New Delhi 110080, India

First published by Juggernaut Books 2022

10 9 8 7 6 5 4 3 2 1

P-ISBN: 9789391165123
E-ISBN: 9789391165246

This is a work of fiction. Any resemblance to persons, living or dead,
or to actual incidents is purely coincidental.

Typeset in Adobe Caslon Pro by
R. Ajith Kumar, Noida

Printed at Thomson Press India Ltd

For Ma, Baba and Budi –
Because after a tiring journey,
'An "ut" is an "ut"'

Contents

Contents

1

Another Term Begins

Boarding schools are not actually prisons – the families eagerly turn in the inmates and sometimes even pay handsome fees to do so. But at the start of every new year, the school assembly on the first day of the term is really meant for those straggling new parents who need the most soothing of anyone. I consider it my job to provide and apply the salve. This is a role I know how to play: I am the consigliere who reassures them that the next generation is in safe hands. Under what other arrangement can adults be set free to pursue careers and social lives unhindered and still be confident that their offspring are being raised at a safe remove, groomed and ready to pick up the reins when the time comes?

Parents who choose to send their darlings to our boarding school are wealthy – at least by Indian standards. Sometimes that money is inherited, but more often than not it is hard won. The parents work diligently on knowing – or becoming – the right people. Their children must ensure that they are picking up a suitable education along with the requisite habits to carry on that momentum. Of course, the kids should be allowed to enjoy themselves, do a smattering of good work, engage in self-discovery and all that, but let us not get too far off track and lose the plot. The responsibility to fulfil aspirations rests on both generations; the kids may just not know it yet. As for me, Suman Ghosh, my goal is that each new parent, heading down the hill sans offspring, leave confident that he or she has made the right decision. I ardently declare how they, dear parents, have come to our institution for the right reasons – honourable reasons, even – and that this is what serious people should do to cement the next generation of their dynasty. I have not yet heard attempts to contradict me.

A façade, you say? But of course! Luckily, there is still some time before I must put on that mask. For now, my walk to school can be relished in solitude. It is a damp morning, but any threat of rain has muttered itself down to a heavy, dewy fog, filling in the spaces between the trees and houses and assuring my privacy. Yes, there are going to be other teachers making their way to school, but for much of my walk I hope to see no one else. Which is how I prefer it. If I do see any flashes of colour or movement ahead, I can easily slow my pace and avoid the awkwardness of walking with colleagues.

In a hill station, like ours, time and distance can appear magically uncoupled. What seems at first to be the most direct route to your destination can become a steep, arduous scramble that taxes ankles and lungs. Of course, you are free to struggle on as long as you wish under the endless canopy of cool, protective greenery, but you may find yourself pulling up short to admire a breathtaking drop into the deep green valley several hundred feet below. At times, the path will simply end unexpectedly, and you must then retrace your steps after you've had your fill of the beauty around you. At other times, inexplicably meandering trails will take you around a blind corner and suddenly deliver you to exactly where you had hoped to end up.

Why is there not a more direct route? That's a flatlander's question and asked only by people who feel confused by the magic. After living in these hills a while, you no longer ask such questions. Instead, you grow accustomed to orienting yourself in terms of outcroppings of rock or the homes of notable residents. You mark your way by remembering those secret views along the way – the ones that provide a private vantage on to an otherwise hidden meadow of flowers or allow you to imagine yourself on an arc that bends up into the sky levitating above the valley below. And should the path prove insufficiently rewarding, you can always take the initiative to create more desirable routes to get to where you already know how to go. Such entertaining pursuits can only take place in the hills. Plain dwellers, flatlanders – people who do not live in the hills as we do – do not appreciate the whimsy of finding new routes to old destinations.

'Oh, hello Manish!' I startle at my own voice. My greeting sounds more chipper than I currently feel, and it surely marks the end of my reverie. I have been too engrossed to notice Manish catching up with me.

'Hello, Mr G.'

'Ready for your first day of school again – eighth grade, now, is it?'

'No, ninth grade, Mr G!' Manish replies emphatically, clearly pleased to be entering high school. There is so little that we can say to each other. I am sure he would rather walk to school alone – as would I – and yet the requirements of basic neighbourliness weigh on us both.

'Can I ask you a question, Mr G?'

'Of course!'

'Do you know who is moving into Craddock – the cottage behind yours? I saw things being moved in when I left, but I didn't want to be late for assembly. It was funny because they moved a piano out and then moved it back in again!'

'No idea, Manish ... maybe our new piano teacher. Did your parents not know?'

'No, Mr G, they have no idea.'

Manish's family and I share the semicircle deep inside our compound. Although their cottage is hidden from mine, and mine from the next, at night their lights twinkle through the trees. It's a reassuring glow that says, 'don't worry, there are friends nearby.' The third cottage on the crescent has been empty for a while now since the curmudgeon of a pianist who lived there moved away. The school and its students proved too much for him. I suppose it's only fitting that the next music teacher also live there.

'Do you know your class schedule already?' I ask. It's an appropriate topic at the start of a year.

'No, Mr G, they'll tell us after assembly. But I know I'm with Miss Little-K!'

'Happy about that, are you?'

'Sure!' he says and smiles. I smile too, and then we both smile but look ahead and walk on. Once you grow accustomed to the alphabet-based naming convention that holds sway at the school, you realize the shorthand is quite useful. Mrs Kalyani, the elder, is our longest serving dorm parent for the girls' dorms and an institution unto herself. She fancies herself something of an elder statesman at the school, though I sometimes wonder if she overplays her hand. She is referred to simply as Mrs K.

Little-K is short for Ms Kalyani, her daughter. 'Little' denotes generational position but could, I suppose, extend to physical stature. The moniker innocently sidesteps any suggestion that, at one time or another, Ms Little-K has likely been the object of ardent, secret affection for many a young man making his way through high school. She is also a dedicated teacher, but that, I am sure, is not what is causing Manish to smile.

It is just as well that the shortcut we are taking now requires us to walk in single file. I can smile freely too – I also look forward to seeing Ms Little-K after the summer break. Manish walks ahead, and it's simple enough to follow his feet at some distance; besides, I know this path well – where the rocks stick out and where the roots can serve as footholds. Ms Little-K stands apart. Her ink-black hair falls about in bouncing tresses, and her perennially mannish wardrobe of kurtas and jeans does nothing to hide the swell of curves underneath. There's just enough from the glint in her eyes and the way the ends of her mouth curl up to know that her natural buoyance and curiosity are genuine – they have not given way to the overly aware artifice of someone who trades on their good looks. The mixture of arresting features coupled with her complete lack of pretence is likely what throws me off. The last time I visited her classroom on some made-up pretext, I must have gawped a moment too long. Her crisp 'Can I help you, Suman?' caused me to turn to see if someone was behind me, and there were several titters and giggles. I've not yet summoned up the courage for another visit since.

Once we emerge on to the main road, the traffic and the need to focus on where one is walking remove any need for polite conversation. Due to the oncoming cars, we walk in single file, and I let Manish go ahead. As we get close to the school campus I can see a straggling line of people – staff, some teachers' kids and other school employees – filtering in through the gates. There are enough of us that I must make cordial conversation with two of my colleagues, though we cover nothing beyond the usual post-vacation banter: how hot it was down in the plains, how so-and-so's parents are ailing but refusing to leave their flat in Bombay. Such intrusions on our lives only occur when we temporarily abandon our hilltop for those lower climes. And we commiserate about the interminable welcome speeches to come and the distracted lovelorn teenagers for whom summer has felt like a lifetime apart.

Occasionally, a new face will stand out. Its newness is not marked by physical appearance – our teachers and students hail from many corners of the world. I can tell from the uncertainty in their steps. This quickly disappears after a week or two, but the idea that you can walk briskly uphill on an unfamiliar trail, round a corner of lush, obscuring greenery, and suddenly find yourself at your destination can take some getting used to. Expecting to see your destination well before you arrive reflects a flatlander's understanding. The change in altitude also creates its own tell. Those unaccustomed to the thin air up here soon find themselves inexplicably breathless and sweaty and are forced to stop to catch their breath after what should have been an easy stroll.

Once we've entered the school compound, the chaos of the street gives way to the organized, manicured paths of the school. Manish and I have both worked our way up to a brisk clip at this point because I don't want to be late for assembly, and I guess Manish would rather walk with me than with anybody else. The act of walking together without speaking is, for me, a gesture of friendship, even if Manish does not recognize it as such. Between a student and a teacher, it shows a willingness to be seen together, even if the difference in age and authority don't permit frank exchange of what's on their respective minds. Manish does not know that I am quietly rehearsing my own little speeches. The one for parents hoping to sit in on a class before heading homeward. ('No, of course, Mrs So-and-so, you're welcome to sit in on my class, even though much of it will be talking through the syllabus.') The one that I have to deliver briefly during the assembly ('Dear friends – welcome, or perhaps I should say, welcome back!'). All clichés, but the students who could have noticed the similarity with last year's speech will be too busy looking up and down their rows of classmates. For the new students and their parents, it will seem as though a fitting speech has just been delivered.

'See you later, Mr G.'

We part ways just before coming into view of the assembly hall. I don't mind – Manish has spotted a few classmates. Rather than walking into assembly with a teacher, it's far cooler to walk in with a crowd of friends instead.

'Heyyy, Manish, how's it going? Good summer?' one of his classmates asks. The boy is ready for the new year – his clothes are new and spotless sneakers flash radiant orange tones. I notice the drawl in the greeting – a usurping of verbal space that marks confidence in one's place in the pecking order.

'Sure, sure . . . how was yours?' Manish replies, hesitantly.

'Great! Went to Dubai for a week because my dad had business there and then to Florida for two weeks. Great golf, man! Where'd you go?'

'Oh, just to Cal for a few weeks.'

'California? Really?' The question is poised on the thin line between disbelief and mockery.

'No, not California. Calcutta.'

'Oh . . . ' The implication dangles awkwardly in the group. No, Manish didn't go to California – the boys already know that. Pointing this out strikes me as wanton. Manish looks over at me, knowing I've overheard the exchange. I muster a beatific smile, as if I've heard nothing at all.

'Come on boys, let's head in to assembly!'

2

Procession Up the Hill

Before the school was a school, it was a hotel. And before it was a hotel, it was the sprawling summer house of a bureaucrat of Her Majesty's administration who had had the initial misfortune to be assigned to Madurai district, with its long, hot summers, its drenched and muggy monsoons and the persistent ministrations to its temple. Providence must have placed the cool, mist-covered hills in these parts for a reason, and the hilltop plied its siren call. Not wishing to spurn such divine benevolence, it was not long before the summer house started to receive a train of regular guests that necessitated the expansion, and it was soon turned into a guest house. By the time the first Christian missionary families had made their way to the hilltop, no doubt with thoughts of saving heathen souls, they did so with the full benefits and trappings of the summer getaway resort that the hotel had become.

To start, there was probably little more than a foot trail

that connected the scattered groups of huts of the people who lived in the hills. We don't know for sure, because in that great, repeating irony, the people who kept the records only accounted for the people worth accounting for. We do know that by the late 1800s there were caravans of coolies and bearers walking up the footpath with some regularity, carrying on their backs the essential supplies for their masters. Over time, they beat back the brush, widened the path and later placed large teak or granite flagstones to mark individual steps in what came to be the coolie ghat. This was the highway of its day, with steps cut into the hillsides that allowed beds, cookware and even cars – hauled on platforms and palanquins – to be raised up the 6,000 feet to the hilltop.

As the area prospered with the growth of tea and oranges in the surrounding hillsides, administrators too became wealthier, and in time they got married. And where else to put their hot, beleaguered families than at this convenient refuge some two days' coolie-ride away? Here the air was cool, the days far more tolerable, and if you dared make the trip up in December, you could even get away with a fire in the fireplace during Christmas – normally unheard of south of Hyderabad.

It was in this milieu that the intrepid Reverend James Erasmus Finley found himself in the late spring of 1874. He had travelled west and south from the Madras Presidency in the hope of establishing a church in a corner of the empire that most needed it. By the time he got close to Madurai, the priests from the temple had heard of his upcoming arrival and warned several of the local businessmen that their harvests would be at dire risk of storm and pestilence if they paid this wandering preacher the slightest heed. And after all, wouldn't it be terrible if they could not pay their taxes to the Collector and went into debt for years to come?

Since travelling Englishmen were rare so deep inside the Madras Presidency, on the evening of his arrival a messenger met the Reverend a half-hour's journey from the town and asked if he would like a ride on horseback to the government bungalow. Finley, having made the trip mostly on the backs of bullock carts, was suspicious at first. But after rereading the clear, flowing script and smelling lavender on paper with Her Majesty's letterhead, he was relieved to comply. Bouncing along on the irritated, undersized pony, the Reverend made a detailed mental recitation of topics of sufficient import to discuss with his future hosts. He had kept detailed notes of his travels since Fort St George, and he had a plan for his ministry, which was no doubt needed in these parts. Too often he had seen a woman with breasts bare walking in the fields beside the cart track. And he had seen flowers and food strewn around haphazardly arranged stones, some not even carved and when they were, shaped into phallic symbols. Whatever the natives here believed, it was clear that these very beliefs were what was holding them back in their state of mortal trepidation. In their eyes he could see no clear sign of hope, no aspiration for salvation.

Having arrived at his guest room in the government bungalow, the Reverend noted with some delight the clean sheets on a bed far softer than any string cot, the shutters thrown open to let in the welcome evening breeze and the concentrated aroma of multiple dishes being prepared in a proper kitchen. This brief reverie was interrupted by a tentative knock.

'Yaaays?' the good Reverend drawled.

'Saar, saapidalaam, saar,' said the voice, a trifle croaky and hesitant, as if not sure.

'Damn it, Pullur!' said an exasperated, clearly English, voice. 'Sorry, Reverend, are you decent in there?'

'Yes, yes, of course!' stammered the Reverend, framing himself quickly in the door as if to allay any fears that he might not be in a presentable state.

A spry, ruddy-faced Englishman with a mutton chop beard and an undone collar stood there, next to a grinning local man easily one and a half times the Englishman's height and width in a girded loincloth tied indecently high.

'I must apologize – Pullur here misunderstood. I mentioned we would be having a guest for dinner and he rushed off to get you. I'm George. George Rumson. Her Majesty's humble servant and local Tax Collector, if you will.'

'James Erasmus Finley – Reverend,' came the reply, in a tone considerably more formal than its speaker had intended. He quickly realized he hadn't spoken to an Englishman for some time and had reverted to the tone reserved for sermons. 'No trouble at all. A pleasure to make your acquaintance.' And they shook hands as Pullur deftly stepped out of the way.

'Well, Finley, do join us for dinner. I'll have a jacket and collar sent over. We usually get a snifter in the main hall before sitting down. Shall we see you there?'

'Of course, it would be my pleasure.' And before he could say more, Rumson had smiled and turned and was walking briskly back down the veranda, presumably towards where the rest of his dinner attire was waiting for him. The Reverend and Pullur stared at each other for a moment. They sized each other up, as men do when they are at close quarters but cut from a different cloth – with care, just not too much. With a flourish, Pullur also turned towards his master and strode briskly away.

The dinner was a fine one – a preparation of poultry and vegetables that Finley had not enjoyed in a long time. The jacket Rumson had lent him fit well in the shoulders but was obviously cut for a man of considerably more midriff than Finley as the lapels crossed easily, closing off any chance of ventilation. Finley ate and drank, but each bite seemed to bring on more beads of sweat on his scalp and forehead which occasionally landed with loud drips onto the teak table.

George Rumson sat opposite Finley, and diagonally opposite sat the younger Mrs Rumson. If it were the younger Rumsons alone he might not have cared as much, but seated next to Finley was the formidable elder Mrs (Adeline) Rumson. She was one accustomed to taking the measure of those who passed through her son's life and had seen to the seating arrangements. A certain steadfastness in her gaze ensured that visitors were made aware of this vigilance; the baleful stare was intended to make those with less than honourable intentions squirm. While Finley did not belong to that category of visitor, his swiftly wilting collar aroused a flutter of suspicion in the elder, and she applied her gaze copiously.

Finally, she could hold herself no longer: 'Tell me, Reverend, what brings you so far afield? Surely there is no flock here to which you must tend!' The question was a fair one, but the emphasis on 'tend' aroused a general pause in mastication around the table.

'Oh come, Mother . . . do let the good Reverend finish his meal!' It was a gentle suggestion made by the younger Mrs Rumson. Although they had been introduced briefly before being seated for dinner, Finley was tired and hungry at the time. Now fortified with several mouthfuls of curried chicken and sips of wine, he caught himself gazing with his mouth in mid-chew at her warm, generous smile. But it somehow hurt to look for too long – like staring at the sun – and he noted quietly that he had not seen an Englishwoman his own age, or any age for that matter, in quite some time. And he recalled his manners.

'Quite, quite . . . Mrs Rumson,' mumbled Finley – his mouth still half full. 'I come to establish a ministry where it is most needed. Is it not a more worthy challenge to tame the wild wood than to plough the fertile field?'

There was no immediate answer; the elder Mrs Rumson had not pondered before the choice now laid before her. Finley sensed this and held forth, telling of the depraved and ungodly things he had seen on his travels between the Presidency and his arrival in Madurai.

'There is so much work to be done! So many souls to guide gently to Christ! They do not know the ways of civilized modesty or of Christ's teachings. And they have no way of knowing. How would they? There are so few of us here and so many of them!'

An approving relaxing of the eyebrows on the woman's face was all that was required. And soon, she was painting a picture of a chapel – no, a proper church – that could be built locally, to which all the surrounding administrators and their families might come to worship. And with them they would bring the prominent local Indian families, who must surely wish to learn of Jesus Christ.

'So you approve of our guest, then?' George teased,

facing his mother squarely with a smile. The elder Rumson grimaced and seemed on the verge of being embarrassed but waved the feeling quickly away with a gesture of her hand.

'At any rate, Reverend, it appears you certainly had the correct answers to Mother's questions!' The younger Mrs Rumson smiled. 'Is that not right, Mother?'

'Indeed!' the elder Rumson agreed.

'A rapid and fortuitous change of heart, then!' the younger Mrs Rumson continued.

'Do stop your teasing, Eliza . . . ' the elder snapped, though it was a friendly rebuttal.

'Very well . . . but you should feel honoured, Reverend Finley. George and I are always pleased to make new acquaintances as they travel through Madurai, but Mother is often not quite so engaging.'

Over the next several days, Finley and Mrs Rumson paced and plotted and planned in the rooms of the administrator's bungalow as to what shape this church would take. However, with the heat of April turning to the full-fledged baking of May, Rumson decided it would be a good time to send the family 'up the hill'.

'You will be accompanying us, of course, Reverend Finley.' Coming from the Rumson matriarch, this was not so much an invitation as a statement of fact. And so, the Rumson household, with a newly attached man of God in tow, set off up the hill. It was a journey of three days, and one that tired the body but not the spirit. The first day was devoted to making the move from Madurai to the foot of the hills, but it was mostly an exercise in logistics and avoiding the heat. The group started at four in the morning, and pushed on till noon, after which the baking heat and unrelenting sun forced the Rumson women into a canvas tent set up specifically for them by the edge of a water tank where there were enough trees to procure shade.

There was no danger, the path was well known, and the locals were friendly, if bemused by the procession that passed slowly through their midst and up into the forest paths. Occasionally, the more well-travelled stretches on the hillside had been marked with steps cut from rough-hewn logs or pieces of stone, but most of the walking was on dry mud paths cut out between the small trees and coffee or jackfruit plantations. When they had to ford a small stream or navigate an especially unpopulated area, the bearers would go ahead to make arrangements and clear the leaves and creepers that had taken over since the last return procession nine months ago. Elephants could be heard calling to one another but never seen. For all their massive size, they were unnervingly good at hiding and moving quietly past.

The second night's camp was in an open field slightly overgrown with taller elephant grass but not of the same variety one saw down in the plains. Already, the vegetation had changed, taking on a rambling aspect; it was a brighter green and more thickly overgrown. The air was clearer and lighter, and less burdened with the moisture and dust of the plains.

'Finley, come have a dekko at this!' It was Rumson calling out. Finley tromped over, a touch reluctantly, given that he had just sat down after several hours' walk. Standing up in front of them, about the height of a grown man's head, was a platform hewn entirely from stone, supported on either side by similarly hewn stone rectangles. 'We have our own little Stonehenge here! There are three of them spread out across this field looking down into the valley. Still haven't figured out what they are or for what purpose they were built. Coolies don't know a thing about them.'

'Perhaps a gate of some sort?' Finley ventured.

'Yes, but where's the rest of the wall? Or path? There's nothing else here. They are well suited for loading and unloading the horses or elephants, but there's no path anywhere.' And it was true. There was no path leading up to them or through them. 'I can't even imagine how they put them together,' Rumson continued. 'And the natives are no bloody help; they don't even keep track of their own history, so there's no telling why they made these.'

'Fascinating. And it's not even a temple of any kind – there's no statues or offerings or flowers in sight.'

'Exactly! I just wanted to show you. We don't often travel up with guests, and so I have not been able to show these off to another gentleman in a very long time. Once we tried to take one apart, but the locals would have nothing to do with them. Refused to even help budge the stones. Can you imagine the mantelpiece that would make?'

Finley pondered this. He was admiring the shaping of the stone, and no, he had not considered what a mantelpiece it would make. The stone piece across the top appeared to be deeper and wider than any of the steps that had been cut into the path, and somewhat precariously balanced, except that the sheer weight of it removed any concerns about the lack of stability or permanence. It would probably take two elephants at least, pulling at the same time, to dislodge the top stone. It was the first time after the temple in Madurai that he had seen anything resembling a certain kind of forethought or unexplained planning. And there the priests had been reluctant to let him in, so he had not seen inside the inner sanctum. Here there was nobody to say yes or no to walking under, through and back again.

'Well, come on. Let's get back to the tents for dinner,' chimed in Rumson. The man had obviously spared whatever wonder he could but now wanted to get back to the routine of the day. And so they walked back over to where the tents had been pitched and sat down for an early dinner. A bit further away in the field near the more easterly stone structure, the coolies had set up a small fire and were roasting their ragi porridge, squatting in a circle and possibly conversing about the day's journey ahead.

Morning brought dew and markedly chilly weather. After so many days on the plains, the need for a sweater or vest had not even occurred to Finley. Mrs Rumson must have noticed the pensive furrowing of his brow because as they started back uphill the next day, she remarked: 'Is everything all right, Reverend? Are we troubling you too much with this migration of ours?'

'No, no, of course not,' came the diffident reply. 'I merely hadn't planned for anything quite so much like England, Mrs Rumson.'

'Ah, the cold and damp, you mean! Don't trouble yourself, Reverend. That is easily taken care of.' After which she summoned one of the maids and asked her to fetch some warm clothing from one of the umpteen leather trunks they had been carrying with them. And it was only after putting on a heavier cotton jacket that Finley noticed how all the coolies had girded their loincloths in a different way – they were now wearing them longer. And they had brought out an assortment of shirts with sleeves and vests out as well.

The next several hours of walking had the rest of the party breathing harder, and Finley noted the slight and growing throbbing in his temples as the walking continued. The womenfolk – the Mrs Rumsons (both the elder and the younger) and the English nanny – and the children seemed rather comfortable in their little platform palanquin, but he was starting to understand why the Sub-Collector had entreated him to take a horse yesterday. It seemed ungallant to ask for one now, several hours in. But his perspiration was not like yesterday's, which was obviously because of heat and exertion. Instead, it now had a cold, clammy aspect and was pouring forth in an unsettling manner. After the party had negotiated another upward bend in the trail, Finley, from his perch on his horse, saw Rumson trotting downhill and glanced up to him, perhaps a little too keenly.

'You don't look well, Reverend. Would you want to pause for some refreshment and rest awhile?' Finley did not know what to make of this. He had already enjoyed more than what he considered his fair share of his host's hospitality and making the whole party stop for him seemed an even greater imposition. And somewhere in the back of his mind he noted the alternating address of Finley vs Reverend – 'Finley' when he was being chummy, 'Reverend' when he was in more public locations. That was when he also noticed the mischievous smile playing on Rumson's face.

'Oh, come now, George, give the man your horse!' The younger Mrs Rumson's coolies had just made the turn and her light, fresh voice broke the pause. 'You must understand, Reverend, George knows what happens to a person when we gain so much altitude. He has obviously not informed you of it!'

Rumson had dismounted and was walking towards Finley, grinning and offering the reins. 'Don't feel badly, Reverend. At this altitude, the air is much thinner than in Madurai and it makes walking harder until one has had a few days to grow accustomed. You may be forgiven for suspecting you are about to be taken ill.'

'Much obliged. But what about you . . . ?'

'I can join Eliza and ride part of the way with her. Take the horse, Finley. And while you're at it, have some brandy – it will help,' he said, proffering a flask from his vest. 'Don't trouble yourself too much; Mother is riding ahead of us. You can count on our discretion.'

For Finley, the rest of the journey seemed to take on a different aspect altogether. The mare climbed slowly but steadily on the path, which it seemed to know well, and before long it was obvious that they were travelling along a wider, more frequented track. These grew into roads, lined with hedges and clear ruts where carts had travelled. The scene changed from one of narrow, single-minded ascent along a mountain path, to what could pass for a respectable village green in any country town in the Lake District, with similar roads feeding into it from several directions, each disappearing away into shaded greenery. And suddenly there were more people – not just those who had travelled up with the Rumson party but an assembly of many more natives and, obviously, foreigners.

Down one of the roads on the other side of the green, Finley observed a gate. It wasn't grand, but it stood out only because he had not seen a gate like this since he had left England. And it was the only gate in sight. A simple engraved sign on the left post read: 'Highpoint Hotel'. And on the other post: 'Welcome'.

At this point, Finley realized he was no longer moving on the horse, but that he had commanded it to one side of the road to simply stare at this junction of people who had materialized as if from nowhere. If Queen Victoria herself had paraded by, Finley would have been no more surprised at what lay before his eyes. Over by the gate, he observed a well-dressed, authoritative woman entreating him to come through.

'Well, come on, Finley, Mother beckons,' he heard a voice at his side. It was Rumson, who, having alighted from his wife's palanquin, probably wanted his horse back. As he slid off the saddle, Finley observed Pullur separating himself from the travelling party and quickly taking the reins of the horse, while he and Rumson began to stroll across the cool green grass towards the hotel gate. Once at the gate, Mrs Rumson (the elder) greeted him with more warmth than she did her son, and the three quickly proceeded through.

'New guest, Subedar!' Mrs Rumson scolded a guard. From his position just inside the gate, the man had made a half-hearted effort to fulfil his given role. The guard must have thought better of it because after recognizing the elder Rumson, and seeing that Finley was obviously being brought in under her auspices, he did not press his point.

'Don't fret, mother, I will register the Reverend,' offered Rumson.

'Thank you. Please do. I have much to discuss with him.'

And Finley noticed Rumson veering back towards the guardhouse – perhaps a little too eagerly – and heard him say, 'J.E. Finley, Reverend.' The guard dutifully wrote it down. 'Yes, for the full summer season,' he heard Rumson continue.

3

The Piano Teacher

Assembly is over, and now the real work of the term begins. In the dorms, the happenings and gossip of the summer are rapidly shared. Coteries of friends that existed before the holidays gather at first, and members size each other up for new developments over the holidays – a new hairstyle, an unreported summer romance – before reviving old routines. And then there's what is revealed over the course of the term, once the trust is re-established: the unexpected divorce, or turns in the family business that make this year's school fees a greater burden than they used to be.

There is a pattern, but none of this goes according to plan for any individual. Occasionally, one member of the group will decide that last year's modes of interaction are no longer to their liking. This will result in a shearing of the edges among the cliques. New friendships will spring up to take the place of mere acquaintance, rancour where there used to be amity.

Teachers move more slowly in this regard. The teachers' lounge is the best place to observe who is new, who is re-establishing their social dominance, and who, like me, continues to pace around in the periphery. I prefer to stand on my own and avail myself of a coffee and a distraction from the classroom and my office, as well as several of the very excellent egg sandwiches. The hard-boiled eggs are diced down to the ideal size and accompanied by the perfect level of mayonnaise and salt, all nestling in soft bread baked fresh that morning and with the crust trimmed away. If I sound too eager about this particular snack, it is simply the absence of breakfast in combination with the pavlovian anticipation of my taste buds. The morning break comes and the teacher wants coffee and egg sandwiches. The combination of flavours renders even the most inane teachers' lounge conversations tolerable. And I can always gesture towards the sandwiches and excuse myself from tiresome conversations – most colleagues will empathize with the desire to grab another one.

There is of course the matter of Ms Little-K. Each new school year brings the possibility that something will have changed in the course of our three-month summer vacation, and that perhaps she will now see me in a different, favourable light. Yes – I know this is wishful thinking on my part – and it's not as if I have made any special efforts in this direction. But it's not the first time I have noticed myself entering the lounge after a break and looking around with intent. I try to do this casually so as not to reveal too much. I scan the edge of the room first, along the semicircle of windows with the bright morning sun streaming in. There she is! Same flowing hair – a little shorter perhaps? She isn't facing me, but I know it's her. The pale-blue kurta with the embroidery along the edges and of course the slightly fancy sandals with the leather braiding that wraps around to secure the back. It's not cold enough for sneakers yet. I find it fascinating how the denim of her jeans bunches at the ankles and then stretches invitingly upwards . . .

'Arre, what a speech!' Pandian breaks in, thumping my shoulder with his heavy palm. He is the PE teacher. We were only vaguely acquainted in college, but even then I remember him playing up his physicality; now he trades on some implied familiarity despite our tenuous connection. We had not kept in touch during his intervening years in the army, and I realize I don't actually know for sure that he was in the army – or what it was that he did while there.

'Thank you, Pandian. You know it's the same speech I give at the start of every year,' I reply with a light smile. Having located Ms Little-K, I was now looking forward to my coffee and egg sandwich and had not planned on making conversation before achieving my objectives.

'But it's the delivery, man! Such conviction – even I feel like I'm going to go to class right away to start learning lots of new things.'

'Then you were either not listening, or you have forgotten what I've said many times before. Look at all those parents and new kids. Do you think they want to hear "Oh no – here we go again"?'

'Of course, of course . . . Congratulations, by the way.'

'For what?' I say, a little disingenuously. I know I've been officially appointed high school coordinator – even though I've been doing the job for a few years now. But I guess it is now common knowledge after the vice principal – Jason Chapman – called on me by name in the assembly.

'The high school coordinator job! Arre, JC said it already – why are you trying to be shy about it?' As usual, Pandian's voice had gone from indoor volume to PE-class instruction levels, so the volume and timbre had the usual effect of getting everyone else to quiet down and pay attention. The last to stop were a group of female teachers assembled on a couch in the middle of an animated exchange, but even they quieted down and looked up towards us. I couldn't be sure if it was my news or the loud declamation of 'JC' that caused this. Some took umbrage at this unorthodox use of the Saviour's initials, and there were those who revelled in the double entendre implied in the reference to the school's 'golden boy' vice principal.

Even Pandian realized he had probably gone a step too far. He harrumphed and moved sideways, picking up the last egg sandwich on the tray.

'Yes, good idea, let's do some announcements.' JC had been waiting for a pause in the conversation, and this was his opening. 'Well, welcome everyone to a new school year. As you all know, there are several staff changes and appointments that were decided over the summer, so we should announce and celebrate each of them appropriately. There are also several new faces among us, so let's do the quick announcements now and leave the longer introductions for our staff meeting on Thursday afternoon.

'First, as you may know, Andrew's flight from Canada has been delayed, so God willing, he will be joining us in just a few days.' Andrew Darling is our school principal. That suited JC nicely – he relished playing principal whenever he could; there was no power grab too small for this JC.

'Then, we have a new high school coordinator – Ghosh will be taking on the new role, and I think there's already a line forming outside his office for schedule changes.' Some polite laughter, and a few tentative rounds of applause. I nod into middle distance. I don't pay attention to the rest of JC's announcements. I had found Ms Little-K, the cooks had brought in another tray of egg sandwiches and cheese sandwiches as well as a new samovar of coffee, and since the bell was about to ring in the first period of classes, there was little time to lose. There's lots I could tell you about bells, but the important thing to remember is that there are two bells – the first and the second. The first bell – a single toll – tells you when to leave wherever you are, while the second bell – two tolls – tells you that you should by now have found your way to where you are supposed to be. There are five minutes between the two. At first, this causes some confusion, but within a week, even the most confused students develop a sense of whether the chimes belong to the first or the second. In a few weeks, by the end of second period, the body learns that it's time for coffee, and by the end of the fourth period that it's time for lunch.

I realized JC wasn't joking. Outside my office door stood five students and two sets of parents, all waiting to talk about their academic schedules, plans for college, and possibly why the grades last year were not what they had expected. I like to start with the parents first, so I invited in the ones that were closest to the door, as well as their daughter – a returning student just starting in twelfth grade. The parents didn't spend long on the pleasantries.

'We wanted to come and meet you, Mr Ghosh. We have great hopes for Payal, you see, and we want her to get a scholarship to an Ivy League college,' Mr Singh begins, though it serves both as an introduction and an opening challenge. I study the father for a moment – crisp shirt, very new jeans clearly not worn often. Is that Brylcream in his moustache? The ends are pointy. His lenses on his glasses are thick enough to reflect, but he peers over them at me. His wife and daughter look closely at his expression, as if the next part of the conversation will also come from there.

'Thank you for coming, Mr and Mrs Singh.' I always start friendly. Sometimes the best way to address this sort of challenge is to pretend not to see it. 'What does Payal want to do after school?' Payal's mother's face turns to me in surprise – surely I should already know that answer?

'Medicine', 'law' – the answers come in unison, but the discord is already clear and makes me wince – usually parents will have orchestrated at least this part of the conversation. I suppose it's something that the conversation is not a premeditated one, and Mrs Singh clearly knows her own mind in this matter.

'Whichever, you know ...' Mr Singh continues, casting a sideward glance over the lenses at his wife. If his wife saw the glance, she does not reciprocate. 'It will be one or the other. To get to the point, Mr Ghosh, what I want to know is, how is this school going to assure us that this will happen? We are paying a lot of fees for this international school!'

'Yes, Mr Singh, it is an international school. And I understand that we have aspirations for our children, but the school cannot guarantee admissions to college, of course.' Both parents seem dissatisfied with the response. In the manner of couples who have been together long enough to mirror each other's gestures, they sit back with the same perplexed knitting of the eyebrows. I notice Mrs Singh's are bushier and the thought strikes me as funny; still, I know how to suppress the laughter inside. I turn to the daughter. 'What subjects are you signed up for now, Payal?'

'Well, Mr G . . . ' It's a hard place for the girl to be – three pairs of adult eyes are eagerly waiting for the answer. Two of those pairs know there is a correct answer and a disappointing one. '. . . maybe I need to change the subjects I've signed up for.'

'What have you signed up for?' the father enquires.

'English, history and art at the higher level, and biology, mathematics and something else at the sub level.'

'Something else?' the father asks. Again, it's not really a question. 'What else could there be? Perhaps gardening or basket-weaving?' His volume and pitch are climbing.

My office has a door; I also know it is not particularly soundproof. A sharp knock is followed by a spectacled face poking round one of the panes: 'Mr G, I have to go to a class, so I will come back later, okay?', and the face is gone before I can answer.

'Yes, yes, this is all very well . . . let the student choose, let the girl decide . . . ' her father continues. 'What do we do when she decides on something with no future? Heh? *Iski dekhbhaal kaun karega?*' (Who will take care of her?)

The question hangs in the air, but a sideways glance
from Mr Singh towards his wife does not go unnoticed.
'*Mujhe kya pata?*' (What do I know?) she retorts. The
parents are slowly becoming acquainted with two irksome
discoveries – the sort that first present themselves as a
stiffness in the neck or a twinge in the temples. The first is
that their child has interests different from what they had
imagined. The second is that they don't know what their
child has been up to all this time. Perhaps they have lost
track of who their child is now. Payal starts to shift in her
chair, but she's still looking fixedly at her shoes.

'Payal, Daddy and I will have to talk about this in the
hotel . . .' the mother breaks the silence with a frown.
'This is not why we sent you here – to study art.'

I try not to visibly disagree with the parents, but I
really feel for Payal – she is not raving about medicine or
law, but she's also not the one paying the fees. I imagine
that Payal just wants to get on with her day, be with her
friends, go from class to class in those raucous tangles
of kids that rush around between the bells. I can see the
pressure starting to well up in her face.

'Okay, Mr and Mrs Singh, I understand what you want.
But there are many steps between where we are now, today,
and when Payal goes to university. And then of course she
will want to decide what she wants to study there.' Neither
parent is engaged in the conversation now. Mrs Singh is
fixing her husband with a passing stare – the kind that

makes it clear he has crossed some boundary he should not have. The points on his moustache wriggle under the pressure of her gaze. 'And the nice thing about American universities is that you can decide what to study after you get in! And also UK, Australia, Singapore – these are all good options if you want your daughter to go abroad.'

'Yes, of course abroad! Why not abroad?' Mr Singh has reclaimed his role at the head of the conversation. No parent wants their child's potential circumscribed – unless of course they do it themselves.

'Okay, let us plan for college outside India.' I try to soothe my way to progress. 'Perhaps we can think about your plans for Payal's education? Maybe let us see what her grades are like?'

'But you should know this!' Indeed Mr Singh, I probably should. I go over to the filing cabinets and try to dig up her folder, while behind my back the sounds of shifting in chairs signals mimed family drama. 'Saran, Schuler, Sehwag, Sen, Shenoy, Singh Jaswinder, Singh Payal . . . got it.' I bring the folder over as ceremoniously as possible, and both parents lean forward for a glimpse into their daughter's future – all before I have even opened the file. Their daughter, if anything, leans away. Payal has done very well in English and art, and not so well in the rest of her subjects. I explain this to the parents who look at the paper, then look at their daughter and then back at the paper.

'Payal, how will you study medicine with such low marks in biology?' Mr Singh looks genuinely concerned at his daughter's performance.

'Arre look, she has done well in English! I told you nah, she will be so much better as a lawyer!!' her mother interjects and sits back with a reassured smile on her face.

'Yes, yes, keep arguing, that's what lawyers are good for, no?' the father shoots back. 'And what is this art?' her father asks heatedly. 'Why do you have high marks in art? You should take all this energy from art and put it in biology!'

Mrs Singh has taken a deep breath and is about to cut in with her own retort, when I decide to raise my hand. 'It says here that her portfolio was one of the best in her year,' I add, trying to get recognition for effort, if not for subject. 'Let me read the teacher's comments: *The year-end portfolio Payal presented represents consistent depth of effort across multiple techniques – Batik, oils and mixed media.*' I pause. 'It goes on at some length – very impressive, Payal! Have you shown your parents your portfolio?'

'No,' comes the terse response.

'How come? Didn't you get it back at the end of the year?'

'Yes,' she ventures, but I'm sensing some trouble ahead from the look on her face. 'I burnt it,' she admits.

'Why would you do that?' I blurt out. I had no idea that this is what I would be dealing with in my first meeting with parents. 'You should not have done that! Payal, this is against the rules, you know that!'

'I didn't know what you all would think!' Payal is close to tears now, and I shove a box of tissues in her direction. Mr Singh's eyebrows are reaching up into his hairline.

'No, no, this is too much!' Payal's mother jumps in. 'Bhupinder, dekho, we are not fancy people. We want Payal to get a proper career. But this is too much! Why should my daughter burn her own artwork?'

Mr Singh looks shocked, but also embarrassed. 'Chhoro – let's go back to the hotel and talk.' Whatever conversation happens next, I am not supposed to be part of it. But I don't want to leave them with nothing.

'Wait. Before you all leave, I do want to say something.' I pause. I hope it helps add gravitas to what I'm about to say next. 'I have seen many students finish school here and graduate.' Turn on the schoolmasterly charm. 'They don't all go to fancy Ivy League colleges. But they do find their way in the world, and many become very successful in their chosen career.' I'm not sure my words make any difference. The trio stand up quietly and move to leave the office in a manner that suggests I have placed something ugly or gruesome on the table in front of me. Each face leaves with its unique parting glance. Payal's father's visage is clearly some version of 'you have no idea how much trouble I'm in.' I stand up and give them all the same uniformly beatific smile.

Halfway to the door, Mrs Singh turns back as if she has forgotten something and returns to the other side of my desk, offering her outstretched hand, which I dutifully shake. She looks at my face and nods wordlessly – as if we have entered into some sort of agreement, without being entirely sure of what that agreement is. Mr Singh follows suit with the formal handshake, while Payal stands awkwardly at the door, waiting for them both. I have often wished I could give parents a more reassuring answer – a promise that their child will leave here on the path to guaranteed success. At the very least I could spare the Singhs that dreaded 'lack of academic talent' conversation.

That brief moment of quiet, when I can momentarily savour the pause after dispatching yet another set of parents, is interrupted by a wave of straight, floppy black hair followed by very square black-rimmed glasses peering awkwardly around my door. The head is high up enough that it must be an older student. It appears, then quickly disappears. Then appears again.

'Yes, what is it?' I ask firmly. I don't want students thinking they can barge in whenever they please. Sounds of fumbling followed by a clearing of the throat but still no accompanying person in sight. 'Is there someone there?'

'Yes, yes, David Koshy, sir.' The words precede their speaker into the room. In shuffles a teenager who looks older than all the others I've seen. He's wearing jeans, a very formal white shirt and the thick-framed black glasses rest comically askew on his nose. A large lick of jet-black hair flops forward from his head temporarily blocking his view. He shoves it aside, and his eyes dart around my office.

'You new here, Koshy?'

'Yes, sir.'

'Did you have an appointment with me at this time?'

'No, sir. But your secretary asked me to come right in.'

'Did she, really? Are you in some sort of trouble?' I know there's probably another parent or two standing outside, and I don't want to keep them waiting for some boy who can't make up his mind about whether he should be in my office or not.

'Well, actually, I don't know if you're the right person to ask . . .'

'What do you mean, Koshy? I'm the high school coordinator – what is your question?' And thinking that maybe the reply would not be quickly forthcoming, I decided to trade down to an easier one. 'What grade are you in?'

'Oh, ha . . . yes, that's just it, you see . . .' I did not see. 'I'm not in a grade.'

'What do you mean?'

'No, no. I'm the new piano teacher. And your new neighbour, I think.'

'Oh no, oh dear. I'm so sorry.' I had to jump up from my chair and extend my hand. 'I'm so very sorry. I thought you were a student who had jumped the queue in front of the parents waiting outside . . . Please, have a seat.' I was mortified.

'No, no – please don't worry. Actually, I've just got into town, and the guard at the gate said Mr Ghosh would know where to go. You are Ghosh, right?'

'Yes. Suman Ghosh. I'll have a taxi take you to your house. Have all your things arrived? Do you have a mover with you?' I decided to study my new colleague more closely. He had taken little notice of the change in my demeanour and remained as nervous and diffident as before. I glanced briefly at his hands. The hands of pianists are actually quite varied. They are not, as novels would have you believe, uniformly muscular or dainty. But they are usually confident – in that they stay still when at rest; they don't fidget or wiggle as much as other people's hands. David Koshy's hands rested confidently.

'Well, I don't have many things, really. Since I'm moving into Mr Paul's old house, he said he would leave me the piano. And the rest of it, I have right here.' He gestured to a pile of assorted things on the floor. A big old leather pilot's briefcase, a large coat which seemed odd in this weather. A green canvas duffel bag, which, while large, was not full and sagged listlessly alongside.

'Is that it?'

'Well, yes . . . And I was told it was cold here, so I brought a coat as well.' It was warm enough now, so the coat seemed particularly out of place.

Two pairs of parental eyes peered expectantly around the door. I gestured to them to come and sit down, while I walked Koshy out to Mrs Mani.

'Mrs Mani – this is David Koshy, our new music teacher.' She rose from her desk to greet him.

'Can you please show Mr Koshy the dining hall? I don't think he has anywhere to eat right now.' I reflect again on just how much I enjoy the sandwiches, which will thankfully return to being a regular feature in my day, now that the term has begun.

'Thank you!' he said, with a slightly troubled brow. 'But actually, I would like to see my place first. Where is it, exactly?'

'Of course, of course. You're in Craddock cottage, in Lake Compound,' I inform him.

'What? Crad-what?' He sounds puzzled and frowns. Each eyebrow is now busily engaged with the other, and along with the lopsided glasses Koshy seems comically annoyed.

'Craddock – it's the name of your cottage. It's the house you see as the road takes a sharp right. Just say "Lake Compound" to the driver, and they'll eventually take you to your house. There's only one circular road in the compound. You won't get lost.'

I wave him off in as friendly a manner as possible and mentally prepare for the next round of family standoff. The parents sit and fidget nervously at my desk.

4

Life at Highpoint

So much of what was the Highpoint Hotel might have been forgotten had it not been for the exertions of Michael Wetherby of Wetherby & Sons of Madras/Fort St George. At the end of each summer season, every family would have a sitting on the lawn in front of the flags and get portraits taken. But in the early part of the summer, Wetherby would busy himself getting his equipment 'just right'. In doing so, he churned out – and carelessly left behind – a profusion of blurry but informative imprints of daily life at the hotel. In some, the columns that marked the gate to Highpoint Hotel can be seen quite clearly, with guards in the guardhouse. Another imprint captured the dining room, complete with tablecloths and rattan furniture – rattan being lighter and therefore easier to transport uphill. A whole series of imprints was devoted to the grand sweep of the balcony that looked out over the lawns, the tennis courts and the central green of the village beyond the hotel gate. There were far fewer photographs of the northern sections of the hotel, located behind the dining rooms. That area was known as 'the kitchens' in polite company. In truth, it was a convenient label for where much of the arduous work of the hotel was done, of which only a small portion involved cooking. A dormitory there housed the single coolies and cooks who would travel up for the summer. The laundry was boiled there. And at the far northern end of the kitchens a less grand but well-trafficked gate was set up for the delivery of food and supplies.

Guest rooms were situated along a corridor on an east–west axis, with the western end overlooking the lake. Most rooms were arranged into guest suites – usually two bedrooms and a shared area that served as a family parlour or salon. The proximity of the western suites to the lake established a clear hierarchy among the guests at Highpoint. The Collectors were usually given rooms furthest to the west, with the last suite set aside for visiting dignitaries of even higher rank. Families of more junior ranks made do with the more easterly rooms. As Sub-Collector, Rumson was of senior enough rank to be located on the western portion of the corridor.

The question of where to put Finley created a quandary. As he was clearly not of the Rumson household, it did not seem fitting that they should share a suite. However, as he had arrived with one of the most senior local officials, the manager of Highpoint – the fastidious Mark Harrison – evaluated his options quickly, establishing that he did not need to provide Finley an entire suite on the main east–west corridor. After plying Finley with brandy and tea, he suggested they take a stroll in the magnificent lawns of the hotel. Harrison knew his marks well, and like the elder Mrs Rumson, wished to make his own assessment of where to place this unexpected holy guest.

'Are you tired, Reverend? The journey up can be quite trying, especially when one doesn't know what to expect.'

'Yes,' replied Finley. 'And no! Your tea has revived me, and seeing so much green after so long reminds one of home.'

'Extremely agreeable, isn't it? This is my fifth season at the hotel, and each year I find myself awaiting the summer more eagerly than the last.'

'You've set up some fine grounds here, Mr Harrison, I must say.'

'All courtesy of Her Majesty's honourable servants, Reverend. The Lord has been very generous to us.' At which point they had finished walking down a lengthy flight of covered wooden stairs which opened up on to an enormous field. Scattered around the edges of the field were several cottages. The three cottages on the left were on the near side of the field and seemed newer and better maintained, with fresh paint and glass in the windowpanes. The ones on the right were further away, on the other side of the expanse that the grass and wildflowers had reclaimed. Even though they were distant, from the little brown children playing in front as well as from their relative disrepair, it was clear that these cottages were where the Indian staff with families lived. In between, at the far end of the path, stood what appeared to be a carriage house. But it was too big to be a carriage house, and there were no carriage tracks to be seen.

Harrison, sensing Finley's puzzlement, stepped in to explain. 'And that, Reverend, is our boathouse. Yes, we've even had four boats built. Nothing quite like an afternoon on the water!'

'Really? I can't imagine! Is there a pond here?'

'Pond, Reverend? No pond – it's our very own small but respectable lake! I'd be happy to take you to see it.' Harrison posed this really as a litmus test for Finley. In his view, there are two kinds of guests, and you can tell them apart soon after they arrive at a hotel – those who believe that the hotel exists to immediately serve up every possible entertainment and diversion, and those whose sense of gratitude at the hospitality permits them to enjoy their surroundings in a more leisurely manner. Finley was of the latter variety, and his lack of immediate response suggested a man who was ready to see where he would be resting his head. 'Some other time, perhaps. Let's see to your lodging, shall we?'

Harrison did a sharp about-turn to face Finley. Only

then did the Reverend realize that this wasn't an aimless afternoon stroll after all. 'Up there is the majority of the hotel and her guests,' Harrison indicated with a sweeping gesture.' Finley turned to look. At the top of the covered wooden staircase, draped across the crest of the small hill it descended from, lay the sprawling structure of Highpoint Hotel. 'Down here is where I have my cottage,' Harrison gestured to the second of the three cottages. 'I reckoned you might like the peace and quiet that comes with one of these cottages too!'

'I hadn't even thought of that . . .' began the Reverend.

'But of course! How could you have even known such a place existed?' Harrison continued. 'It's well away from the chaos of the main building, but as you can see, close enough that you can easily rejoin the hubbub if it pleases you!'

A slow smile spread inside Finley – that sense of relief to be alone again with one's thoughts. While he appreciated the warmth of the Rumson household, solitude and time for reflection were not easy to come by. The sentiment must have become evident on Finley's visage.

'I see you approve! Good, good! Why don't we go see your cottage, then?' Without waiting for a reply, Harrison strode decisively towards the last of the three cottages. Finley followed him.

Once across the small front porch, the neatly painted dark red door of the cottage opened up into a simply appointed but tidy living room with whitewashed walls and a large recently refinished table of unrecognizable hardwood and chairs framed from similar wood if not from the same tree. The room was spare and welcoming at the same time, with yellow cotton curtains that did just enough to dull the brightness outside and still threw plenty of light around the room. On one side of the room another door let off to a sleeping chamber. Finley eyed the freshly made bed with some eagerness. None of this would have passed for lavish at home, but to Finley the spare appointment of the room felt reassuring, and he couldn't think of anything more when Harrison enquired after his requirements.

Finley's eyes came to rest on the low hearth built into the wall between the living room and bedroom, but he scoffed at the thought of a fire, having only just escaped the oppressive heat of the plains. As if sensing his train of thought, Harrison piped up. 'Oh, don't worry, we don't use those until November.'

'Really? Does it truly become cold here?' remarked Finley.

'Yes, you would be surprised, Reverend. November and December here are like the Lake District in March – wet and quite cold. The fire becomes very useful for drying off as well!'

'I see no place where I might prepare some food . . .' Finley finally observed.

'Come, Reverend, we are a hotel after all!' Harrison chided. 'If you wanted to do your own cooking, you've come to the wrong place, I'm afraid.' And then, quite unexpectedly, Harrison barked out, 'Cherian!'

No answer.

'Cherian!!' This time with more emphasis. There was a squeaking of a bolt, and a door on the other side of the living room, which Finley had mistaken for a French window, opened. A strapping local man stepped in, blinking to adapt his eyes from the sunshine outside.

'If you need anything at all, Cherian is here. He looks after my cottage, and now yours too. So please ask him for whatever you need.' Although leery of Cherian's intent gaze, Finley could appreciate that the man was trying to work out what manner of relationship linked the two foreigners. Guests did not usually come to these cottages.

'I wonder if I should go and get my things?' Finley queried.

'No, no need. Cherian can fetch them for you,' Harrison replied, turning to face Cherian's observant gaze. 'Get saar's luggage,' he commanded. When Cherian didn't move, he followed up with a simian gesture of hauling bags, one in each hand. And then all was clear and Cherian, after gesturing with downward palms that Finley should stay put, strode out of the room in search of the Reverend's worldly possessions. Harrison intimated that he had duties to return to and also excused himself.

The bedchamber suddenly seemed intensely appealing to Finley, and he stepped in to give it a turn.

When he opened his eyes again, Finley could see that dusk was falling outside, and the sharp shadows of the afternoon had given way to softer light that streamed in from the windows. His luggage lay open on a stool at the foot of the bed, and the clothes it had contained had been hung carefully over a wooden stand. Feeling disoriented by the throbbing behind his eyes, his efforts to sit up in bed were met by a shadow suddenly springing up in the corner of the room. Only after yelping 'Hullo!' did Finley realize that it was Cherian – Harrison's man – who had been squatting in the corner, presumably waiting for Finley to wake up. In two swift steps, Cherian left the room, returning with a glass of water on a small tea saucer. The thought that he was both thirsty and tired finally seemed to catch up with Finley, and he reached out like a child, quickly drinking the water that was offered. The headache receded slowly, and Finley was able to stand up and start exploring what was his new abode.

On the table, Cherian had laid out his books, and the hotel had helpfully provided some sheets of plain paper, ink and several pens. Next to the paper sat a plate of plain baked biscuits, and as with the water, Finley's stomach seemed to rise up in hunger now that the opportunity to eat had presented itself. Finley quickly reached out for one and took an eager bite. Only after the second bite did he turn to see Cherian staring self-consciously into middle distance, as if to purposely avoid noticing Finley's frantic chewing. With the same undirected gaze, he strode past Finley to push back the curtain from behind which he had first emerged and revealed two doors – one that led to the outside, and another that led to a bathing chamber.

Finley had not bathed in hot water in quite some time – perhaps not since Fort St George – and the ablutions left him feeling refreshed and more capable than he had felt in several months. By the time he stepped out, Cherian had laid out his clothes as well as a dinner jacket. This jacket was somewhat tight, likely borrowed from Harrison's wardrobe, given the MGH sewn into the inside of the lapel. With the evening air cooling down from the day, the dinner jacket no longer felt like the imposition it had in the heat of Madurai. It was an appropriate garment for an unexpected rebirth into polite society, so far from home. With a lantern in his hand, necessary given the fading light, Cherian led the way out of the cottage and to the right, up the wooden stairs towards the hotel.

'Reverend, you're able to join us, how wonderful!' a familiar voice remarked. Finley had been focusing on the stairs, which felt more challenging in dress shoes than in the walking boots he had arrived in. It was the elder Mrs Rumson, standing at the top of the stairs, looking down as Finley made his way up. The climb was only a few flights, with landings for rest in between, but by the time he had reached the elder Rumson, Finley felt winded.

'Yes, I was settling into my lodgings,' he was able to reply, more breathily than he would have liked.

'Well, allow me to introduce you to some friends! It's not often that we see new people in these parts, and certainly not a man of the cloth,' Mrs Rumson began. Finley agreed, as it seemed the only appropriate thing to do. Cherian, sensing he was no longer required, quickly walked on ahead and disappeared into the main building. 'I believe some of our fellow guests would be well served to know that you are here!' the elder Rumson added pointedly.

On entering the main structure of the hotel, Finley discovered a large portion of the terrace had been taken over by tables and chairs, with a pair of waiters rushing back and forth from a small but well-stocked bar. Below, the area in front of the flag green had been transformed into a promenade of sorts, lit with lanterns strung up so that the gathering dusk did not interfere with guests greeting each other, remaking acquaintances from summers before.

'Good evening, Reverend Finley!' the Rumson kids chorused as they ran by, trying their best not to drop the pieces of fruit they were carrying. The ayahs followed in close pursuit, bearing glasses of lemonade for their little babas.

'Hello, hello!' Finley replied, surprised by the commotion.

'Walk, children! Walk, please!' admonished the elder Rumson.

'Finley, come join us!' called out the now familiar voice of George Rumson. He was seated at one of the tables closest to the perimeter railing of the terrace, looking down with amusement at how his mother had taken charge of Finley.

'Not yet, George! I need to make a few introductions . . .' replied the matriarch. And with that Finley found himself shunted from group to group along the promenade. What followed was a frenzy of shaking innumerable hands, and bowing and smiling to a succession of Her Majesty's officers in south India and occasionally to their wives or mothers too. By the time Finley and the elder Rumson reached the table at which his hosts were seated, Finley was in desperate need of a libation of some form. This was rapidly provided – an ample whisky and tonic water – and eagerly consumed, just in time for the dinner gong. And with a coordinated urgency, the entire crowd on the terrace and the promenade below turned in unison to briskly make their way to the main dining room.

It was here that Finley could finally make a full tally of the guests at the Highpoint. Perhaps sixty adults in all, and then thirty more in the form of children of varying ages. The littlest ones with their ayahs were seated along the wall closest to the inside of the hotel, with some of the older children able to occupy their own tables nearby. As with the residences, a strict seating order helped organize the room. Guests of highest rank were seated closest to the porch, and therefore most able to partake of the view outside, had it not already become dark. The fact that everybody seemed to know what table they should go to considerably expedited the process of being seated. The waitstaff appeared to have grown in number, and there was a rushing around of trays of food, carafes of water and lemonade, and additional cutlery and crockery. The Rumson family occupied one of the tables in this exalted row, and as Finley was still being treated as a de facto member of their household, he was shown to their table.

The clamour of excited conversation died down almost immediately once the appetizers had been served – curried egg on toast points, lightly spiced chicken kebabs, mutton skewers and cream of onion soup – and the diners eagerly narrowed their focus to what lay served before them. At around the same time, the elder Mrs Rumson stood up. Seeing her do so, a few of the gentlemen at adjacent tables gallantly stood up as well, but it was only after George gave him a quick nudge did Finley realize what this was about.

'We have clergy in our midst now . . .' began the elder Rumson in a dignified, but shrill tone. 'And so it seems appropriate that we should begin with a prayer for the opening of the season.' Indistinct grumbles emanated from various corners of the dining room. Finley, sensitive to both his own rapidly cooling soup and the effects of several drinks on empty stomachs all around the room, surmised that this benediction had better be a rapid one.

'Thank you, Mrs Rumson,' he began hesitantly. 'I have only recently been introduced to many of you and hope to better make your acquaintance soon. At this time, allow me to offer a prayer of thanks.' Changing to a less quavering tone, he began. 'Lord, we gratefully receive this nourishment in these bountiful surroundings. It is provident indeed that . . .' A sharp pain shot up from his ankle, and Finley struggled for words to complete the sentence. He looked down to see George's shoe receding backwards under the table. '. . . we are able to partake of such wonderful company. God save the Queen!' It was the best Finley could do to draw to a rapid conclusion.

'A trifle brief for the occasion, wouldn't you say?' the elder Rumson glared as Finley resumed his seat. With the ankle still smarting, Finley looked up just in time to see Eliza Rumson smiling into her soup. Her eyes glanced briefly in his direction as she raised her spoon, but as soon as Finley met her gaze she quickly lowered her gaze and gulped down a mouthful, pursing her lips. Finley could not tell whether it was from suppressed laughter or because the soup was still too hot.

'Indeed, Mrs Rumson. I shall reserve more complete remarks for a future date.'

'I should think so, Reverend. We are as examples here, to the children and the natives around us. And I suspect many of them learn far more from us than they appear to.' Finley made a mental note to ensure he had prepared remarks close at hand from now on.

Following the brief prayer, the entire room descended into a mood of reverent mastication, the food before them being delicious and the first properly prepared food that Finley had had in days. In between mouthfuls of stuffed chicken, he was able to surmise that the same was probably true for many of his fellow diners, as there was no banter for the first several minutes. Only the ayahs appeared to be doing any talking, exhorting their young charges to take mouthfuls of chicken and buttered potatoes.

The rest of the dinner proceeded uneventfully, but being called to deliver pastoral ministration at short notice left Finley wary and uneasy. For a pastor hoping to establish a congregation, this was not an auspicious start. He felt himself wince upon hearing the clinking of a knife against goblet and hoped he was not going to be called on yet again. Thankfully, he was able to discern Mark Harrison raising a glass, standing on a dais in front of where the waiters had lined up the food. He was clearing his throat and holding up a glass.

'Ladies and gentlemen . . . ' Harrison began in an authoritative tone. 'It is my privilege to welcome you, Her Majesty's subjects, to the Highpoint Hotel for the summer season of 1874. We are honoured to have with us for the third year, Mr Andrew Haight and family, Collector for Cochin region; Mr George Rumson and family, Sub-Collector for Madurai region. Luckily for the Rumsons, they have the shortest journey of us all! (followed by polite laughter); Mr Bryan Cadbury and family, Sub-Collector for the Trichinopoly region.' And so it continued, for another eight or so introductions. 'And this season we have the good fortune to welcome our first man of the church, the Reverend James Erasmus Finley, who comes to us from Fort St George. It is his first time with us, so do be gentle as the good Reverend gets his mountain legs. You will all have the chance to meet him when he leads the services on Sunday next.' Polite applause followed.

'Don't worry, Finley,' George Rumson mumbled between mouthfuls of food. 'That gives you two full days to get the sermon ready, so you need not sweat about it now.'

'The good Reverend is not sweating . . .' cut in the elder Rumson. 'I believe you have one written already, do you not?'

Finley paused, mid-chew, to consider this. While he had many thoughts and observations noted in his diary from the last several months, he had not paused to craft these into a cogent missive. 'I believe I have sufficient material, Mrs Rumson,' came the careful reply.

'Good man,' added George, so as to bring this particular topic to a close as quickly as possible. 'Shall we let the Reverend enjoy his meal?' he added, followed up with smiles and approving nods to the occupants of nearby tables between mouthfuls. Something in his manner suggested that a schoolboy's impishness had overtaken his normal gravitas. Perhaps a few too many whiskies before dinner. He seemed to focus rather too intently on the food before him and did not engage in conversation in his usual manner. Perhaps, Finley speculated, out of fear of blurting out something inappropriate. The genial George Rumson did not re-emerge until coffee had been served, and it was finally time to step away from the tables and take a turn on the terrace.

'Care for a cigar, Reverend?' George enquired. 'We typically leave the ladies to their own devices and repair to the terrace for brandy and cigars.'

'Thank you, yes,' Finley replied, relieved to be standing up again and away from the enforced quiet of the dining table.

'I ought to have warned you, Reverend,' Rumson added. 'Mother has a way of rather taking the fun out of the whole operation if allowed to. And my apologies for my under-the-table signal – everyone was quite hungry!'

'I gathered! You did save me from carrying on . . .' Finley replied. His ankle had stopped smarting some time ago.

'You know, all that "We are as examples . . ." approach
to being at Highpoint. No, no, Finley! We are here in
this small emerald corner to enjoy a respite from our
regular burdens. Not to drag them up the hill with us!
Don't let mother corner you into being too responsible.
Although I suppose having real pastoral guidance will be
an improvement over her Sunday blandishments against
wickedness and debauchery.'

'I see . . .' Finley replied.

'No, I don't believe you do see. Yet. But you will. In these
short months, with no daily administrative duties, we can
all imagine that we are ever so briefly on home leave.
Albeit with a motley subset of our fellow countrymen.'
As the men lit their cigars on the terrace, Finley began
to understand what Rumson had in mind, and a certain
manner of post-prandial camaraderie ensued, in a way
that had not been possible earlier.

'Before we go much further with this ribaldry, gents,
may I introduce the Reverend James Erasmus Finley,'
George offered graciously.

'Finley, eh?' Haight grimaced, over what might easily
have been his fourth or fifth whisky of the evening.

'A pleasure, sir,' Finley replied, offering to shake
Haight's hand.

'Ah, come now, Reverend. Let us dispense with these
formalities. There's nobody watching us here!' With this
he put a heavy, leathery arm around Finley's shoulders.

'Welcome to Highpoint, Reverend. We come here every summer to have a grand old time, and I do hope you won't begrudge us that.'

'I assure you I had no such plan,' Finley replied demurely.

Haight was a strapping man in both height and girth, and he knew it. 'Good, good. Chester here can be relied upon to observe the requisite confidences,' he said, nodding towards the lone man behind the bar. 'He's my valet, Finley, so his services are always timely and priceless.' Releasing the heavy grip of his arm on Finley's shoulders, Haight bellowed, 'Fetch the good Reverend a drink please, Chester!'

Finley made his own way to the bar where Chester sized him up while enquiring after his fancy.

'A port, Reverend?'

'Yes, thank you. I'm afraid I've had rather a lot to eat.'

'I have it on good authority that the altitude amplifies the effect of liquor,' Chester replied.

'Does it really?'

'Unless one is accustomed to regular consumption in sufficient quantity of course, and even then, the effect can sometimes take one by surprise.'

'I'll keep that in mind, thank you.' And then, as an afterthought, he said, 'Tell me, Chester, is this a normal evening here at Highpoint, or is it because it is the opening of the season?'

Chester considered his reply for a moment. 'Well, sir,' he launched in, 'there is a dinner service of this nature every night, but lighter fare such as sandwiches can always be sent to rooms. Was there anything specific sir had in mind?'

'No, nothing specific. Just wondering if we always gather for dinner in this manner.'

'Yes sir, we do. Although not everyone attends dinner every day. Some families may choose to dine en suite. After a full day's boating or hill-walking, not everyone desires the full dinner service.'

'Ah, good, good. Then one would not be remiss if one were to not attend every dinner service, perhaps?' enquired Finley. It had dawned slowly on Finley that the exercise of dressing for dinner and the long procession of alcohol and food was more than he was accustomed to.

'Not at all, Reverend. In fact, in the interests of moderation, one would be well served to not make a daily habit of this,' he replied, indicating the rowdiness on the terrace with a nod of his head.

The group on the terrace grew louder. Cadbury had cracked some sort of joke, and there was bellowed laughter from Haight and the others. Finley observed this from a distance, not sure as to whether – or even how – to join in. The joke was about a bachelor civil servant who on his first post out in Cochin had very nearly fallen off his horse upon seeing a group of native women with their uncovered breasts. The young man, unaccustomed to such sights, had leaned rather too far over to the right with his telescope, and the horse, detecting a shift in weight and a movement in the shadow behind him, had bucked and galloped forward with some speed. Cadbury returned to giggling over it after retelling the story to Finley.

'They really are sending out the wrong sort of chap nowadays,' Haight observed. 'Observe closely and sate your curiosity if you must but leaning out of the saddle – unforgivable, really.'

Cadbury continued. 'The man does not seem to have received basic riding instruction. Wonder what he will do when he sees an elephant or, heaven forbid, a tiger!'

'What should one do? If one sees a tiger, that is?' enquired Finley. His upbringing had covered neither riding lessons, nor tiger-handling ones.

The question created an uneasy pause in the collective mirth. 'Well, Reverend,' Rumson ventured, 'I imagine you should call for help or shoot at it, if you are able. Tigers do not reveal themselves easily, so it is either unable to hunt, or about to attack. And whatever you do, do not turn your back to it!'

'And if all else fails, pray!' Haight guffawed. 'Yes, that's it, Reverend, pray!' he repeated, the laughter gurgling forth at his own wit.

'Come now, sir . . . ' began Rumson, observing the conversation had taken an unexpected turn.

'Sorry, sorry, yes of course . . .' mumbled Haight. 'Naughty joke, Reverend, my apologies. Especially on a first meeting like this. I expect it's the mixture of fatigue and altitude that's making light of your question. Do forgive me, Reverend.'

'You're not far wrong,' Finley offered generously. 'I imagine praying is exactly what I would do!'

The evening wore on in a similar vein, with Finley able to appreciate only fragments of jokes and double entendre in the conversation. There was much talk of ledgers and crooked government clerks that took too fondly to their peons, or worse, their peons' wives. And how hard it was to tell the natives apart unless you had them as part of your staff for a while. After the second port it occurred to Finley that he was very tired indeed and should turn in for the night. Having made this decision in principle, he found himself working hard to translate the decision to action. Finally, he stood up in a jerky motion, declaring to the remaining threesome: 'Gentlemen, I believe it is time for me to retire.'

'Why, yes, Reverend, judging from your list, I believe it is!' replied Haight cheerfully.

'What list is that?' Rumson enquired sleepily.

'Whatever list it is, clearly I'm not on it,' Cadbury tittered, like a schoolboy having discovered something he should not have.

'Careful, Cadbury,' Haight warned. 'You may not be on the list today, but you could be tomorrow!'

'Goodnight, Reverend,' replied Rumson. His fellow guests were not being as good hosts as they should have been and were making merry at Finley's expense. 'And remember, Finley, do forgive us our trespasses,' he added, waving Finley off into what had turned into a quiet, dewy night.

'I'll walk you down, sir,' Chester said quietly at his side, holding Finley's arm in a firm grasp with one hand and carrying a lantern in the other.

'Thank you, Chester. Thank you. I feel I need some assistance with the navigation at this stage of the evenings.'

'Yes, sir. Given that it is your first night here, the stairs can be tricky.' Finley immediately realized what Chester meant. Once they had turned off the terrace, there was little light and the stairs seemed to disappear downhill into a bank of fog. Climbing down it was only possible to make out the faintest trace of where the edge of the step was after the next. The sound of voices from the terrace receded, first into incoherent words, and then completely into muffled sounds that seemed to bounce and squeak through the air. Which was why the sound of a young woman's giggle surprised Finley. It came from somewhere below on the other side of the staircase, followed by the sound of a man clearing his throat.

'Who's there?' enquired Finley boldly. The mysterious noise and the lack of visibility in the fog had suddenly made him very alert. 'You heard that, surely, Chester?'

'Some of the children, I imagine, sir,' Chester offered.

'Children? At this time of night? Why aren't they in their beds?'

'Indeed, sir,' Chester replied, more loudly this time.

'Chester? Is that you?' a prim young lady's voice enquired out of the fog.

'Yes, miss,' Chester replied, not breaking step on his steady march assisting Finley down the stairs.

'Well, you won't tell, will you?' The young woman asked. Without waiting for a reply, she continued, 'Goodnight, Chester!'

'Goodnight, miss.'

Finley was confused by the exchange, but could not formulate the appropriate question to ask. Chester seemed to know his way around, and soon they were inside the cottage assigned to Finley. Cherian had prepared the bed, but Finley thought he might sit up and remove the shoes and jacket first.

'Can I help you, Reverend?' Chester enquired.

'No thank you, Chester. You have done enough. I could not have made my way down those steps without your help.'

'You will be well accustomed to them soon enough, sir. Was there anything else you needed?'

Finley thought for a while. 'Where are you from, Chester?'

'England, sir.'

'Of course, Chester, but what part of those fair isles do you call home?'

'Cornwall, sir. My family has been with the Haights – Lord and Lady Eversham, that is – for a few generations now.'

'Good Lord. So Andrew is of the Cornwall Haights, then?'

'Yes, sir.'

'Well, that is fortuitous! I am a Cornishman myself. My father is in Her Majesty's Postal Service. I chose to take Holy Orders instead.' Finley paused. 'A truly strange turn, is it not? Two Cornishmen here in this corner of Her Majesty's empire.'

'Indeed it is, sir.'

'What brings you so far from home, Chester?'

'I came with Mr Andrew, sir. It became necessary for him to go abroad, as it were, and Lady Eversham and my father decided it would be good for him if a part of home were to see him safely on his journey.'

'Necessary to go abroad?'

'Indeed, sir.' Chester did not care to elaborate further. 'I'll leave the lantern here for now, sir. I should return to the guests.'

'Yes, of course. Thank you again, Chester.'

'Goodnight, Reverend.' And Chester stepped nimbly back out into the fog, closing the red door behind him.

5

Unexpected Garden Creatures

On campus, students and colleagues feel free to break in on my time as they see fit. But the walk home from school transports me away from that tumult, past gangs of rowdy tourists and into the quiet of Lake Compound. Once I am in the compound, I am assured of only seeing one or two people walking in either direction. As I make the last turn towards Penrose – my own cottage – I can be reasonably sure that there is no one else nearby. The only person I could run into is my maid, Sivakumari, but she has usually cleaned, cooked and left the house by three o'clock. And if my neighbours do appear, I can get away with just waving to Manish or his parents.

The first few weeks of term are behind us. We slip once again into the comforting rhythm of lesson planning, classes and meetings that form the unglamorous, gratifying pieces of a schoolteacher's life. One of my classes today veered into a particularly productive discussion that I had not anticipated. The question: where do we learn to show love as we get older? How do we figure out how to express it appropriately? And how do we learn what is not appropriate? Of course, mention the world 'love' in front of a group of high school students anywhere in the world, and you elicit a mix of titters, giggles and spectacle-fogging confusion. There are always the few students who will try to make it awkward for the teacher by asking purposefully probing questions: 'Mr G, why are we talking about love?' Or, a more thoughtful attack: 'Mr G, do you mean Kama Sutra-type love? Or King Lear-type love?' Those are the smarty-pants identifying themselves. There are also the students who take every opportunity to play out the drama happening in their own lives: 'We should ask Akshay about love, Mr G. He might have something to say about it!' Akshay, in the meantime, cowers in a corner, trying to duck this barb from his irate girlfriend.

The students that don't say much are the hardest to work with. They are often the ones with the occasional incisive comment, the kind that could make a discussion really interesting, but they are normally reticent. Perhaps their shyness comes from being told at a young age, as I was, that they should listen more and talk less. They noiselessly doodle their frustrations upon page after page of paisleys and rock-band logos – I've noticed AC/DC and Iron Maiden are particular favourites. You have no idea whether they are listening or not, but every so often one of their kind will surprise you. This moment is what keeps me in the classroom after so many years. That instant when you realize that the child, after enough doodling, fumbling and turning the thought over in her head, has broken ground on a new level of understanding. That happened today as well.

'We all think we learn about how to express love from our parents,' she begins. 'But it seems that here we actually learn it from each other.' This from a girl who had not spoken in class for almost two weeks. 'At least that's what it seems like every evening if you walk around the basketball courts or the piano practice rooms. People making out everywhere!' Titters start all around the room. 'Or maybe, it's just that we're expected to only show one kind of love here. But there are many kinds in the world – we just don't see the other types at school.'

It seems a bad time to ask what her name is, so I let the comment linger, unanswered. You can tell when someone's moved the air around the classroom in just the right way. It is marked by the rare pause when everyone stops to think.

'I think love has to be part of being recognized – as a person,' offers another girl.

'Wait, wait! I can recognize a teammate on my basketball team. But I don't have to loooove him.' This from the class wit, followed immediately by laughter and guffaws.

'But I think that is exactly the point she was making,' I cut in, trying to return the conversation to a productive path. 'What's your name again?'

'Maya.'

'Yes, Maya. Maya did say there were many kinds, right?' I prompt. And then the discussion breaks loose.

'So, we're not just talking about love in the Hollywood movie sense? I thought that's what you meant, Mr G!' another student adds.

'Well, you can say many things. People love books, their pets, their parents.' A second one chimes in. The discussion is gaining momentum.

'. . . I really miss my dog . . .'

'. . . I really miss good hamburgers. Does anyone else miss hamburgers?'

'You know, I think you can love places too. Or be very drawn to places, at least.'

'But between humans, individual people. Is love just an extreme case of recognition of another individual?'

'Good question, Akshay!' I reply. And then the bell rings. As usual, just as the class discussion begins to ascend towards the profound, it is time to stop. The last few minutes of a good class are always too short.

I catch myself as I walk over the cattle trap. The pine needles become very slippery when wet, and even though my foot is large enough to not go through, it's easy enough for it to turn and get a nasty twisted ankle.

Once I am through the gate, I am in Lake Compound, and the buzz of motorbikes and buses falls away. Today, since it is still light, I take the steeper, shorter way home. It tickles me to think that I am likely the reason this path exists at all, since the grass and moss are only too eager to come back in and recolonize the exposed rocks and rich, red soil. It's also a good way to work up a sweat and get in some deep lungfuls of fresh air before retiring for the evening. The calf muscles also get a workout. So far, I have found two very different ways to accomplish an uphill climb. You can do the dreary slog, hands on knees, preserving energy, as an elderly person might. On long hikes, or when you don't know when the uphill ends, this method can be useful. But for the walk home, I try to skip up the hill, flexing the calves at the end of each step to get that little bit of bounce before attacking the next step. I know that it will take exactly twenty-six such steps to get me to the top of the hill, and from there it's all downhill to Penrose Cottage.

The time to be careful is when it has rained, because the small rivulets that form leave behind slick mud with little traction. At such times, there is a real possibility of falling face first in the mud. And moving off the path on to grass or moss is not helpful either, as rain will make those surfaces slippery too. I am then forced to take the paved, gradually sloping road that leads home. I arrive just as the sun is dipping below the hills that form the horizon. They are not far – four or five miles as the crow flies – but the fog that collars them gives the impression that their summits are floating, detached from the worldly concerns below. The sunset's colours are reflected on the patterned leaded glass of the door, and I admire the scene for a moment before entering my house.

The distracting beauty of the walk home has a cruel side effect. On especially pretty days, the moment of entering Penrose Cottage makes the awareness of being alone even more acute. I've learned to anticipate this, of course: the trick is not to imbue that moment – the tightening chest, the shallowed breath – with any significance. It's just a moment, a transition between what came before leading into what will come next, which is dinner. Sivakumari has left me the usual delicious dinner on the stove, ready to reheat quickly and eat before too long. In the five minutes that it takes to heat the dal, bhindi and chapattis on the stove, I can quickly freshen up and change into pyjamas, firan and slippers. I then create my preferred concoction – a generous thimbleful of Old Monk with a half glass of Thums Up – and sit down to savour my meal. I realize I have no ice today, so will have to drink it at room temperature, which is when the pungence of the rum comes through more clearly.

I favour the seat by the window. There is another chair, but from that one you can't see out of the window and your back is to the door. I don't like how that feels – if a visitor were to enter unannounced, then I would not be able to see him.

In case you think me odd for expounding on such things, let me tell you, surreptitious visitors are a very real concern. The last time such a guest arrived, it was not of human form but a close relation. An intrepid Rhesus monkey, probably the leader of the pack, or an up-and-coming male, had made his way in and was halfway across the room before the screen door slammed, scaring us both. I turned, and for a moment we held each other in an enquiring, tense gaze. The monkey knew he was not invited. He made a grimace, showed his sharp, yellowed teeth and made a swift leap towards the door. Unfortunately, his exit was blocked by the mesh screen, and the monkey fell backwards onto the floor. This gave me time to stand up from my chair, and I yelled 'Get out!!' The monkey pulled himself off the floor, with a scowl that suggested I had said something rude, and opened the door and scampered out to rejoin his pack. The rest of the troupe had been observing closely from the other side of the door. Loud verbal commands may not have been the best approach, in retrospect, but I was operating with a teacher's instinct. If the monkey had thought to further test my mettle, he might have learned that there was very little testing required. I had already planned to lock myself in my bedroom and escape through the bathroom door that leads out of the cottage. This is why I no longer eat alone with my back to the door.

Curious megafauna are not salves for loneliness, either. When I had first moved to the school – and there was no Sivakumari to ensure that I returned to an ordered home and a delicious meal – perhaps the troupe of monkeys could intuit that I was completely alone. No alpha male in this dwelling. They seemed to take peculiar joy in growling at me while playing on the lawn and on the columns of the porch. They especially enjoyed making a loud, crashing noise using the corner of the porch roof where the corrugated aluminium had come loose. They could also – with little warning or ceremony – copulate, as if that were a natural transition activity between sliding on the roof and picking lice off each other's backs. Their communal revelry had a way of underscoring my own solitude. Over time, I found my routine, and theirs, seemed to have moved on from Penrose Cottage. Even so, if I am walking home with fruit or vegetables that are visible, the troupe seems to detect an opportunity. A few of them will stride boldly forward to test me and see whether I will give up the treasure. Mostly, we have achieved a working truce.

I remind myself to enjoy the evening meals when I can, and enjoy those times when I can gaze peacefully upon the lawn, with the sunset splashing colour in haphazard angles. Every few weeks there will come a stretch of time when I have to stay at campus for meetings or activities. At those times, the calm, restorative meals alone feel very far away. If I get stuck on the school campus for too long, I also begin to wish that the troupes of teenagers that wander all over school would transform into monkeys, just for a while. They could then helpfully disappear into the trees, and then I would no longer be responsible for their behaviour or welfare.

After dinner, I feel as if I haven't spent enough time outside for such a beautiful day, so I go down the whittled stone steps and on to the lawn. I stretch and look up at the emerging stars wheeling above in the quiet evening. Between the eucalyptus and pine trees, I can see that my new neighbour, Koshy, has moved in. The light from his living room window has not been on all summer, but is now glimmering through the failing light. It's not far. In fact, I can hear the faint sound of the piano skittering through the trees. He's obviously working on some sort of phrase, since it keeps playing and stopping. And repeating again slowly, and then at normal speed. He must be teaching himself a new piece.

I should invite him over for dinner. But let's wait till he's settled, I suppose. I don't want to appear too eager. And as the high school coordinator, inviting him over won't feel like a friendly gesture, it will be 'now you must eat with the boss.' At least, that's how I'd see it if I were in his shoes. And maybe he doesn't want to have dinner with the boss. At least not yet. In any case, the rest of the week is taken. The regular staff meetings begin again later this week. I am on to chaperone activities this weekend, so Friday and Saturday are spoken for. And I'd like to keep Sunday night to myself, thank you very much, before the rumpus of the week begins again. So that's that. Koshy will have to wait.

The next few days are uneventful. Because I know the walk home in such detail, I easily notice slight changes in the trees and woods inside Lake Compound. I know when the school gardeners have been around and cutting the branches and trees that gradually encroach on the paths. Or when they have swept away debris, and the edges of roads and paths stand out more clearly.

The downhill section that leads towards my very own Penrose Cottage is flanked on the left by a clearing, beyond which a channel of thicker woods separates the compound from the well-marked tourist attraction of Finley's Walk on the other side. As a child, I would imagine that meadows and gardens were like moats that grown-ups had invented to detect when trolls or robbers were approaching. Even now, I check open spaces for approaching malcontents or wild animals. Not that this is a serious concern here; we are too close to habitation for the panthers or deer to stop by.

Except that today I am not alone anymore. I feel it before I know why. On the uphill edge of the clearing, perched almost so I would not see them, a figure is kneeling in the grass. I stop to look, and the person – because now I can be sure it is a person – continues to stare into the flowers that have bloomed in the clearing. The flowers don't look as if they belong here – I am sure I've never noticed them before.

'Can I help you!' I ask, more statement than question. Every so often a particularly curious band of tourists will enter the compound and use it as their own private Eden. They'll set up a picnic or I'll sometimes catch them in ridiculous poses, with one of the party trying to capture the moment on a camera.

'Aaah!' The figure leaps back and stands up with a cry. She is wearing jeans and a sweatshirt. The camera slung around her neck bounces up and hits her in the stomach a moment after. She seems to be a student from the school.

'Mr G! It's me! You really startled me.'

'Maya? What are you doing here?' I am surprised to see her here.

'We have a photography project due, Mr G. So I'm collecting the material,' she replies, pointing to the flowers.

'At six thirty in the evening? I don't think you're even allowed to be here! There's no going off campus by yourself at this time! Did you come alone? Did you get permission from your teacher?' I realize that my rapid questions are not giving her a chance to answer.

'Oh, I didn't know that Mr G. I was just taking photos.'

'At this time of the evening? What are you even taking photos of?'

'The flowers,' she said, pointing at the bunches of flowers that cover a large section of the clearing in front of her.

'Come over here,' I order. She walks gingerly around the stand of blooms and joins me on the path. 'You're not supposed to be off campus at all. Especially at this time and especially by yourself!'

'Well, it's the closest bloom I know of, Mr G.'

'What's so special about those flowers? We have flower beds all over the school!'

'That's a very special kind, Mr G. They bloom only once every twelve years, and I think I'm very lucky to be here to see it.'

'Really? I had no idea. Are you making this up?'

'No, really, Mr G. Look!' and fishing out a notebook she carefully enunciated, '*Strobilanthes kunthiana*, commonly known as the kurinji flower.'

I took a step back to think about this. Normally, being caught off campus, especially so close to 7 p.m., when all the students were supposed to be in their dorms, would have been grounds for disciplinary action. But she seemed to be quite unaware of these restrictions.

'How long have you been doing this?' I asked, gesturing at the flowers. This seemed to cause a break in the conversation and required more cogitation than I thought it would.

'Well, I've been taking a lot of photographs. Maybe two rolls of thirty-six exposures – one colour and one black-and-white ...'

'No, I meant how long have you been here off campus today?'

'Well, probably since late afternoon ...'

'You know you're not supposed to do this, right? You cannot leave campus without telling anyone.'

'But I did! Miss Little-K said I should grab some pictures for my project.'

'Right, but did you get an off-campus pass?'

'What's that, Mr G?'

'It's a piece of paper that your dorm parent has to sign that tells them ... Oh, forget it! Next time, you have to tell your dorm parent to sign something so they know where you are. And for gods' sake, don't go off campus alone, bring a friend or something!'

'Okay, so should I go back now? Am I in trouble?'

'No, you won't be in trouble. Run back, you'll make it in time for the 7 p.m. curfew.' And realizing that this could turn into an even bigger mess, I followed up with 'What's your dorm again? I'm going to call to make sure you're back by seven, so don't muck about!'

'I'm in Haight House. Sorry, Mr G. I didn't know I wasn't supposed to be out.' I would have taken that at face value, had it not been for the extra twinkle in her eye. That suggested it was the first time she had been caught, but perhaps not the first time she had gone on a walkabout. And there was something in her manner that suggested she may be beyond this kind of admonition, and perhaps she was just humouring me by playing along. On arriving home, I waited a few minutes and then got on the phone.

'Yes, operator, can you connect me to Haight House? Yes, the dorm parent's phone, for Mrs K.' After a few clicks and buzzes, I was connected. 'Hello, Mrs K?'

'Yes, who's speaking?'

'Mrs K, this is Suman Ghosh here.'

'Oh, hello Suman. How are you?' I'm talking to Mrs Kalyani, the dorm parent at Haight House, one of the older girls' dorms. She is unhurried and warm in manner. But she will not suffer fools and wards off any overreach with a well-practised raise of the left eyebrow.

'I am well, Mrs K. Sorry for calling so late.'

'No trouble, Suman, no trouble at all. The girls should just be getting ready for homework hours. I don't have to do much right now. So, what can I help you with?' I have been warned to be careful of her interfering ways, so I proceed cautiously.

'Well, actually . . .' as it dawns on me that however I pose the question, it might seem improper.

'Yes, Suman?'

'On my way home this evening, I saw one of the girls from your dorm in Lake Compound. It was near the field just above Finley's Walk. I told her to go back to campus at once. I just want to make sure she got home okay.'

'Really? There should be nobody off campus at this time of the evening!'

'Yes, that's what I thought too. It's Maya Chatterjee. I was on my way home when I saw her, so now I just want to make sure she got back.'

'Of course, of course, let me check . . .' She must have put the receiver down, because I could hear her steps receding from the phone, her lilting voice calling out 'Maya . . . Maya?' She obviously received the answer she wanted, because in a minute she was back on the line.

'It's all right Suman, she's back in her room. She said she was out taking photographs.'

'Yes, she was, that's exactly where I saw her. But she didn't have an off-campus pass or anything, and it was starting to get dark.'

'Oh dear. I'll have to have a chat with that girl. She may not have realized. She's an exchange student, here for the semester.'

'Really? No wonder . . . I knew I hadn't seen her last year, because she wasn't in any of my eleventh grade sections. Why would someone come for just a semester in the final year of school?'

'Well, things are different with her, you see. She's already got into some sort of combined programme for college and graduate school. But her parents are going through a very difficult divorce, and the situation at home has become very rocky.'

'Oh really? I had no idea.'

'Yes, yes. You know, the usual story. Parents both went to America when they were young, worked hard, made lots of money, paid for the best for their kids. And then, with the thought of the child leaving home, they suddenly realize they can't stand the sight of each other.'

'How does it help her to be here, then?'

'I don't know, Suman.' Mrs K seems exasperated by the question, and I begin to wish I had not asked it. 'Maybe she needed a change of scenery. Or maybe she had a break of some kind. I only listen when the girls reveal things to me. Within reason, I try to give the young ladies their space.'

'Well, will you tell her about the dorm-pass system, please? It seems a shame for her to be in trouble when she's here so briefly.'

'Yes, I will. It's funny, you know. She is an adult – I think she'll be nineteen by the time she starts college. I remember Lila at this age – constant bickering about how she could dress and move about as she pleased once she turned eighteen. I'm glad Maya isn't like that.' It's endearing how Mrs K will conflate the behaviour of her own daughter, Lila, with that of all the other girls that come through her dorm. 'But you know, they're all different, of course.' I'll have a chat with her. Of course I

can't legally tell her to do things because she's technically
an adult, but I'll break it to her as a 'rules of the community'
sort of thing.

'Thank you so much, Mrs K. I am glad to hear she's
safely back in the dorm.' At this point, I want to turn
to my dinner. 'Of course, of course, Suman. And yes,
between you and me, I would say it is not worth the
trouble to take any disciplinary action. She seems a
mature sort – I believe she will see that she has to play
by the same rules as all the other girls.' This is more
statement than clarification. So, this is what I had been
warned about. No disciplinary action of this kind would
go anywhere if Mrs K did not see fit.

'I agree. Have a good night, Mrs K.'

'You, too, Suman. Thank you for calling and checking
up on us.'

6

Unexpected Garden Creatures – Retrospective

For the first few days, Finley stayed close to his hosts. The Rumsons being well established in this circle, it served Finley well to follow their routines. Mornings were devoted to correspondence – the matters of empire never ceasing to require daily attention – and Finley would enjoy the quiet camaraderie of Her Majesty's able administrators in the small library that had been constructed off the terrace. The tables were interspersed with newspapers and ashtrays, and a samovar of coffee was always kept hot. Outside, beyond the terrace, one could hear the children playing and the admonitions of various nannies and ayahs, but the inside of the library was strictly adults-only. Whereas the newspapers that arrived were several days delayed, they arrived like clockwork. One simply adapted to the knowledge that, beyond the ambit of these hills, the world was progressing several days ahead of one's awareness of it.

Finley's sole obligation of the week was to lead the service in the small chapel near the bottom of the flag green. Sunday services were usually well attended, but now even more so out of curiosity about the new prelate. The simple benches, upright piano and makeshift altar were ample, and congregants did their best to rise up in wholehearted worship each Sunday. His first sermon, Finley reflected, should be one of gratitude for the bounty of their surroundings, both the natural aspects as well as those wrought by human hands. He made sure to quote Blake, leaving out the parts about satanic mills:

And did the Countenance Divine
Shine forth upon our clouded hills?

It seemed a fitting opening, and after the service many of the guests came to thank him for expressing their own sentiments so well. They had all travelled up the hill recently and appreciated being away from the heat and dust of the plains. The cool weather and the varied, generous foliage, flowers and green lawns, were an ideal balm for which every guest could be thankful. Finley occasionally chafed at how that gratitude for the Lord's benevolence – for all the natural beauty and wonder that surrounded them – was sometimes replaced with self-congratulatory airs among some of the guests, but these moments were fleeting. His congregants lauded British talent and foresight in securing for themselves this wonderful corner of empire. Perhaps he should wait a few weeks before pointing out the folly of this excessive self-regard.

Once unburdened of his weekly duty, Finley was able to turn his time and attentions to his environs. And it did not take long to bend the rhythms of Highpoint to his own predilections. His routine soon included an early morning stroll down to the boathouse and – with the aid of some brief instruction from Harrison – a daily row in one of the three wooden skiffs moored there. There were no other takers so early in the morning, and Finley was soon able to scud along the longest straight line in the lake. When the fog came in close and large sections of the bank were hidden from view, Finley could almost convince himself that he was on calm water, close to home. Only the missing smell of sea salt, and the absence of the cries of gulls kept him from completing the illusion. Once he had worked up enough of a sweat, he would pause in contemplation by lodging his boat among the dense congregations of lily pads at the ends of the lake's many fingers.

The solitude of the early morning row could be a stark contrast to the rest of the day. After tea and toast, brought down from the kitchens by the ever-prompt Cherian,

Finley would dress and stroll up the wooden steps to partake in the activities of the day. Finley understood from his earliest interactions that he was something of a novelty, both because he was new at Highpoint and because he lacked any formal role within Her Majesty's administration. This meant that he could move between various groups without attracting much attention. Who, after all, wants to deny the solitary vicar a seat at their table?

It was usually after lunch that George Rumson and several colleagues would take to riding into the hills on horseback. By this time of day, the light was good and the fog from the morning was sure to have burned off. While the men fancied themselves part of a hunting party, the progress through the thick, knotted forests was slow. As a result, the party was often constrained to tracking the pugmarks of a panther that had wandered close to a muddy stream bank or attempting to locate an especially scenic overlook remembered from previous years. There were several of these, and over the course of a few weeks Rumson had taken to asking the porters to run ahead and cut a semblance of a trail to ease the most desirable routes. The porters saw little point in this, given that the routes would not be travelled frequently enough and the vines would grow back quickly, rendering the paths as impassable as before. Pullur was enjoined to partake in several frustrated discussions in translation – far lengthier than would normally be required to convey 'cut a path that way.' Despite not understanding their language, Finley sympathized with the porters' frustration.

After a few such excursions, it occurred to Finley that horseback may not be the ideal mode by which to explore such unpredictable and hilly environs. Having grown up close to the sea, he knew that the coastal cliffs are also best traversed on foot and not on horseback. Finley knew that horses have a well-developed sense of danger, particularly in matters of sureness of footing, and moving on horseback meant restricting oneself to following streambeds or relatively gentle terrain. If one were, instead, to set out on foot, one could more easily traverse the sharper inclines without fear of falling off one's mount or the horse losing footing. So Finley took to exploring on foot, much as he had done as a child. His efforts quickly bore fruit. Not far from Highpoint, after a short walk along one of the paths that led out of town, one could scale down the side of the hill for about twenty feet and then stand on a natural path along the side of the mountain. To the right the hill would continue upwards towards the sky, but on to the left lay an unencumbered vista down into a valley below where no man had left any visible mark. And at the end of a short walk on this narrow path, the hillside flattened and broadened itself into a large platform of soil layered on top of rock that jutted out over the valley floor below.

The exposure of the outcropping and the thinness of

the soil made it difficult for larger trees to grow near the overlook, though a few had launched tentative roots as if to explore the possibility. Among those roots lay a thick carpet of moss and grass, each growing as if trying to outdo the other. The mosses had gained purchase over the farthest edges of the cliff overlooking the valley, but the grasses held their position on the landward side. Interspersed among the grass and the moss, not wanting to choose sides, stood bunches of green bushes – taller ones towards the hillside and shorter ones as they approached the cliff.

The first time he made it as far as the platform, Finley could not figure out how it had been created, and he very much doubted its stability. He pressed in as far as he could on the hillward side and marvelled at how such a sudden indentation could even exist in the side of a mountain. It later dawned on him that a landslide may have brought down that large outcropping of rock which now rested as a promontory over the valley below.

Reclining near the edge of the overlook, Finley reflected on what manner of chance had brought him here, so far from home. There was no specific reason for him to be in this particular emerald corner of empire. He had simply wanted to choose the path of ministry, to spread the word of Christ among non-believers in a part of the world where it may not have taken root yet. Like this rock, perhaps his teachings would find their own place to come to rest and take hold. To achieve this, he would have to excavate, and then set the foundations of Christian practice. In between these contemplations, Finley realized that within this single vista, he could squint up at the sun and into the depths of the green sea of the valley below. In a place so beautiful, what need was there for human ministry? And if that were the case, Finley decided, perhaps he should take his leave of it to find a place where his work was needed more. With this righteous course set in his heart, Finley walked back along the narrow path, scaled his way up the side of the hill and back to the hotel. He arrived just in time for dinner.

'Good Lord, Finley – where have you been?' Rumson started upon seeing him.

Finley quickly realized the problem. Not only was he not dressed for dinner, but his trousers also had several green and brown stains from clambering across the moss and earth. He decided to make the best of it.

'I have taken a very satisfying exploratory walk,' he found himself replying. 'There are truly impressive vistas, just beyond the town.' He gestured in the general direction of his discovery.

'You should take someone with you, Pullur or Cherian. Wouldn't want to have to send out a search party in these hills. Some very treacherous terrain if you're not careful. And panthers, of course . . .'

'Yes, I know. I shall be more careful.'

'Please do, Reverend. Wouldn't look good for me to report the Reverend missing!' It was the only time that Rumson had been in any way short with Finley, and it seemed to take them both by surprise. 'Sorry, Finley. I should explain. We have heard of panthers and groups of elephants nearby, and neither take kindly to being surprised.' Finley nodded his understanding and stood himself behind one of the chairs at their table. Rumson's eyes looked a bit more harried than usual. Finley did not have to wait long for an explanation.

'Truly, Eliza, I should really have thought not!' hissed the elder Mrs Rumson, with more heat than her usual tone with her daughter-in-law.

The family was being seated, and the elder Rumson was about to receive a reply from the younger, when George fixed his gaze on Finley and opined, with uncharacteristic firmness: 'Perhaps it would be better for everyone if we all enjoyed our supper more peacefully!' Finley's immediate question – more peacefully than what? – remained unasked.

'An excellent idea,' added the younger Mrs Rumson. With a series of glares exchanged over their respective bowls of peppered mulligatawny soup, they bowed their heads in silent chewing. The children, Alice and Andrew, followed their parents' example and said nothing. The heightened strain of the silence at the table prompted Finley to study each face more closely than he might have otherwise. George's face, like his mother's, revealed little more than the presence of a cloud, yet both seemed firmly resolved to march through the meal as there was little conversation. Eliza's features betrayed something of the events of the day, whatever they were. Her normally relaxed mouth was now pursed in a severe line. Their glances met briefly, and she replied to Finley's raised eyebrows with a twinkle of the eyes, while the generous upturn of her usual smile almost leaked through at the corners of her mouth. Since the exchange was followed by a prolonged downward gaze at the soup in front of her, Finley realized it was not the time to ask more questions.

As the meal wore on with its unusual lack of Rumson family banter, Finley tried to fill the gap with a retelling of his day's discovery. 'It is as if someone created a small lawn and suspended it over the valley floor below . . .'

'Truly remarkable,' added the younger Mrs Rumson, restoring some normalcy to the conversation. 'Perhaps we could all take a stroll there?'

'We should put up a plaque – "Finley Rock"!' Rumson added, resuming his usual good humour.

'It is very well for you to humour the Reverend now, but we must maintain our standards, lest we should fall further than we already have!' the elder Rumson cautioned, loud enough for the tables nearby to hear. Curious heads turned and glanced over, with pauses in their respective conversations.

'We shall, mother, we shall,' George soothed. Alice's lip began to quiver, and she sniffed.

But the elder would not be placated. 'Perhaps you do not appreciate the gravity of the situation, George . . .' she continued.

'Perhaps, Mother, you do not appreciate that this matter should not be addressed in public over dinner!' hissed the younger Mrs Rumson, with a directness Finley had not seen before.

'I think we should repair to the terrace for coffee, don't you?' suggested George. The comment, while addressed to everyone at the table, ended with a pointed glance at Finley. Sensing this was a signal of some urgency, he quickly excused himself to join George.

'Sorry, James,' George whispered as they walked over to the terrace. 'Mother is out of joint because she has become aware of some goings-on and insists that we do something about it.'

'Goings-on?' Finley enquired.

'Well, and I am sharing this in the strictest confidence, I might add, it appears that Ms Haight and Master Cadbury were seen in flagrante.'

'Ah.'

'There's more to it. My Alice was supposed to join them for an afternoon's picnic on a boat, but she discovered them, shall we say, in a quiet section of the boathouse. And since she appears to have a fondness for Master Cadbury, she is out of sorts as well.'

'I see, a delicate matter, to be sure. What will you do about it?' Finley ventured.

'Do about it? I'm not sure I want to do anything at all!' Rumson replied, helping himself to a slowly collapsing meringue. Cadbury is my equal in rank, Haight is several rungs farther up the ladder. And I don't want to be seen as interfering in – how to put this – personal or family matters.'

'But surely you must do something to remedy the situation . . .' Finley opined. 'What if the young lady involved had been Alice instead?'

'Well, then, I would sit Cadbury down and tell him what's what,' Rumson replied in a tone that suggested he may not actually have done that at all. He changed tack and continued, 'You see, Finley, here we are, in beautiful surroundings, with ample time for leisure . . .'

'Yes, I consider myself most fortunate that you invited me here,' Finley replied.

'You have missed my point. We – you and I, Haight, Cadbury – we have our duties to attend to. Administrative in my case. Spiritual care in yours. There is a sense of duty that marks our days. But this is not true for everyone, is it?'

'I'm afraid I fail to grasp the . . .'

'You will force me to lay this out for you, I see. Well, you and I were also in the bloom of youth once, Finley. Physical urges easily set aside now used to be less tame at one time. Do you comprehend, Finley?'

'Ah, so you are referring to the children?'

'Yes, of course, Finley! And Master Cadbury is no mere child and not yet a grown man. And with little demands on his time, idle minds . . .'

'Are the devil's workshop – indeed!' Finley finished Rumson's sentence with some relief, having at last grasped where this exchange was headed. 'If I may be so bold, why are these children not in schools in England?'

'You may have noticed, neither are Alice and Andrew,' added Rumson, and he seemed irked by the implication. 'As it happens, the last time we had home leave at Windermere, both children were taken ill to such a degree that the doctors assured us that the warmer climate here is far preferable for them.'

'Is that so?'

'Well, yes, although nobody thrives in the blasted summer heat on the plains. But with Highpoint for the summer – and some excellent tutors we have secured in Madurai – both children seem to be flourishing. Setting aside the recent developments, of course.'

'And what of Miss Haight or Master Cadbury?'

'I have not ventured to ask,' Rumson replied. 'And given current sensitivities, I do not intend to.' And after a brief pause, 'Pardon me, I should not trouble you with such familial cares.'

'No trouble at all, George.' Finley felt restless, so he put down the coffee and motioned Rumson over to the edge of the terrace in the rough direction of his walk. 'While exploring out there today, I realized that there is not much need for my ministry here. Familial cares – as you put them – are the first chance I have had to lend a sympathetic ear. You have brought to mind the original reasons for my journey to India.' After a pause, he added, 'Though I may not have been of much use in this particular matter . . .'

Rumson's attention had already veered towards a group of colleagues gathered around a central table on the terrace. They were now entreating George and Finley to join them. 'Come on, Rumson and Finley, time waits for no man!' Haight yelled. Rumson strode over to the merry group, having apparently set aside his worries; Finley followed tentatively after.

By the second glass of port, the exertions of the day caught up with Finley, and he excused himself before returning to his cabin. He need not have bothered, as the group sat in thrall of Haight regaling them with yet another story of an embarrassing punting 'accident' that had befallen a fellow Canterbridgian, who was now ensconced as a toothless functionary somewhere inside the home ministry. Finley reflected on how it was not sufficient to merely enjoy the grandeur that surrounded them, but that man alone must have the need to further embellish his own reality with baubles, reminders that others have not reached so exalted a state. Perhaps these retellings served to create common cause among men who would otherwise not have felt bonded together. Finley, ever leery of large groups, preferred to think of himself as a lone sentinel or scout, content to be watchful of his environs and entirely comfortable in his own company.

Rather than turn in right away, Finley decided to take a gentle stroll along the perimeter of the field in front of the cabin. Though the light was fading, he could see enough of the lawns and the boathouse that it seemed a good time to stretch his legs. The evening air was turning chilly and heavy with moisture. Walking in a pleasant doze, he did not expect to hear rustling in the grass to his right. At first, he thought it was a snake. But snakes tend to make themselves scarce when given the chance. And then he heard a giggle, followed by voices whispering to each other. Finley thought about continuing on, and then stopped.

'Hullo! Is there anybody here?' The grass was of medium height, so surely it would have been easy to see. Finley wondered if he was imagining things. He was just about to continue his stroll when he heard a twig snap, followed by more giggles.

'Who is it?' Finley demanded more firmly.

Two figures unfurled themselves from the ground and stood up. One was holding a lantern, which the other was trying to light, with little success.

'Hello. I'm Reverend Finley.' He could not think of a more appropriate opening, given the circumstances.

'Evelyn Haight – wonderful to meet you, Reverend,' said one of the two figures, having given up on lighting the lantern and now striding confidently towards him through the grass. Once she moved forward, the fabric of her garments catching on the blades made it clear that this figure was a woman. Tall and physically self-assured – much like her father – it was only when she was sufficiently close that Finley realized that he was looking at a young lady. Her cheeks were ruddy, and a warm, toothy smile accompanied her outstretched hand. Finley realized quickly that he didn't know who her companion was, and that this young woman should probably not be where she stood now.

Evelyn, appearing to sense Finley's curiosity about her companion, helpfully pointed out, 'And this, Reverend Finley, is Master Oliver Cadbury.' A young man rushed forward through the grass, his hand extended, and almost crashed into Finley. Evelyn giggled.

'Oliver Cadbury, Reverend. A pleasure to meet you.' The young man was slightly built but carried the family resemblance. As he had recently been dozing on his feet, Finley felt himself expending great effort into what to make of the present situation.

'Good evening! I was just out for a stroll before turning in,' he added helpfully. And then it dawned on Finley that, as the elder in this meeting, he need not account for his own actions. If anything, the dynamic ought to be reversed, but Finley had little to fall back on in these matters. 'It is getting quite dark. Perhaps you should return to the hotel, before the fog from the lake comes in?'

'Yes, Reverend, that was exactly what we were going to do,' Evelyn replied quickly.

'Do you not have a chaperone?'

'No, I told ayah she could go back to her lodging.' Evelyn gestured to the cottages at the far side of the field.

'And you, Master Cadbury?' Finley enquired of the young man.

'Well, I had just come out for a walk with the lantern. But it has gone out, and I seem not to be able to light it.'

'Let me help you,' Finley offered. And the three of them gathered round while Finley expertly struck the flint and the lantern sprung into flame. From the light, Finley could observe that Evelyn's hair had come loose and was out of place, and the top of her corset was untied.

'Thank you, Reverend!' Evelyn cut in, expertly taking the lantern in one hand and extending her arm so the pool of light moved away from her body. 'Come on, Oliver. We should return to the hotel. Goodnight, Reverend!'

'Goodnight, Reverend,' Oliver added as he followed after her. The two of them made rapid progress down the path and towards the stairs that led up to the hotel.

'Goodnight,' said Finley, but it seemed evident that the pair were not waiting for his reply. No longer sure as to whether to continue his walk, Finley retraced his steps over the field and headed back towards his cabin.

The next morning, over mouthfuls of Cherian's punctual toast, Finley considered the previous evening's events. His mind kept running back to the glance from the younger Mrs Rumson. Perhaps it was the fleeting smile or the full-eyed look that reached Finley and shifted something during the brief exchange.

He also reflected on his encounter just before turning in. Cherian's grasp of English was spotty, and also, Finley suspected, selective. After all, one of the few privileges the natives retained was how much or little they revealed of what they knew about their masters or their guests. Finley thought he should try anyway.

'Cherian, do you know Haight?'

'Haight saar. Yes, saar.'

'What about his daughter? Evelyn?' Finley gestured using both hands curving down either side of his head and shoulders to express the feminine form.

'Evelyn miss. Yes, saar.'

'What about Evelyn-miss and Oliver Cadbury?' he ventured. He felt awkward asking the question.

Cherian's response was telling. His eyebrows and eyes rolled upwards in a quick gesture and he made a 'tssk' sound of clicked disapprobation. 'Bad manners,' Cherian added. As if realizing he might have overstepped, Cherian started moving briskly about the cabin attending to the fireplace, which did not need attending to, and disappeared into the bedchamber to make the bed. The conversation, inasmuch as it was one, had come to an end.

Finley spent the next few hours occupied with reading the Bible and preparing for the next Sunday's sermon. He scoured chapter 7 of Corinthians 1 for instruction, but the verses did not provide the lessons he sought. He felt the need to convey that now was the time for sowing the seeds of chastity and discipline, which would bear fruit in the years to come. That it was not the time for improper relations between those too young to be man and wife. It was proving to be a difficult search. Besides, the sermon was not solely for the wayward Haights and Cadburys of the community; it was for all the attendees at the tiny chapel. Upon further reflection, Finley decided that he was truly irked by this recent turn of events. After all, how much was it his own responsibility to shape the conduct of these children over whom he had no control? But then again, were we not all God's children? And if so, did he not have a duty to minister here, even if his congregants were not, as first envisioned, drawn from the throngs of heathen non-believers? Having tied himself into knots over the sermon, his current understanding of what was truly his duty and God's plans for him, an irritated and peckish Finley stepped out into the sunshine to make his way to lunch.

He was beset by unexpected company almost immediately. Andrew, Alice and Mrs Rumson, the younger – having spent the morning rowing on the lake – were also making their way back up to the hotel for lunch. 'Good morning, Reverend!' trilled the two children, flush with their morning activity and eager for the meal ahead. They quickly made their way past Finley on the path as he mumbled his initial reply.

'I'm sorry, Reverend. You seem preoccupied. I hope we didn't startle you,' smiled Mrs Rumson as they walked in a more sedate cadence towards the stairs.

Finley wanted to pause for a moment and study the wind-blown wisps of hair waving from the normally well-coiffed head and the twinkling gaze underneath the bonnet. Eliza Rumson was a handsome woman with a languid stride and a curvaceous build that drew attention away from the beauty of her face. As they walked side by side, her large eyes with their steady, generous gaze gave Finley the distinct sense of being watched – or studied. 'Preoccupied – yes . . .' he replied, sounding distant even to himself. 'Good morning, Mrs Rumson,' he added afterwards, remembering his manners.

'Is something wrong, Reverend?'

'I'm not sure,' he started, although he was in a mood to unburden himself and did not particularly care who the audience was. 'I'm starting to believe that we may have a serpent in the garden.'

'Well, you should tell the gardeners, or tell Harrison. They have experience with such things and will take care of it. You should not try to do handle it on your own.'

'Ah, no . . .' Finley corrected himself, smiling. 'I did not mean it so literally. It seems that some here are taking liberties with the bounds of appropriate conduct.'

'Surely not, Reverend!' Mrs Rumson replied in feigned surprise, a twinkle dancing in her eyes. 'What could have led you to believe such a thing?'

'This is no trifle, Mrs Rumson,' Finley replied, feeling as if he were being toyed with. 'George – Mr Rumson – shared his knowledge of the circumstances with me, and at first I too believed there was little to be concerned about. In the matter of young Miss Haight and Master Cadbury, that is.'

'Ah,' came Eliza's tart reply. The twinkle had disappeared. 'We should tread carefully here, Reverend.'

'But later that evening . . .'

'I prefer not to dwell on such matters, Reverend. We all know what is said about casting the first stone . . .' Mrs Rumson warned.

'It's just the impropriety of it all!'

'You are beginning to sound like my mother-in-law, Reverend!'

'But they were unchaperoned! In the grass! In the dark! And I do not believe it is an isolated incident.'

'Oh dear, Reverend. I'm afraid you must have had quite the shock!' Mrs Rumson continued, the glimmer of a laugh returning to her face.

'It is no matter for mirth, Mrs Rumson.'

'Indeed, Reverend. It is not.' Her face grew severe, but the rapid reappearance of her charming grin showed that she was doing her best to humour Finley – and failing. 'Surely you remember what it was like to be their age?'

The comment caught Finley unawares. First, he had not considered that there may be a more sanguine approach to be taken in this matter. Reflecting on his own youth only served to highlight its solitude. Finley's comfort with being alone had its origins in necessity – he had grown up without siblings or cousins or friends nearby. Much of his adolescence had been spent walking alone and gazing out at the sea or observing the animals that lived on the rocks and cliffs. Only now, seeing that this other kind of childhood was possible, did Finley perceive any lack in his own experience.

Sensing his unease, Mrs Rumson quickly added, 'I didn't mean to cast aspersions, Reverend. Merely that for those in the bloom of youth, a certain curiosity about such matters is only to be expected.'

'Perhaps, Mrs Rumson. But are we to simply look the other way?' It was an earnest question from Finley, but it prompted Mrs Rumson to wrinkle her nose in annoyance.

'What is it that you fear, Reverend?' she asked.

'Fear is too strong a word. I worry about the impropriety of it all. The potential for ruined virtue. And that a young lady, particularly of her social provenance, should be brought low through youthful indiscretion.' Finley could feel a gathering momentum in his words, despite the slowing progress up the stairs. 'And is it not our duty, as guardians of our community, to see that such dissolution not take root here?'

'Perhaps, Reverend. Perhaps it is.' They were approaching the top of the stairs now and found themselves among more of the guests, all moving with purpose towards their midday meal. 'Perhaps we should trust that the young lady of whom we speak also knows her own mind?'

Signalling that there was no more to be exchanged on this topic, she called ahead: 'Alice! Andrew! Straight to the table, please!' She was about to place a gloved hand on Finley's arm but seemed to think better of it, modifying it into a more distant, placating gesture. 'Do not trouble yourself too much over this, Reverend. Sometimes the resolution simply appears with time.' Finley was about to reply, but Eliza and the children had joined the throng of eager diners.

7

The Photograph

'There's an emergency staff meeting, Mr G.' Mrs Mani pokes her head round the side of my door. 'In the staff lounge, in fifteen minutes.'

'Really? It's 5 p.m., Mrs Mani! Are you sure?'

'Yes, Mr G. All teachers and administrators need to attend.'

It had been a full day of classes and midterm tests, and I knew the weekend would be taken up with corrections and grading that I could no longer postpone. I was looking forward to the quiet walk home and some solitude. But apparently, that was not to be. The corridors are quiet except for a few students walking through on their way to and from various activities. On the way to the meeting, I walk by Manish.

'Hello, Mr G.'

'Hello, Manish. How's your term going?'

'Quite well, Mr G. Glad the midterms are over! Going to basketball now.'

'Well, have a good time.'

'Thanks, Mr G. Oh, can you tell my parents I will be at the basketball courts? I heard they have a meeting, so we're not going home yet.'

'Oh, yes, of course.' I had not realized news of the staff meeting had spread so quickly.

'Do you know what it's about? I thought staff meetings were usually on Thursdays.'

'Yes, they are, usually. And I don't know what it's about.' The boy was curious, sometimes precocious to a fault. 'And you should mind your own business!' I add, with a smile.

'Oh, I know, I know.' He runs away, grinning.

In the staff lounge, the air is one of tired curiosity. Most of the teachers, like myself, were wrapping up for the day and had not anticipated this meeting at all. Only Darling and Chapman, the principal and vice principal respectively, seem peculiarly engaged. Their eyes patrol the room, mentally taking attendance as to who has heeded their last-minute summons.

'Right, ladies and gents, let's get started!' Chapman begins. The light conversation that had permeated the room stops. Chapman looks around the room. It is that strange pause that administrators use to signal the importance of what is about to be said. I begin to suspect that Chapman uses it as a device to reassure himself of his own importance – 'look on me . . . and despair as I fritter away your time.'

'It seems we have a disciplinary problem in the school. It has come to our attention that students are taking inappropriate pictures in Ms Kalyani's photography class.' I start looking around the room to find Ms Little-K. Her normally relaxed features seem set and her lips are pursed. She looks towards Chapman's face with glazed eyes, but the furrowed forehead suggests nervousness. 'We must put a stop to this,' Chapman continues. 'It does not meet the standards of behaviour we expect of this community, and we worry about the reputation of the school if these things become widely known.' This unexpected scolding from Chapman leaves the room quiet, as if we are all somehow to blame but nobody is quite sure how. Knowing Chapman, that is likely the intended effect. I had suspected he was one of those administrators that extracted obedience through vague aspersions about unspecified, but possibly career-threatening, shortcomings. Now, sitting on his side of the table, I am sure.

'So, we need to figure out who is doing this and take appropriate disciplinary action,' adds Darling.

'We know that the student is in eleventh or twelfth grade,' Chapman continues briskly, seizing the gap between the half-formed thought and whatever sound is about to emerge from Darling's mouth. 'Because the evidence was found in Ms Kalyani's lab in the dark room. And only those two years are allowed to take photography.'

'Ms Kalyani, do you have any idea of who it could be?' asked Darling.

'Well, no, to be honest,' Ms Kalyani replies, blinking herself away from some unshared speculation. She seems put out at having to answer the question in such a large forum. 'The storage cupboard where we keep old prints and negatives was getting full, and I was trying to free up space when I found it. I haven't done that in at least, oh, maybe two years!'

'Well, if it has been two years, perhaps we need not pursue the matter now. The students involved may have graduated and left,' Darling follows up, with eager relief that the matter need go no further.

'Yes, but what if there are others?' enquires Chapman.

'Others?' Darling starts.

'Yes, other photographs. Or other students involved. How can we be sure that the student is no longer here?' Chapman's thoughts seem to be gaining speed.

As he starts to piece together the implications, Darling's face grows rapidly less sanguine and a scowl forms. 'Ms Kalyani, why did you bring this to our attention? Are you concerned that there could be more of this going on?' he asks.

Ms Little-K is clearly not prepared for what should normally have been a conversation held in private. She uncrosses her legs and plants her feet more firmly on the ground. 'Should I not have mentioned the photograph?

It is the first time in the four years of teaching the photography class that something like this has happened!'

'No, no, of course you should have brought it to our attention!' Darling snaps and then, catching himself, goes on with saccharine patience: 'I think we are just trying to gauge how serious the problem is, you see.'

'Why don't we just find out who took the picture?' Chapman enquires. 'Is there a way of doing that, Ms Kalyani?'

'I checked all the negatives and cameras that are being used right now. If the picture was taken recently, the negatives have been removed.'

'Maybe the picture can provide a clue?' Darling ventures.

'Well, I suppose . . .' Ms Little-K is rubbing the gold locket between the cream-coloured beads on her necklace. I find the gesture endearing – it calls on the part of me that makes me want to jump up and comfort her, but she is now scanning the room in an odd way.

Darling reaches over to a yellow manila envelope in front of Chapman, opens it and takes out what is clearly a black-and-white photograph print. It is larger than the regular sizes you see at photo shops. His head slides backwards on his neck and his eyebrows arch high. Any of the remaining teachers who might have been staring distractedly out of the window or peering at their own papers now sense the break in conversation.

Everyone cranes forward to take a look at what this evidence might be.

'Oh wow!' declares a voice, louder than the others. Pandian had been standing behind Chapman and Darling, and his location affords him a full view of the picture that Darling holds clinically between his thumb and two fingers. 'Can I take a look?' and without actually pausing for an answer, Pandian helps himself to the print, adding, 'I say . . .' In his usual demonstrative manner, Pandian very visibly considers who to give it to next, while Ms Little-K starts to raise her hand as if she were a student in class. Not seeing her hesitant wave, Pandian passes the photo to his neighbour in the other direction. The teacher, expecting neither the photograph nor its contents, shoots it a horrified glance and quickly passes it on to the next person. While Darling emits brief bleats of protest, the photograph makes its way quickly around the room. The lounge begins to buzz.

By the time the photograph arrives in my hands it is considerably the worse for wear, with several fingerprints and smudges intruding into the developed area of the printing paper. Whoever had developed it had not taken the time to trim the edges yet, but in the centre of the image is a pair of generous, round breasts. They are slightly out of focus, as neither their shape nor the areolae are clearly defined. Their nipples raised, the breasts extend forward as their young owner holds up a book of some

sort to hide the top half of her face, while the bottom half
reveals parted lips captured in half smile, half surprise. The
book, held sideways, is actually sheet music, with notes
arranged in arpeggiated runs. The composition of the print
is beautiful. If taken by a professional, it would have been
considered a work of art.

'That's quite enough gawking, Mr Ghosh!' cuts in
Mrs Kalyani, standing immediately next to me. I feel my
cheeks grow immediately hotter.

'Of course, here you go,' I reply, quickly passing it on
to her. I can sense tittering around the room, but I did
not want to look up to check the source. For the next few
moments, I feel the need to focus on the intricacies of the
carpet at my feet.

'Well, now that everyone has seen the . . . evidence,'
Darling begins, 'perhaps we could establish if there is
anything to be done about this. Do we have any ideas?'

'How do we go about identifying who this is?' Chapman
enquires, with perhaps too much relish. 'Could we start by
interviewing the girls in Ms Kalyani's photography class?'

Mrs Kalyani, the elder, had obviously had enough.
'Ask them what?' she cuts in. '"Are these your breasts?"' Or
should we ask: "Do you know who this is?"' A murmur of
surprise runs through in the room. She continues.

'Is it not enough that we pass something private like
this around the room, and we all gawk and stare? Is it
really for all the staff in the high school to stare at one of

our students' breasts and now wonder "Who could it be?" These children are our responsibility! They are not here for our gross curiosity! For all we know the person has graduated and left! And we do not all need to bother our heads about this!'

The force of the delivery, if not the argument, seems to snap the room back to a sense of purpose once again. 'All right,' Chapman begins. 'Along with Principal Darling, Ghosh, Mrs K and I will figure out what is to be done in private.'

'Yes, yes. Thank you everyone!' Darling adds. And the room empties rapidly, with the teachers alternately eager to get home, or to chew over this latest turn of events with close friends.

Turning to make my own exit from the lounge, I find my path blocked by Mrs K. 'Sorry, Suman, I didn't mean to cause you embarrassment with my comment . . .' Which only seems to make the problem worse by reminding me. 'There are very few teachers I can call on by name like that, and I wanted the passing-it-around nonsense to stop. Don't worry, you did nothing wrong.'

The apology is genuine, and didn't need prolonging. 'It's okay, I understand.'

'Shall we get this over with now?' she gestures to the table where Darling and Chapman sit with Ms Little-K. As we settle down at the table, it is clear that nobody has any clue how to proceed. Ms Little-K's kurta today is a light green colour, and it contrasts deliciously with the smooth brown skin of her forearm. And I can't tell the type of shampoo, but I know it is her gorgeous curls creating the smell as I pull up a chair. She gives me a wide-eyed look with the up-and-down of the eyebrows. Her gaze makes me nervous at the best of times, so I can only reciprocate with a weak shrug.

But Mrs K clearly has an opinion. 'Look, we cannot let this happen again. It is not right for a student's private mistake to be blown open like this across the entire teaching staff.'

'I don't see any alternative. How else would we know who it is?' Chapman begins.

'Know?' Mrs K interrupts. 'What is it that you want to know? Which girl's chest we were all staring at? And what will you do when you find out?'

'I think disciplinary action is called for. This reduces the standards that we have to live by as a school!' Chapman continues.

'Perhaps. If you saw that in a museum, we would call it art. If you saw it in a teenage boy's bedroom, you would call it pornography. And now? Now that every single teacher here has taken a good look, what shall we call it?'

'Well, what would you propose? Should we just let it go?' Darling beseeches, grasping at any available route to escape this awkwardness.

'How about this . . .' Ms Little-K interjects. 'Maybe I

tell my class, please don't take any nude photographs. I've found one, we don't want to make a big deal of it, but in future I can't teach a photography course if I have to deal with inappropriate material. How about just that?'

'That sounds wonderful!' Darling is ready to depart now.

'But it does not solve the problem at hand! Surely you agree, Suman!' Sudden entrapment in conversations, when I am content to say very little, is a Chapman favourite. It forces me to confront whether Chapman truly wants a new perspective or if he is just looking for rapid acquiescence.

'Can you tell us, what is the problem here really?' I hear myself saying, and realizing instantly from his tightening jawline that that is not what Chapman wanted to hear.

'Think of the school's reputation! What if it got out that there were dirty pictures circulating in the school? There are parents who would withdraw their kids immediately!'

'But are there such pictures circulating? I've been doing this for a few years, and it's the first time I have ever seen such a thing in the developing lab.' Ms Little-K provides her own reply with a worried pout. Her long, dainty fingers, usually slightly stained with developing chemicals, are interlaced and wriggling against each other in the most distracting way. I try to imagine what it might look like if I could interlace those fingers with my own.

'Mrs K, you've been a dorm parent for the older girls for a long time. Can't you just look around and see who it is?' Chapman presses on.

'How should I do that, Mr Chapman?' she counters. 'Ogle the girls in the shower or while they are changing?' Chapman seems on the verge of nodding his assent but reconsiders. 'I would never do something like that!'

'Then we must investigate in some other manner,' Chapman commands. 'Ms K, can you please make the announcement to your class and recheck the cameras and negatives to see if there are any other cases of such photography in previous years?' She nods agreement. 'Ghosh, I think you and I should think about how we can handle this administratively.'

'And do be careful!' Darling adds. 'Wouldn't want word getting around – this sort of news is sure to travel.'

'Okay, so for now, Ms K, please make your announcement and do your checking,' Chapman concludes, clearly dissatisfied that there was no more to be done. 'Suman, can you please take care of this?' he adds, handing me the envelope. 'I have to go home now, and I don't want to be walking around with it.'

'I'll just put it in my office filing cabinet,' I reply. I don't want to be responsible for this either.

'Yes, fine, fine. Just don't lose the "evidence".'

All through the corridors, students in various stages of post-games perspiration make their way to the dining hall for dinner. The envelope feels like an unwelcome parcel of guilt in my hand. Being in possession of such a thing makes one look differently at the world. The groups of teenage boys and girls, to whose company I am so accustomed, now seemed strangely distant, as if behind a one-way mirror. The image of the breasts, at once enticing and unavailable, seem completely unrelated to the students around me. I had seen something of one of them that I was never meant to see. I have nothing to share in return to restore the imbalance. Placing the file in the bottom drawer of my desk, I gather my bag and papers and decide to walk home, avoiding the dining hall and the more heavily frequented corridors.

All along the walk, there is little of the usual relief of leaving the campus behind. It has grown darker, and where normally I could have observed the trees and the sunlight, I now had to focus closely on the path ahead. Roots and rocks tend to assert themselves more virulently in low light. As the light fades in the deepening tree cover, I grow more annoyed at the image of the breasts floating before me. In their supple, generous proportions and the accompanying smile lay the promise of sensuality and intimacy. Except that the promise was being made to someone else, not me.

By the time I reach home the fog has beaded up on my hair. In the dark, the less welcome a thought, the harder it becomes to push away. It leaves room for the mind to project all manner of imagery in those spaces normally occupied by the fuller distractions that can be seen by daylight. But no, the photograph does not bother me. The breasts do not bother me. That someone else would enjoy their warm embrace does not bother me. But the stinging awareness that there is no such embrace waiting for me – that is what makes that out-of-focus black-and-white print so unbearable.

8

Honest Labours

On Sunday morning, Finley awoke from clouded, unsettled dreams, in which he had struggled to row across the lake, but no matter how hard he tried to balance the oars he only succeeded in moving in slow, frustrating circles. The panicked thought of never being able to reach the shore was what eventually woke him up. As a trainee pastor, he had taken easily to the study of scripture and reflection. But the act of instructing others on how to comport themselves made him uneasy. As to the morning that lay ahead, he felt a weighty fatigue at the thought of preaching piety to those who were already saved. A beggar who is starving gains great nourishment from the first mouthfuls of bread and water. But that very same life-giving nourishment means little to a man that has already eaten his fill. Christ sought to minister to the weak before the strong, did he not? Perhaps he needed to work that into the sermon.

Fortified with tea and toast, Finley bantered with the families in attendance. He appreciated that Haight, so obviously nursing a headache from the night before, had gamely made the effort to attend along with his family. Haight greeted Finley with a friendly smile and a nod that required the bare minimum of movement. The Rumson family were all in attendance as well, apparently more at peace than at the last meal he had taken with them. Seated in the benches on either side were the Bentinck family, Wetherby with wife and son – no photography equipment with him for once. And Mrs Attlee, but no Mr Attlee or Master Attlee. Harrison might have thought to attend, but perhaps duties at the hotel were making this impossible. Making his way to the front of the room, with the sun streaming in through the open windows, flowers on the altar and white curtains flapping in the breeze, Finley reflected that there was much to be grateful for.

Taking a deep lungful of air, he began: 'Ladies and gentlemen, I bid you all a good morning! For today's sermon, we turn to Timothy, the first chapter. "If a man desire the office of a bishop, he desireth a good work." Let us turn our thoughts now to discern what is this "good work" in the Bible. And how are we, mere mortals in a land so distant from Christendom, to comprehend and remember what constitutes that good work?

'That good work is the great enterprises of which we all partake in some measure. And in which we hold together with our fellow man. Like the embrace of the Lord, the good work binds us in an embrace using two powerful arms. One arm is to exemplify the message of Christ – through our own word and deed, through honourable acts and sincere repentance when we fall short. The other arm requires us to raise this land and its peoples, that they too may live as good Christians.

'Every soul in this house of God, in their own manner, feels the strength of this embrace and the promise of salvation that comes with fulfilling this duty. But the full reward of salvation lies not only in one's own striving. While that is good and necessary, striving for oneself alone breeds pride and vanity. The value of salvation lies also in giving aid and succour to those who strive alongside us, inasmuch as that striving moves us all in the direction of Christ's teachings. When our neighbour becomes wayward, digresses from the path that the Bible has laid so clearly before us, then it becomes our burden, our shared responsibility, to rescue our neighbour from their wanderings and return them back to the righteous path.

'The Lord, in His infinite wisdom, has provided the document, the blueprint for such striving. But the blueprint must be read repeatedly, considered carefully, for the same words that contain the plan for your life also contain the plans for your neighbour, your friend, your servant. How, then, do we divine our plan, for the words on the page ever remain the same?

'Let us turn to Timothy again. To desire the "office of a bishop" is to also become worthy of that which is greater than our current being. And on this, the Bible states clearly:

> A bishop then must be blameless, the husband of one wife, vigilant, sober, of good behaviour, given to hospitality, apt to teach; not given to wine, no striker, not greedy of filthy lucre; but patient, not a brawler, not covetous; One that ruleth well his own house, having his children in subjection with all gravity (for if a man know not how to rule his own house, how shall he take care of the church of God?); not a novice, lest being lifted up with pride he fall into condemnation of the devil.

After interpreting this passage for his congregation, Finley's speech finally wound around to the prescription he hoped would benefit specific people in the room. He looked up and paused, noting that Ms Haight was staring distractedly out the window.

'Finally, "if a man know not how to rule his own house, how shall he take care of the church of God?" For the church of God is but the single penultimate expression of the devotion that is required to Queen, to country and to God. And here Timothy provides us true instruction, for he speaks of "having his children in subjection with all gravity." Of maintaining appropriate order not only in our own conduct, but in the conduct of those for whom we are responsible, in the manner that parents are responsible for the conduct of their children. What do we say of the man whose children gambol as wild animals and display their idleness, grow wicked and dissolute?

'We say: There goes a man who should not hold the title of "bishop". There goes a man who has parted ways with his fellow man and shunned the enterprise with which we are entrusted. And such a man becomes a burden to his fellow men, for he must then be assailed and his attentions and efforts turned back to the righteous path. And the same must be done, if necessary, for his wife and his children. For if we cannot deliver our fellow man who strays momentarily, how then can we save the multitudes of heathens who have never beheld the path even once?'

At the mention of children who gambol as wild animals, Evelyn Haight appeared to have re-engaged with the sermon. By the end of the section, she was glaring directly ahead and her cheeks and neck were starting to turn a bright red. Finley couldn't tell if Oliver Cadbury had registered the implication in its entirety. Oliver was also watching Finley's face closely and nodding along in polite agreement, as if Finley were referring to a matter completely in the abstract. He couldn't dwell on this single aspect of the sermon too much longer, so Finley continued on with his prepared remarks, ending with a resounding 'God save the Queen!'

Finley closed the heavy book in which he had inscribed the sermon with a bang. This startled several members of the congregation, including Haight. His nodding neck quickly straightened up and his eyes fixated on some distant point past Finley's right shoulder. Two faces to Haight's left, Evelyn's mouth was drawn tight and her eyebrows were furrowed, even as the blushing had abated. Finley stood flushed with a sense of completion. Despite Evelyn's concerned expression, he caught her gaze and smiled back. Casting his eyes over the rest of the audience, he could see calm thoughtfulness, punctuated by forceful nodding from the elder Mrs Rumson. Finley could not actually see her face, but the movement of her hat and feathers suggested emphatic agreement. After the obligatory hymn and a delightful piece on the chapel piano by Alice Rumson, the congregation stood up and dispersed into the sparkling August sunshine.

'A fine sermon, Reverend!' The elder Mrs Rumson was the first to congratulate him. 'You will grow into a fine shepherd yet, Finley!' She did so in that avuncular manner of elder relatives which, while aiming to congratulate, feels condescending nonetheless. 'If only some of us were able to heed the message!' she added, within earshot of several other congregants, who were waiting to offer Finley their own greetings.

'This is varied terrain, Mrs Rumson. Each must find it after their own fashion,' Finley replied, trying to be as agreeable as possible.

'Yes, yes, fashions are all very well, Finley. All very well,' she went on. 'But some things are beyond fashion or taste, and must simply be held to account!' With that summary judgement she strode purposefully towards the refreshments that had been set up on the lawn.

The Wetherbys approached Finley next. 'Thank you, Reverend,' Mrs Wetherby offered.

'Yes, a good message for us all, Reverend,' her husband agreed politely.

'You are most kind.'

'Your services, Reverend, are a most welcome addition to life here on the hilltop,' Wetherby went on. 'I have a rather different perspective, as it were, than most. For I am able to capture not simply portraiture but also that which occurs when the subjects are unaware.'

'I'm afraid you've lost me, Mr Wetherby.'

'Consider our native servants, Reverend. When we sit at table, or partake of our evening entertainments, we devote our attentions mostly to one another, do we not?'

'Yes, certainly, I can attest to that myself,' Finley agreed, while taking a few steps in the general direction of the refreshments himself. Wetherby followed.

'But are you aware that there is, at the very same time, a parallel set of conversations and interactions going on, of which we observe little?' And glancing up at Finley's confused expression, he tried to clarify. 'Let me be clear. I spend much of my time printing the images I have captured. And on closer observation, I am able to notice the interactions of the natives who accompany us as well. Those who stand by our side with trays of refreshments, or clear away our plates, or make our beds.'

Finley confessed that he had not paid attention to such things. Wetherby continued: 'Do you know that there are five cooks in the hotel's kitchens? And that only the head cook is allowed to sample our food as part of the catering operation? The others dare not because they lack the priestly dispensation that the head cook has received to do his job! The others can only gaze on as the head cook samples the dishes that they have laboured together to create. And do you know how I learnt of this?'

Again, Finley was at a loss. But he was certain that Wetherby would elaborate. 'I had asked Harrison if I could take photographs of his fine facilities, including the kitchens. Upon setting up my camera in the window of the kitchen, I was able to occupy that spot for many hours. The cooks and labourers finally grew tired and stopped regarding my every action with suspicion. Once they returned to their work, I was able to surreptitiously capture many exposures. There is a choreography to what takes place behind those windows and walls. In one frame the arrangement was very much like the painting *The Last*

Supper. Two cooks on either side of the head cook, each man's visage raised expectantly as the head cook sampled the fare. All this, Reverend, is part of what we could easily look at, but we do not see.'

Finley had just taken his first bite of a cucumber sandwich and was unable to answer Wetherby's next question: 'Why, you may ask, am I telling you this?' Finley nodded assent – he was indeed wondering why. 'My system of lenses and tripods also allows me to see things which were never meant to be seen. An indiscretion here. A peccadillo there. And so, Reverend, I agree with you most heartily.' Wetherby paused, tapped on his nose and drew his face closer to Finley's. 'We must indeed have our houses in order. For we truly never know who it is that observes and learns from our every move.'

'Mr Wetherby, you have truly grasped the true essence of my message this morning!' The first few bites of the cucumber sandwich, washed down with coffee, had a calming effect on Finley. He sought to pass this sentiment on to Wetherby: 'Perhaps I should have borrowed the analogy of your printmaking before I wrote the sermon.'

'No, no, Reverend. Far be it for me to assist in matters of the Church . . .' Wetherby mumbled. 'But thank you for lending an ear, Reverend. Most illuminating. Most illuminating.' And he politely walked away, leaving Finley to wonder who was illuminating whom.

'Well, hullo, Finley!' He knew this was Haight, without even looking. 'Splendid job. Rumba job, as they say, you know!' Haight seemed pleased. Although Finley could not see the reason why. Perhaps the fog of the previous evening's carousing had lifted, and Haight was turning back into his energetic self. 'Good of you to remind us to stay on the straight and narrow, what?' Haight said, with the attitude of one who has been told this all his life. He clearly regarded it as a suggestion that one may or may not wish to ultimately take on board.

'Yes, Reverend. Thank you for the reminder. We must seek to always be at our best,' Mrs Haight agreed. Evelyn Haight said nothing, which her mother chose to remark on. 'Did you find the sermon instructive, Evelyn?'

'Father, do you feel like you have Mother and me under a suitable degree of control?' she asked Haight with a grin.

'Come now, poppet!' Haight replied.

'Evelyn!' Mrs Haight exclaimed.

'I am very sure that Timothy did not intend subjection in quite that manner, Ms Haight,' Finley replied.

'Please excuse the impertinence, Reverend!' Mrs Haight cut in. And turning to her mischievously grinning daughter, she said, 'Come on. Come with me. We have other matters to be attending to.' She took Evelyn by the arm, and mother and daughter strode off towards the hotel.

'Rum thing, Reverend. But my Evelyn may be right. We don't expend too much on controlling what the children are up to here, do we?' Haight was reflecting. It was a rare occurrence for him to opine on matters other than administrative duties or ribald recollections about youthful escapades. A distant smile played on his face. 'Now, if this were me at Evelyn's age, I shudder to think of all the tamasha I could get up to.' And perhaps realizing he should not have shared that aloud, Haight quickly added, 'Never mind, never mind. There was something else I wanted to ask you about.'

'What's that?'

'Well, let us walk a bit away from the crowd, shall we?'

'Of course . . .'

So, Finley and Haight strolled up the gentle slope towards the flagpole and down the wooden stairs towards the boathouse. 'We needn't continue much further, Finley. I only wanted to get away from the crowd.'

'We can stop here, if you wish. Actually, my cabin is just a few steps further on the path to the boathouse.'

'Why don't we just amble around the field?' And turning towards the meadow, Haight slowed his stride. Less purposeful and less characteristic of his normal, bounding pace. 'It's a bit delicate, this matter. But unfortunately, I have little by way of time to myself where I can ponder, so I would appreciate your counsel.'

'Certainly.'

'And your discretion. I'm not Catholic, but if we were, we would be having this conversation in the confessional, you understand?'

'I understand, Mr Haight.'

'Andrew, please. I think we have spent sufficient time around each other to dispense with the formality.'

'Yes, Mr Haight – Andrew.'

'Has to do with Oliver. You know, Cadbury's boy.'

'I see.'

'Well, I'm not sure how you would see. Apparently, Oliver and my Evelyn have been spending rather too much time together. Unchaperoned, as it were. Just like your sermon said.' He turned to gaze at Finley with the pained air of one who has lost his moorings. 'They grew up together, you see. When the hotel barely existed, they would climb those trees together in their little white sailor suits and play hide-and-seek in the boathouse. But the time for these things has passed. If you understand my implication.'

'I do, Andrew.'

'And yet you do not seem surprised. Perhaps you are already aware of my predicament?'

'In a manner of speaking, yes, I am. Quite aware.' And Finley was about to carry on, 'Why just the other day . . .'

'Yes, quite, James!' Haight cut in. 'I was young once too, and we need not dwell on the specifics of the matter.'

Finley was embarrassed, but the distraction of strolling

along the edge of the field allowed for a sufficient pause in the conversation.

'Well, what is to be done, then, Finley?' Haight began again. 'Is there not something in your godly book of instructions that we can call upon?'

'Such as? What did you have in mind?'

'Well, I'm sure Jesus or one of the Apostles had an answer. The Romans were not celibate saints, were they?' And then realizing that perhaps he'd overstepped, Haight added, 'I do not mean to offend, Finley. This has me at my wits' end. I can indeed command legions of men, but have little sway over my daughter.'

'Perhaps we can provide a diversion of some sort?'

'Such as?'

'I don't have an answer, Andrew. Something that improves the mind, as it were. And distracts from untoward desires.'

'Physical activity, perhaps!' Haight seemed pleased that he had landed on this solution himself. 'That's right. Boat races. Make them row up and down the lake twenty times, and they won't have much left in them past dinner time! Splendid idea, Finley!'

Finley, acutely aware that boat races were not in fact his idea at all, chose to let the conversation continue in this vein. 'But someone could go overboard, and that would not do. My Bernie – Mrs Haight – would create a horrendous fuss if that were to happen. No, Finley. You must amend your idea and conceive of a similar, but less fraught plan.'

'Perhaps an exploring party in the nearby hills, Andrew.'

Haight looked over quizzically. 'On horses, Finley? They can take the horses out whenever they want!'

'No, I was thinking something more physically rigorous. Perhaps the chaperones could be on horseback, but the older children could walk. We need not go far . . .'

'Capital idea, Finley!' said Haight, clasping and rubbing his large leathery hands together with evident relish. 'The Reverend's Walk! An activity to build character and knowledge of our environs. Required for all children over age twelve!' And having thus convinced himself of the merits of the idea, Haight turned to Finley with an outstretched hand and said, 'Come, James! We have a course of action at last: the Reverend's Walk. Your excellent idea will begin tomorrow. I will have Harrison arrange for refreshments and bearers, and you shall have your walk!'

And so began the tradition of the Reverend's Walk. At ten in the morning, the party would assemble just below the flag and then tramp out together through the Highpoint gate, across the green in the middle of the intersection beyond, and disappear into the forests and hills beyond. Cherian, being the most locally oriented of the staff, would plan out the walk with Finley. Planning was perhaps too strong a word. Around the table in his cabin, Finley and Cherian would take several attempts to navigate the incomplete, but most current, contour map that the last surveying team had left behind. Between Cherian and Finley, the exchange comprised mostly gestures to indicate cliffs, water, thick forest or difficult walking.

The first occasion of the Reverend's Walk was well attended, even though Haight had to be called away at the last minute. Evelyn Haight, Oliver Cadbury, Alice and Andrew Rumson, Jonathan Wetherby and Harold Attlee were all able to go along. The younger children had been asked to stay behind, but Andrew Rumson had cajoled his sister sufficiently to be allowed to accompany them at the last minute. Outfitted with water bottle, pith helmet and walking stick, each of the children ended up somewhere between intrepid explorer and costume party caricature. Mrs Haight, accompanying on horseback, would be the parent chaperone, and Michael Wetherby would come along with one tripod-and-lens set-up to commemorate the occasion at the turnaround point. Lest the party should be overcome by hunger or thirst, Cherian had enlisted one of the coolies, Sivarajan, to bring food and drink and a few durries, on the back of a mule.

Unbeknownst to Finley, the logistical execution may have been rather too thorough. Cherian had not only gone ahead and marked the walking trail the previous day, he had even taken care to ensure that Mrs Haight would not be inconvenienced on horseback. As a result, while Finley and Cherian began gamely enough at the start of the walk, they were quickly overtaken by Evelyn and Oliver who, with their youth and curiosity, strode quickly ahead, only to have to be called back each time they disappeared beyond the next turn in the trail. Cherian's thoroughly executed trail markings only emboldened them, and soon all the children had scampered ahead, while Finley, Wetherby and Mrs Haight, on horseback, were left to bring up the rear.

The trail ended abruptly in an overlook. Two barely visible footpaths continued sharply downward from the overlook, but they would not have accommodated travel on horseback. Taking a quick count of the party, Finley realized in the same moment as Mrs Haight that her daughter and Oliver were missing from the group. After some hullo-ing into the surrounding bushes and vines, the top of a pith helmet popped up from one steep downhill trail, soon followed by the sheepish visage of Oliver Cadbury.

'Go on, keep climbing!' the strong voice of Evelyn Haight rose from below. And soon enough, its owner also climbed into view. Both looked flushed, although it was not clear whether from exertion or embarrassment.

'Well, children! This is most improper!' Mrs Haight began.

'But Mother!' interrupted Evelyn. 'You didn't tell us that the trail markings stopped here! We merely continued to follow the trail down. And we turned around after realizing that we had not seen Cherian's trail flags for several yards.'

'Is this true, Oliver?' Mrs Haight enquired of the young man.

'Yes, Mrs Haight,' he replied with some hesitation.

'Good god, Oliver!' Evelyn began. 'You look like a lamb to slaughter! It's only Mother.' And she started giggling mischievously. Oliver permitted himself a smile.

'Well, all right, the pair of you. I don't want you to leave my sight until we get back to the hotel. Is that understood?' They mumbled their agreement. Much of this excitement was soon forgotten as Sivarajan, unaware of the fuss all around him, had unloaded the mule with Cherian's help and was passing around sandwiches and lemonade.

After the group had devoured Sivarajan's refreshments, Wetherby announced that a photograph was in order: Inaugural meeting of the Reverend's Walking Club. It was a serious undertaking for Wetherby to set up his equipment. He had started as soon as the party had arrived at the lookout point, but Sivarajan had placed the mule too close to the frame of the picture. With comical gesturing, and translation from Cherian, it was made clear to Sivarajan that while he was welcome to join the picture, the mule needed to be moved outside the shot. By this time, Mrs Haight had rounded up most of the party, making sure to insert herself between Oliver Cadbury and her own daughter.

'For goodness' sake, child, look at your hair!' she admonished.

'Mother worries about my prospects. You won't parade this imprint around Fort St George, will you, Mr Wetherby?' she enquired loudly to discomfit her mother. Wetherby looked up and emitted some incoherent mumblings.

'Stop it at once, Evelyn!' Mrs Haight scolded. 'The man is trying his best to commemorate the occasion.'

Mrs Haight placed her arm heavily on her daughter's, making sure that the daughter and mother were standing arm in arm in the very centre of the visual frame. 'Come, Reverend Finley!' she trilled. Mrs Haight played hostess when it suited her, and she understood how mutually beneficial the rapport between a man of the church and a senior administrator's family could be. Finley felt beholden to the Rumsons though, and did not want to seek Mrs Haight's patronage. He edged closer.

Secretly, Finley also harboured a distrust of this new invention. Even as a modern man of God, he felt unnerved by how it captured the detail of expressions, which, while fleeting in real life, remained etched forever on those imprints. This was of no concern when the imprints depicted scenery or wildlife from hunting expeditions, or grand buildings. But Finley wondered what aspect of a person – what portion of the soul – this contraption might unwittingly trap. It discomfited him further that Wetherby was the one who got to have the first close look at the imprints. Did he secretly examine the lines and expressions on his subjects' faces once the imprints were created, interrogating them through his lenses and chemicals? Or did he admire the shape of a bodice, the places where plump flesh pushed out and those parts where the concavities curved in? Finley felt that Wetherby must collect, and keep for himself, some token of his subjects. A piece of their personage or memory that had not been inventoried, just for Wetherby's private satisfactions. Everyone had finally assembled inside the frame, and Finley made sure that both Sivarajan and Cherian were included as members of the party. He felt particularly grateful to Cherian for having scouted the path ahead and noted that he should express this praise to Harrison.

On the walk back, Evelyn Haight made a point of walking with Finley.

'Reverend, I would like to thank you for arranging this outing for us. I don't remember ever being allowed to explore so far beyond the hotel. And there is so much to see!'

'I'm glad you enjoyed yourself, Ms Haight. These are delightful environs we live in,' Finley agreed.

'Could we do this again? Perhaps we can even create our own maps – like true explorers?'

'I should certainly hope so. There is much to see and explore here.'

'Very good, Reverend. I will hold you to your word! Do

you know, Oliver and I found a stream coming out of the hillside further down?'

'Really?'

'Yes, Reverend.' Oliver had caught up and was walking on the other side of Finley. 'Cherian even took a drink from it, so we knew it was safe. And the water was nice and cold!'

'Cherian was with you?' Finley asked, surprised.

'Yes, of course. He's the one who showed us the water gushing out of the side of the hill,' Oliver added. 'I don't know that I would have noticed it on my own, though maybe I would have.'

'He said there's a bigger stream further down, too,' Evelyn went on.

'Perhaps we should take a smaller group and explore there some day,' Finley smiled.

The green patch in the centre of town now appeared before them, and the three stopped to take a breath and let the others catch up. Finley turned back to the rest of the party as the centre of town came into view and shouted: 'Almost home, everyone!'

'Wonderful! Come on, Oliver, let's find something to eat!' Evelyn gave Oliver's shoulder a shove, and soon Ms Haight and Master Cadbury were rapidly making their way through the hotel gate and up the slope that led to the dining room. Finley waved to the guard and stood aside to wait for Mrs Haight and her horse.

9

A Witless Voyeur

A teacher that claims to enjoy midterm exams and grading is either a liar or a masochist, or both. One must truly grit one's teeth to confront the reality of what meagre share of instruction has found purchase in the students' minds. Was it always this way? Perhaps Einstein's teachers also shuddered as they sat down to grade their tests. I have to remind myself that Einstein did not do well in school.

It is rarely the gifted or capable student that taxes one's patience. Those taking the correct approach can be dispatched quickly, even if the numbers are not quite right. But there is a multitude of ways to be wrong. For me as a teacher, providing useful guidance means that I must now follow every twist of tortured logic far enough to point where the wrong turn occurred. The most trying cases are the ones who fervently believe that they understand when actually they do not. A student whose belief in his own correctness exceeds his understanding of the concepts will struggle to admit that a wrong turn was even taken and will go to great lengths to convince you of his correctness. Therein lies the greatest burden of the high school teacher.

Ultimately, it is a trench of mud I have to wade through. And the weekend will pass with cups of coffee and stacks of papers in various states of correction scattered all over the dining table. I've observed that I almost prefer that the weather be foggy or rainy outside when I have to go through this exercise. It makes the indoors brighter and seems to convince me: 'go on, keep grading, nothing to see out here.' And while I'm at it, I play little games with myself. Five questions, forty students, two sections. Maybe I should do all of question one first. But let's not do them in the same order because I already know who the students are that may end up doing well, as well as those who may not. Tarun M – likely to do very well. And I'm starting to recognize his handwriting, so best to stick that in the middle, otherwise everyone else will feel like a disappointment.

I like to choose problems that test comprehension first. It helps to identify quickly which students read the problem and developed an intuition, as opposed to diving in and solving it through rote recipes. Consider the problem at hand now: find the maximum volume of liquid that can be safely contained in a trough that can pivot up to 30 degrees around an axis. In this case, the diagram of the trough shows that one edge is higher than the other. But the rotation is symmetric; the trough can rotate backward by 15 degrees towards the long edge, and forward by 15 degrees towards its short edge. When tipped towards the long edge, no more liquid could fall out than what already fell out when the trough was tipped the other way. Grasp that, and you know you really only have to solve the case where the trough is tipped over as far as possible towards its short edge. Any liquid above that level will fall out.

I start with Manasi R. At the end of this exam, she looks like she's coming along with steady progress – a B plus. Could have paid more attention early on, but clearly grasps the core concepts. Akshay D – I feel bad for him. Every time I grade anything of his, it's a solid D. Any time I discuss a problem in class, I notice the glazed look in his eyes. This is not done to offend; I know he would prefer to be anywhere else. Sarita V – a very happy surprise. Very quiet student, with little class participation. I have no idea if she pays attention or not, because she is often looking down or staring out the window. But she has obviously been paying attention, because after tallying up the points, she gets an A. And Tarun M – great potential, but still an A minus because of sloppy calculation errors. I really need to talk to him about this. I noticed he was done earlier than everyone else, and there was a lot of looking around the room and daydreaming. He should have been using that time to check his numbers!

Sivakumari is busy in the kitchen. I can smell her cooking, now that the prep is done and the real cooking has begun. Since she takes Sundays off, she does a larger batch of cooking on Saturdays so it lasts me for whatever intervening meals I might want. I sit back with a sense of accomplishment. I've put a big dent in the grading. I don't have to grade the essays for my applied philosophy class until next week. Yes, it is unusual for a single teacher to cover both subjects, but Perkins left in a bit of a hurry, and the powers that be in school recognize that I'm enough of a polymath to cover both. Somewhere deep down, I'm sure they are also happy to hire just one teacher who can handle both subjects, rather than two separate teachers, and be the high school coordinator too. Probably a good time to stretch the legs. I put on some sneakers and head out the back door, letting Sivakumari know on my way out. She suspects I am in a rush and tells me that my meal will be ready soon.

The fog is still brooding on the lawn outside, but it's not as cold as it could be. I've come to learn that there are many kinds of fog. There's the heavy, warm, wet fog. It creates a lot of condensation and makes things slippery. It smothers and is hard to walk in if you're congested with a head cold. There's the chill, stationary fog that hangs around for a long time. It's dense, and sound gets muffled. Finally, there's today's variety – a cool, flowing fog that means the clouds are moving around us and we are getting in the way. This is the most entertaining to walk in, as it moves noisily like the wind and can suddenly create gaps to reveal things. Just as quickly, those gaps will close up as more fog rolls through. This is not so amusing if you have to drive in it, though, because the usual visual markers can appear or disappear in a disorienting manner.

I often make a loop of Lake Compound when I need to stretch my legs. The path climbs gently uphill, passing the walkways that lead off to individual staff cottages and over to the gate of the compound. If I keep going, the path will eventually loop back around and return me to Penrose. I typically don't use that returning section of the path. There are more neighbours on that stretch, and I prefer to keep my own company. On a Saturday like this, I'm unlikely to see anyone.

As I stroll, the fog has parted slightly to my right, and I notice the path that leads over to Craddock, Koshy's house. He seems to have settled in okay, but I had not heard much from him since his arrival. His students seem to like him and he has several lined up to perform at the upcoming school concert. Buoyed by my progress with corrections, and since I did not have any plans for the evening, I thought it might be nice to invite him over for dinner today, after all. Why not? I had intended to several weeks ago, and then the usual preoccupations of school had taken over.

The path leading up to Craddock is marked with large

flagstones. With no houses beyond the cottage, it does not receive much use, and moss and grasses have grown over the corners of each stone. The sound of my footsteps dies away as I turn on to the path, and I can see that it approaches the house from the flank, then wounds around on to the front lawn. The deep porch looks out to the tall eucalyptus stands on the hillside that falls away at this edge of Lake Compound. With the dense, moving fog, I have to keep looking down to make sure I don't trip over the retaining wall of the front lawn. That's not the sort of entrance I want to make. I pause at the point where the path curved to join the front lawn. What I can see from this vantage confuses me.

A very large figure sits on the porch, much larger than Koshy. It is seated in a rattan armchair, the kind one finds all over the lounges at school. The figure seems to be writhing in a slow, repeating motion. Perhaps the fog is playing tricks with me, so I lean in for a closer look. And then I realize it is not a single figure on the chair, but two.

Both are seated facing the trees and fog. A woman's arms reach overhead, her hands pull and run through the straight lengths of Koshy's hair. Koshy whispers something to her and nibbles gently along the rim of her ear, the lobe and on to her neck. His hand reaches under her sweatshirt at the waist and pushes gently upwards, revealing the smooth, bronzed skin of her torso. For a moment, all motion pauses as his hand reaches up, cupping the breast, gently tracing the contours of its shape outside the fabric of the bra, pulsing pressure on forgiving, welcoming flesh. The woman sits up for a second, reaches around behind her back, unhooks the clasps of the brassiere, and leans back again, once again enveloping Koshy's head and hair in her hands.

And then it is released, the fullness of the breast tumbling out and sideways. The skin of the torso has gathered goosebumps, the nipple stands erect, and Koshy's long fingers gently stroke it, bending the nipple with each pass, circling the areola. The woman's torso rises up, her back arches and her mouth opens slowly, saying nothing. Koshy's left hand appears, wrapping around the woman's body, the fingers searching for the same breast, and the slow writhing resumes. The right hand disappears, first into the waistband, and then further down still. Her hips rise to meet his fingers and add to the friction. The writhing is gaining speed and building up to a rhythm. Her hands tighten on his locks of hair, her back arches, her hips push further upwards and quivers in a momentary staccato. Then her figure collapses back on to Koshy's body, and she turns towards him, nuzzling and hiding her face in his neck.

My feet are rooted to the spot. I stand there figuring out whether and how to turn around. My face feels warm and there is an unpleasant constriction in my trousers. I was not supposed to have seen this, but I had stood and watched. Should I stay to see what comes next? The pair continue their embrace, heads together, sharing a secret conversation. The foreheads nuzzle close to each other, and the hands tousle Koshy's waves of hair more playfully now. This is not the time to be making neighbourly invitations. I try to retrace my steps as quietly as possible, and soon the fog has restored its thick curtain between the lovers and me.

I am disoriented enough that I find my way home by the shortest route, and not by the loop I had planned on taking. Sivakumari had finished her work and left for the day, which is just as well since I need the privacy to take care of the throbbing. My mind finally slows enough to take in the room and the shifting grey light pouring non-committally through the windows. From my prone position, out of the window I can see the silhouettes of the larger eucalyptus trees shifting gently in the passing fog. I can follow their blurry shadows around the room, alighting on the bed, on the table strewn with papers, the framed photographs. On the shoes arranged neatly in the corner, awaiting an inspection that will never come. I keep thinking back to the image of those hands, first frenzied and taut, then relaxed and stroking Koshy's hair after the climax passed. No hands to stroke my hair here; life measured out in coffee spoons indeed.

Having dozed awhile, I wake to the same scenery – the light is the same but the shadows have changed position.

It is now mid-afternoon. The food that Sivakumari had set out has grown cold, but I peck at some of it to stave off a gnawing headache. A cup of coffee later, I am back at the table, ready to finish grading the remaining set of papers. But it does not start. Each paper that I begin to read makes very little sense beyond the student's name. Outside, the wind has picked up and blown some of the fog away. Whoever I am grading now has clearly forgotten to evaluate the integral at its limits correctly. Incomplete answer – five points off for that. If the monkeys outside were capable of portraiture, they would surely depict me as an Indian adaptation of that picture of a scowling Beethoven. He could hardly be blamed for feeling out of joint. A whole life of training and then suddenly unable to partake of the very thing you are responsible for creating. A chef who cannot eat. Or maybe a maths teacher who cannot follow the solutions to his own exam. Was it jealousy? That Koshy had someone? That I had no one? Or was it that lurking sense that something – or rather, someone – was missing?

I do not like to ponder these questions, so I decide to find some music that will take my mood from brooding to a sense of purpose. Soon, I am treating myself to the booming crevasse of the opening bars of Elgar's cello concerto. I conjure a picture of a man laid low. By observing the flight of birds soaring and the sky above him, he finds a way to stand and bring himself up again. It does not happen all at once – the cello must make room for the oboe and clarinet. The man must make several attempts before standing tall again. And when the crescendo plays, it exhausts the high notes a cello can achieve.

Eventually, my mood is restored sufficiently to return to the task at hand, and the agreeable lilting of the second movement is the backing track to my return to grading. Elgar accompanied me while I finished my work, meting and doling out the points as I saw fair. I must have become absorbed in it, because soon enough, the tssk-tssk noise of the record player reminded me the concerto was over. I continued to work on the grading in silence, and soon dusk was gathering outside.

With the events of the day as they were, I no longer wished to stay at home. The image of the fingers holding tightly and desperately to the waves of hair, and the relaxing their hold and stroking gently, taunted me. Koshy engaged? He never mentioned being marri partner – perhaps just a convenient arrangement unattached but each nevertheless meeting needs. Of course, I had heard of such of convenience. But invariably someone g balance is never quite fair, and the one who c less always has the upper hand.

The possibility of intimacy, engagement, marri they do break into my thoughts sometimes, esp when Ms Little-K is around. I was even suppose arranged with someone, once upon a time. My parents had set up the meeting after some lengthy conversations. Or rather, my mother had, and my father indicated that I should humour her and go. Unfortunately, on the day of the meeting, a city wide bandh had preoccupied most of Calcutta, and so the introduction was postponed. There may have been a change of heart on the bride's part soon afterwards, because neither party offered up a new date. Out of curiosity, I once asked my mother what had happened, but was shooed off with 'there are many fish in the sea'. That particular fish had obviously changed direction and chosen to swim elsewhere.

I decide to walk back to school. Walking to school as dusk falls is a different kind of experience. I know the paths well enough to not trip or fall. There is a special way of putting each foot down so as to anticipate the errant ~~se~~ stone or root; one treads lightly, anticipating the ~~bility~~ of a rolled ankle or lapse in grip. But I know ~~he~~ big falls might happen, and as long as there ~~ding~~ light, or bright moonlight, I have grown ~~moving~~ briskly on these walks. The fog has

crisp air is settling in
must be more
he road,
the larger
risk because they
to drive confidently

happily
arrangements
the other's
gets hurt. The
res slightly
Was
fed. A
ge. Yes,
cially
o be

Saturday nights are a busy time on campus, with activities happening for several different groups all at the same time. But the happy melee of the children is a perfect antidote to a day spent brooding over gaps in one's life that cannot be easily filled. In the din of the dining hall it is easier to forget the image of caressing hands. I can sit with some of the other teachers who will soon be on duty, or maybe even with some of the students. Then there will almost certainly be an activity or two that I could drop in on, or chaperone, to distract myself. I can think of several teachers who would be only too happy to be relieved of this responsibility.

In truth, I enjoy watching the older kids play basketball. It's usually several vigorous half-court games happening all at once, but it's also a subtle jockeying for social currency. The social leaders aren't always the best at the game, but they have to be good enough to be credible. The star players are obvious – this is their world. And then there are the quieter ones, hanging around the periphery, watching and waiting to be invited when the game requires more players, but never starting a game of their own or ordering anybody else off the courts. I look for them, I suppose, because they are like I was. Watching. Trying to figure it out. Not really sure if they even want to.

Of course, I cannot watch for too long. There is a permissible amount of time that a teacher can watch students in unstructured activities. I would put it at about five minutes – longer, of course, if there's a really exciting game on. Occasionally, I join in. It quickly becomes obvious how much faster a sixteen-year-old boy can move in unexpected directions, but experience and anticipation help my case. Tonight, one of the chaperones is happy to be relieved of his duty to oversee the weekly dance that takes place in the auditorium. I wave him off, and he thanks me profusely, promising to return the favour soon. I can't be too obvious that he is doing me a favour, too. I find longer stretches of time at home by myself unsettling, but particularly on a day like today when it seems that even Koshy has managed to find himself some company.

I'm a lazy chaperone. The kids dance in little groups, while some of the couples split into pairs. The song very much dictates who stays or leaves the dance floor, some songs being more amenable to social dancing, while a few are geared towards a more intimate interaction. I am still not sure why we allow the latter kind. I'm supposed to tell them not to dance too close to each other, but at some point it really becomes a question of judgement; and of willingness to intervene constantly, because at any one time there are always one or two couples getting entwined in some quiet corner or wandering off from the auditorium to find a dark, private spot. Do I follow them? And if so, which one? And then, do I tell my fellow chaperone where I'm going? It all becomes too cumbersome too quickly. I pacify myself with the thought that the students know who I am. They know I won't intervene unless something truly egregious is going on.

With each change in song, some kids will walk in while others will trickle out of the auditorium. A few of my students wave to me as they walk in or out, and occasionally they will stop to chat. Ultimately, I have learnt to trust them to be themselves. They are figuring themselves out. They are figuring each other out. There's a group of kids who will firmly believe that who they are in this short, frenzied stage of their lives is who they will always be. And there's a quieter, less visible group that realizes that things will not always be the way they are now. Do they enjoy that, or look forward to the change that comes after school? I don't know, but I suspect they see it with some trepidation. Another couple leaves the dance, arm in arm. I make a visual note that they have turned towards the darkened driveway that passes along the side of the auditorium. 'Not too far, you two!' I call after them, and they quickly spring apart and look back at me. They pause and pretend to walk slowly back, deep in suddenly intellectual conversation. I typically don't do any more than this. After all, one wouldn't want to become known as another Perkins type.

The story of Perkins is a primer in what not to do at a residential boarding school. He was a strapping, devout man who coached girls' softball, and taught religious education and applied philosophy. I also suspect he mixed the subject matter from the two classes up quite a lot. Though he meant well, in truth Perkins often took the desire to do right by his God and his church too far. There was the incident where he had stormed into a joint yoga session for students and alumni, holding his cross out before him and beseeching participants to renounce the ways of the devil. And then there was his predilection for assisting in the girls' baptisms rather too enthusiastically; there was no risk of drowning and the girls were definitely old enough to not need help drying themselves afterwards. But he lost the sympathy of his colleagues entirely when he tried to intimidate a veteran teacher during a staff meeting by standing nose to nose and shouting, 'Who do you think you are?' A mincing apology followed several days later.

What really destroyed his last shred of credibility was that – on nights like this one, with the school buzzing with student activities – he had taken to following wayward teenagers around the darker corners of the school's campus. It turns out he would spy silently on them, allowing the heavy petting to progress to an obviously inappropriate stage before suddenly shining his flashlight on the pair of teens, catching them in the act. It never dawned on Perkins that his surreptitious methods jeopardized the possibility of taking any disciplinary action afterwards. After all, how could he possibly have caught the errant teenagers if he hadn't been standing there watching for a while? Pointing this out to Perkins did not curb his eager vigilance. None of the administrators believed the students who complained about Perkins's behaviour either.

So it continued until that one fateful night. Perkins had shimmied his way up into a tree branch to ensure a suitable vantage point, but his movements to locate and aim his flashlight must have proved an unbearable stress on the limb. It snapped loudly; Perkins, flashlight and branch fell a distance of almost ten feet, and the two teenagers – who had been busy fondling each other up to this point – found themselves thrust into the position of temporary medics. The other canoodling couples in the vicinity, who had also been enjoying the relative privacy, all emerged slowly with the goal of 'helping', but it was up to yours truly and a few other teachers to ultimately transport Perkins's substantial personage to the dispensary. For a year afterwards, chaperones checking to make sure students were not behaving inappropriately would be met with a gleeful 'Perkins?'! After that incident, Perkins was hard-pressed to explain his injuries. One thing led to another, and soon even the muscular evangelism of his well-funded Kansas church could not save him from the ignominy of explaining the facts to the local police officers. With some hilarity, the policemen informed the school that while this could become a police matter, they would prefer not to have to deal with foreign staff members with such unusual proclivities. Perhaps the school would like to handle the matter internally? Darling and Chapman quickly agreed that they would very much like to do so. In a letter to students and parents, it was soon clarified that Perkins would be returning home to Kansas with great urgency for some unspecified reason.

At least Perkins made an impression – if only being good for a laugh. On days like this one, when I am left to my thoughts despite the activity all around me, I do wonder what I will be remembered for. Or, for that matter, how this year could be made more memorable than any others that came before. Perhaps I should finally do something about Ms Little-K. I wonder what it would be like to have her company on my porch, and sit and watch the fog together. Or how we could lie together, and how much I would like to trace the shape of her body, and hold each other close while the shadows of the day moved around my room.

The image of the hands, clinging ecstatically, returns to me. It seems the evening's efforts to distract myself have been in vain. Can I even conjure the image for myself? Ms Little-K's silver-stained hands tousling my hair? I put one hand up to see how it feels, but that doesn't do it at all. For now I'm a grown man, standing alone outside a high school dance on a Saturday night, scratching my head and hoping to conjure a feeling that doesn't appear.

10

Plans and Providence

The success of the inaugural Reverend's Walk, or Mrs Haight's eager recollection of it to all who would listen, established Finley's reputation as an outdoorsman. For his part, Finley realized that this reputation brought with it significant advantages. He was now able to take time to privately scout out new trails. These outings were ripe for quiet rumination, a time to gather and parse the raw material for upcoming sermons. He now had ample opportunity to reflect on how the hand of God, His art as it were, was present in all things. The complex, intertwined growth of the forest might be seen as an impediment – and for many of the farming estates seeking their fortunes in these hills, perhaps they were. But they might just as easily be seen as a protective cover – the best kind, which supported a wide range of fruiting trees and flowering plants as well as wildlife in the form of deer, panther, monkeys and assorted colourful birds – all while protecting from heat, rain and even lightning. The forests, Finley noticed, were resilient; they did not catch fire, they held the earth tight when torrents of rain made the soil of the estates prone to landslides, and even in the hottest weather they retained a cool stillness that could not be found elsewhere. Surely, Finley wondered, Eden may have appeared similar to Adam and Eve as they wandered through it. Perhaps God had Himself felt some remorse in having to expel the wayward pair. Of all the trees and all the fruit in Eden, would Adam or Eve have been drawn to that particular fruit if God had simply omitted to mention its existence? Did God not bear some responsibility for drawing special attention to that particular tree? Surely, telling a child 'Do not touch this' is what plants the seed of curiosity in the child's mind. Perhaps God should have pursued a path of distraction, or planted the apple tree on some distant, remote outcrop within Eden where neither Adam nor Eve could find it. From this line of thought emerged Finley's next sermon on how, even in our failings and Original Sin, the Bible had provided the lesson to 'lead us not into temptation'.

Finley would usually be accompanied by Cherian on these private explorations. He had paid mind to Rumson's chiding about not necessitating a search party. Who better to bring along than the man who best understood the nature of these hills. On more than one occasion, Cherian would find Finley a path that skirted around a precipitous drop or a particularly difficult climb. And he seemed to possess an innate grasp of how to pace oneself, especially when exploring new routes. This was especially true when the climb on the way out from the hotel in sunlit, favourable conditions would change dramatically, and thick fog or driving rain soured their return journey. Cherian also educated Finley on the importance of making noise and talking or whistling, especially in fog or fading light. Snakes and bear do not take well to being surprised. Elephant herds can disperse unnoticed over large areas, and one does not want to find oneself unwittingly near a juvenile – the mother is likely to take aggressive measures against any interloper. The experiences of Finley's youth, while physically vigorous, could not have prepared him for these concerns, and he was grateful for Cherian's guidance. Cherian, in turn, had found out he could be of service by marking the trail while Finley made sketches and detailed notes on hand-drawn maps.

Perhaps there was another purpose at work here as well. Sometime ago, Cherian had grown tired of the domestic chores that consumed most of his days working for Harrison at the hotel. While he might have sought other work, Cherian knew he was too old to join the sepoys; whatever rank he could now achieve would not pay what he earned at the hotel. And the risks to life and limb were far greater in that line of work.

Cherian knew where he stood in this current

employment arrangement. He was supposed to know enough English to understand commands and requests, even surprising the guests sometimes by appearing to intuit what would be needed next. Harrison could count on him for the confident and timely dispatch of the many duties that he could not entrust to anyone else. Crucially, Cherian also knew when not to reveal any further understanding of what was being exchanged. He studiously ignored the subtle undercurrents of a too-curt greeting; the lecher's gaze towards other men's wives following the fifth or sixth whisky; the quiet comings and goings of domestic staff who had spent time alone with their masters or mistresses in ways they should not have.

What shocked him deeply, for a man who otherwise prided himself on his grasp on the world, was the gaze of boredom with which a husband and wife could sometimes regard each other: the shared but unspoken realization between two people, while yoked together, that if given the choice they would choose to have nothing to do with one another in a private life of their own construction. It seemed a great tragedy that such a fate should befall two people at once. He worried that this may unexpectedly creep up on him too. Consequently, Cherian had no family, and apart from the occasional tryst with a woman in a village several hours' walk from the hotel, had no aspirations of starting one.

Given all this, Cherian was only too happy to accompany

Finley on his explorations. The walking was not always easy, but he could usually anticipate the patterns of the trails that would lie ahead. Most of the trails were narrow and created by goatherds. Cows could not travel as easily through the thicker jungle or handle the steeper rocky gradients. Over time, a new pattern of interaction emerged between the two men. On one occasion, he had to grab Finley by the arm and pull him back as Finley began to descend a root-covered piece of ground that curved downhill in the fog. Cherian showed him how to pick up a small stone and throw it ahead; if it made no sound back through the fog, there might be a steep drop-off in that direction and it was unsafe to move forward. Only if the stone made the sound of hitting nearby ground or wood should they proceed.

Finley had initially turned red from annoyance at being grabbed suddenly by the arm, and then blanched when Cherian showed him the test with the stone; Finley quickly grasped the implication of what Cherian was telling him. 'Thank you, Cherian . . .' Finley said quietly. And the two sat down for a while with their backs to the hill, staring out into the blank wall of fog that surrounded them. 'Why don't you walk ahead of me for a while?' After this incident, when alone, both men would drop the formalities that had to accompany their interactions when being observed by others. By tacit agreement, the formality would return upon their re-entering the town and the hotel compound, or during walks where others were present.

In a short time, the Reverend's Walk – usually Tuesdays or Saturdays, and in some weeks, both days – had become an institution. The only person this did not please was Harrison, who found it an encumbrance on two fronts. First, his valued foreman had been whisked away by Finley on pointless exploratory jaunts. And then, with the Reverend's Walk becoming more of a fixture in the hotel's calendar of weekly events, there was a new set of catering responsibilities to be accounted for. Finley did not appreciate the extent of Harrison's irritation until one evening, when he commented on what an invaluable assistant Cherian had become.

In an attempt to recognize Cherian's efforts in this matter, Finley opined to Harrison, 'Your man Cherian is proving a most capable squire on our walks!'

'That's just as well, Reverend! I certainly notice his absence with regard to his responsibilities at the hotel,' Harrison replied, a little more quickly than would have been natural.

'Ah, I must confess, I had not anticipated that Cherian's absence would create a difficulty for you.' Finley felt suddenly beholden in a way he did not like. 'I was merely praising the fine training he has received in your employ.'

'Fair enough, Finley. I reckon he knows these hills well and can serve as a very able guide. Perhaps we ought to craft a more predictable arrangement so that he can also discharge his duties here at the hotel.' Harrison seemed to have prepared the arrangement well in advance of this conversation.

'Certainly, Harrison, he is in your employ, after all.'

'Would it constrain you terribly if we restricted his off-compound activities to two days of the week at most? Perhaps one for the planning and then another day for the occasion of the Reverend's Walk?'

'That would be most generous . . .'

'An acceptable arrangement, then!' Harrison replied, rapidly closing the conversation.

Finley felt strangely outmanoeuvred. He had not wanted to impose upon Harrison, but had obviously done so. Perhaps he was wearing out his welcome at the hotel. Now might be a good time to attend to his original goals of ministering to souls beyond Her Majesty's British subjects. But how should he do this? It was in this pensive frame of mind that Finley got up to leave the terrace and walk towards the stairs down to his cabin.

'Reverend!' The voice was shrill and commanded attention. It was Mrs Rumson, the elder, and she was making her way up the lawn with some haste. A grim and purposeful scowl set on her face.

'Yes, Mrs Rumson?' Finley retorted, startled by the force of her summons.

'Reverend, I must seek your advice. Truthfully, all sense

of propriety is being tested in the most unacceptable of ways!'

'Certainly, Mrs Rumson. I was just about to . . .'

'It's that wretched Evelyn Haight. Would you believe she has convinced our dear Alice that she must behave in a similarly shocking manner to attract the attentions of young Master Cadbury!'

Finley realized that he would not be repairing to his own cottage as he had planned. 'I am afraid I do not follow.'

'No, of course you don't, Reverend. It's not for a man of the cloth to be preoccupied with such trifles. Unfortunately, the rest of us must attend to them in some form. Really, I thought by having two sons these matters were behind me at my stage in life.'

'Perhaps you would care to elaborate from the beginning, Mrs Rumson?' Finley added helpfully. There was little else he could say. The pair walked back again to the main buildings and took their places under an awning on the terrace. And Mrs Rumson held forth as to what it was that had so agitated her.

It turns out that Evelyn Haight had been providing Alice Rumson, her junior by almost three years, advice on attracting the attentions of Master Cadbury. The asymmetry lay not only in the difference in age and maturity, but the fact that Evelyn had, for some time, it seemed, been trifling with young Cadbury's attentions, knowing full well that Alice also fancied Master Cadbury, but in a more wholesome and innocent manner. She had now sought to provide some elder-sisterly advice, announcing that as she, Evelyn, was soon to leave India and be presented to society in London, it wouldn't hurt if Alice stepped up and made herself more obvious to young Cadbury. But it was the substance of Evelyn's advice that caused the matriarch the greatest consternation. In fact, Mrs Rumson had caught Alice in the act of loosening her bodice so as to reveal more of her décolletage. And on being pressed, a flustered Alice revealed that Evelyn had suggested this course of action, as it was most likely to garner young Cadbury's attention. Evelyn could after all claim, with some authority, that young Cadbury paid more attention to what was high up and in front, rather than under hoop skirt. Having now grasped the bones of the grandmother's concern, Finley was irritated as to why this was being brought to his attention. Or, truth be told, how he could possibly be helpful in such matters.

'Here is what it comes to, Reverend,' Mrs Rumson went on, moving from narrative to directive. 'This is the natural folly and mischief of youth! These children have far too much latitude and insufficient instruction in the productive manner in which to spend their days.'

'Surely, Mrs Rumson, this is a matter for parental guidance, is it not?' Finley was thinking of the last time he had ventured to comment on this to Eliza Rumson, and how he had been left feeling distinctly out of his depth.

'One might suppose that, Reverend! But parents can achieve scant discipline when they are preoccupied with their own affairs.' And then realizing the implication of what she had said, she quickly added, 'And by that, I mean their own duties and daily tasks! This is why we have nannies and tutors, and when they are older, we send them off to boarding school. There, the teachers and administrators are free to shape youth's follies with a firm hand and guide them away from this moral turpitude!'

Finley sat silent. There seemed little to add to this very sound proclamation, and he had no reason to disagree.

Sensing that there would be no useful retort from Finley, Mrs Rumson threw down the gauntlet in a huff. 'Reverend, then I must put it to you that the shepherd should tend to the needs of the flock he has before him and not the one he wishes for at some future time!' And with that, she turned and strode into the hotel's corridors, leaving a perplexed Finley in her wake.

'An aperitif, Reverend?' Chester stood at Finley's elbow with a glass of sherry. In his purposeful absence of facial expression, Finley was able to discern that Chester had overheard the conversation, and that perhaps Finley needed some steadying. 'Would the Reverend prefer something stronger?'

Finley smiled. 'The sherry will be fine. Thank you, Chester.' Chester retreated with a bow, the smallest smirk of a friendly smile in his eyes. 'Would you be so kind as to bring some sandwiches down to my cabin in twenty minutes, Chester?' Finley said this quietly, but purposefully. Chester was not his valet, but Finley surmised that the man had seen enough of Mrs Rumson and her sort to provide useful counsel in her handling and care.

Finley moved briskly down the wooden steps to the field and towards his cabin. His feet seemed to work by themselves to carry him rapidly away from the scene of the exchange with Mrs Rumson. Arriving at his cabin, he closed the door and drew the curtains. Luckily, Cherian was not in the cabin, and Finley felt that even the bright sunshine outside was too much of an intrusion at this point. He sat down heavily and slumped his head, as if in prayer. A heavy, tightening sensation had begun to take form in his chest, and he could tell that its source lay in the elder Rumson's parting comment. So now he, Finley, was no longer a passing guest or prop in the scenery. Mrs Rumson was challenging him to play a part – play *his* part – in shepherding the flock. Were the weekly sermon and Reverend's Walks not sufficient?

The cabin, the hotel, the people in it, even the beautiful surroundings, had been in cahoots; conspiring together to ensnare Finley. To take his youth and vitality and attentions and bend it to their designs. After all, what was it that made the rich, dark soil so fertile, the surrounding forests so lush and green, if not the gradual surrender of all living things? Life piled on life. And now, despite his intentions to dedicate himself to spreading God's word, he was to be curtailed; his plans of ministry turned on the misdeeds of errant children and their cajoling, chiding grandmothers. And all the while, he could see that duty and reciprocity required it. After all, had the Rumsons not opened their home to him? Had they not brought him to this beautiful outpost in the hills and shared of their treasure? And had Finley forsworn all this? No, he had not. He had even made a home for himself. Carved himself a purpose on Sunday mornings and Wednesday afternoons. Perhaps, unbeknownst to him, God had intended this to be Finley's path, after all.

A crisp double knock on the door brought Finley's reverie to an abrupt halt. 'Come,' he replied.

Chester stepped in nimbly, bearing what was indeed a plate of sandwiches, which he placed on the table. He took a step back, staring into middle distance. 'Your sandwiches, Reverend.'

Finley briefly studied the man's waistcoat. The buttons were polished; his boots were polished. Chester either had no idea of the turmoil in Finley's mind, or had become expert at revealing nothing of the things he knew.

'Chester, do sit down!' Finley barked.

'Yes, sir.' He seated himself carefully on the edge of the chair, ready to spring to a standing position at any time.

'And stop calling me Sir! "James" or "Finley" will

suffice. Or "Reverend Finley", if we are in public and you wish to avoid familiarity.' Chester nodded assent. 'For now, let us dispense with the proprieties, Chester.' Finley launched into a retelling of the many things that burdened him. He considered his fellow Cornishman an automatic ally and assumed Chester felt the same way.

Chester waited till Finley had stopped talking before replying, which he did in very careful measured tones. 'Sir. Finley. If I may.'

'You may, you may . . .'

'I have been with the Haights a long time. My family has been so even longer. I came up as a little boy on their estate. And I have seen several churchmen come – and go.'

'I fail to comprehend, Chester.' Finley felt himself becoming uncharacteristically brusque. Perhaps Haight's manner was influencing him. He tried to soften his tone. 'Do continue, Chester. I am momentarily not myself.'

'These families. Haight, Rumson. Them that has. They see themselves as visionary heralds of civilization. To bring light where there would be darkness otherwise. What they fail to consider is that the brightest light, except for that moment at high noon, also casts the darkest shadows in which to hide.'

'Go on.'

'If I have grasped your quandary, Finley, then you wish to be of service to something worthwhile in the eyes of God. You cannot square how ministering to Englishmen, or their wayward, mischievous children, in the far reaches of Her Majesty's dominion fulfils your own desires to bring Christ to the heathen.'

'Precisely, you have grasped the very essence of my concerns!'

'If you will allow me, I would like to share something that may place a different perspective on your situation.' He paused for a moment to shuffle his feet, and sat back a little further on the seat of his chair. 'The same wayward youth who once pursued the milkmaids from his horse, is now Mr Andrew Haight, Her Majesty's Collector for a substantial tract of southern India. Perhaps you have heard of Archbishop Norcross?'

'Norcross, yes . . . A most revered name in the church.'

'Archbishop Norcross was once Reverend Norcross. And as a young chaplain he stayed with the Haights in Cornwall for a period of seven months. He rode and walked and argued with young master Andrew for all that time. And at the end of that visit, Andrew Haight forswore the dalliances that had once so distracted him, choosing instead to join Her Majesty's government in the East.'

'I did not know that the Haights and Norcross were well acquainted, Chester. But what has this to do with my situation?'

'Permit me to complete the narrative. With master Andrew now on his way to becoming a respectable young man, his parents felt greatly indebted to Norcross. And Norcross, like you, had ambitions beyond pastoral care in sleepy village estates across England. Lord and Lady Haight endowed him with a purse to travel to the Indies and Barbados. And it was there that Norcross worked with Reverend Dr Coleridge, establishing schools for slave children. He even established the first school for training clergy in those parts. Coleridge went on to become Bishop of Barbados, and Norcross served under him before returning to England and becoming bishop himself.'

'Norcross must be industrious indeed. He richly deserves the honours accorded to him!'

'I fear you have missed the thrust of my story, Finley. Norcross came to be recognized because of his tutelage of younger charges. These charges, in turn, grew into the members of society that their parents and pedigree required. That, in time, afforded Norcross the ability to spread the word of God in more distant soil that had not yet received that seed.'

The faintest traces of Chester's message began to take shape in Finley's mind. 'Ah, I see, Chester. You wish to suggest that Mrs Rumson's exhortation to tend to this flock would allow me to establish ministry for the native heathens that live around us?'

'Perhaps, Reverend. We certainly have a precedent. And it would become a question of imagination and assiduous application of one's energies. Any counsel that could tame the likes of Ms Evelyn and her peers would be favourably regarded by their parents.'

'I see ...'

Chester permitted himself some levity. 'And consider, Reverend, the guests at the hotel ... Can you see a more capable shepherd than yourself?'

Finley felt the grip in his chest loosen. He turned to the sandwiches Chester had brought and helped himself to one. The first mouthful was delicious. Realizing he had forgotten his manners, Finley quickly pushed the plate towards Chester. 'Please, do help yourself!'

'Thank you, Finley. I normally would not, but I believe I shall now.'

Finley rose and pulled back the curtains. The sun streamed back in through the windows. And the two men sat for a good time, contemplating the delicious flavours of the cucumber inside the sandwiches.

'I should return to my duties.' Chester sprang up from his chair. 'Reverend, please do not think me impertinent, but I would appreciate if you treated our exchange with the appropriate discretion. The matter of Reverend Norcross is not widely known in these parts.'

'Of course, Chester. I understand.'

With the afternoon sun continuing to cheer brightly outside, Finley decided to take a walk and clear his mind. He preferred to avoid most of the hotel, and its occupants, by walking to the boathouse and turning left to take the path that ran alongside the lake. As he approached the boathouse, he could see the lily pads were in full flower, bright whites and purples stippled with yellow, sitting on leathery green pads.

'Reverend! Reverend Finley!'

He turned to see Eliza Rumson waving from a boat in the middle of the water. It would have been blocked from view by the boathouse, but she was rowing vigorously to draw alongside him on the water. Finley stopped to wait for her.

'Be careful, Mrs Rumson. Those lily beds have a way of entangling the oars.' Her ayah sat at the bow end of the boat. Andrew was leaning over one side at the stern, clearly entranced by something he had seen in the dark green murkiness.

'Speaking of entanglements, Reverend . . .' and for a while she struggled with her own hair that had come loose under her hat and was blowing over her face. In that brief moment before she could look up, Finley noticed how her skin was flushed from the effort of rowing, and how her cheeks glowed. He studied the slight upturn at the end of her nose and the fullness of her lips. She looked him full in the face and Finley felt an unsteadiness in the ground at his feet. It hurt to look directly at her.

Eliza must have seen him wince. 'Are you all right, Reverend?' she asked, concerned. Her eyes twinkled and the mouth could not resist breaking into a smile. Finley didn't know how to reply. He could not form the words, and his chest felt a different kind of tightening. He managed to nod in response.

When Finley nodded, she continued: 'I wanted to thank you, Reverend. Alice and Andrew thoroughly enjoyed the Reverend's Walk. Perhaps I may accompany you on some future occasion?' Observing that her son's curiosity might lead him to fall in, she added, 'Andrew, for goodness' sake! Say hello to the Reverend!' The boy's head sprang up from the water and he turned and saluted.

'Good afternoon, Andrew,' Finley replied.

'Well, I will leave you to your walk,' Eliza continued. 'I must return and dress for dinner. Do please invite me to chaperone a future walk, Reverend!'

'Thank you, Mrs Rumson. That would be delightful.'

Taking leave was awkward. Finley detected something in Eliza's flushed glance that suggested she had more to say. But perhaps it was the struggle with the oars as she turned the boat towards the centre of the lake. Finley thought it best to doff his hat and continue with a purposeful stride, not looking back for several moments. By the time he allowed himself a glance, the boat was making steady progress across the path of the sun and back towards the centre of the lake. Continuing to the other side of the green, Finley traced his steps away from town and towards the short scramble on to the narrow walking path he had discovered. This was where he would come to contemplate. On days when the fog rolled in, he would have to keep one hand on the hillside so as to not make a misstep towards the valley below. Today the sky was clear, and even though he was no longer on the sunward side because it was late afternoon, the shadows had not yet lengthened. Most of the valley below was illuminated in bright green.

With the bright light, he could have made brisk progress along the ledge that curved around the hillside. But the events of the day demanded a slower cadence, and Finley reflected on how the rocks on the path, some loosened from the soil but most stuck firm in the mud and roots underfoot, supported him on his path. It was his responsibility to walk around or over the obstacles. Mrs Rumson's challenge, to tend to the flock in front of him, still rankled. Perhaps recent events were also mere obstacles – a large rock in the road to steer around. Or perhaps, as Chester had suggested, this was an opportunity. A hill to be climbed that would open up vistas beyond that could not be seen from where he stood today.

The 'flock in front of him' – surely Mrs Rumson had meant the guests at the hotel and their children. But should the flock not also comprise the staff, the people in the kitchens, their children? Would not Christ's love and teaching be even more valuable to their souls? Finley chided himself – perhaps it was possible to be overly ambitious or gluttonous, even when it came to saving souls. He was not, after all, gathering bales of hay. Perhaps it was best to begin with that which was most familiar. Perhaps he should tend to the young souls of the guests at the hotel first.

But how? He was loath to give up his private walks around the hills; they were the closest he had come to seeing God's art and sensing His presence all around. And addressing the very specific matter that the elder Mrs Rumson had brought to his attention seemed overly intrusive; how would one begin such a conversation? No, there had to be a more constant, powerful way of sharing the teachings of Christ. Incidental conversations or whispers about improprieties would not do. Whatever lessons he, Finley, wished to impart, had to be brought into the light, dragged if necessary and shown in their full glory. But when would he impart such lessons? How could he hold an audience with the children in a way that would have them sparing him their attention without distraction?

The answer, once it presented itself, seemed obvious! He would offer to conduct some summer lessons – in the correct subjects, of course. The Bible. Rhetoric, and some mathematics, could also follow. And he could understand what stories were most readily taught and absorbed. This could be the foundation for future ministry with the natives nearby! Finley's chest felt as though it would leap forward and off the hill at this final thought. It was as if the pieces of a puzzle, covered in grime and long ignored, had been magically dusted off and had rearranged themselves voluntarily into a picture of a ministry that could be.

It occurred to Finley that of all the signs of God he had seen, this day might be taken as one such. The sparkling afternoon sunshine, the clear path, the pristine view of the valley below and the unhindered view of the plains that lay beyond. It was rare to obtain this uninterrupted view from such a great distance. Finley pondered the nature of grace and what manner of foresight a creator must have to make such a reality possible – rich in both what was allowed to exist, but also in matters of fortune, timing and happenstance. And because he was looking out over the plains, Finley failed to notice what was right in front of him. On his favourite promontory, the bushes once nestled together in browns and greens had burst forth into a carpet of brilliant purple. The surrounding greens added to the contrast, and Finley staggered back in surprise. His breath and the tightness in his chest seemed to escape all at once, and he sank down on the moss. If ever God had wished to make a gesture, then here, surely, was that sign.

11

Back for Another Look

After so many years, I am still not inured to the shock a student feels upon learning that she may not be able to go to college because she cannot pay for it. For me it creates a sour and irritating heartburn. Of course, the aspiration is sparked early in life, stoked over the years by parents and relatives, sometimes even by other teachers. To be then handed a massive bill seems a cruel deception that only reveals itself years after the product has been talked about, dressed up, desired. It is the least rewarding thing any teacher must do, to inform a talented and motivated student that, for reasons entirely outside her own control, she should now lower her sights. Whenever possible, I try to avoid doing so, even though the notion of managing one's expectations does not easily take root in a teenager's mind.

By the time the first round of applications is dispatched in late October, an adaptation will have occurred and the disappointment stings less. In prior years, I have tried to dodge these painful conversations, but what is the worth of a teacher who abdicates when a student needs him most? Some students, perhaps due to earlier troubles with their grades or precarious family finances, will have already had the tough conversations with their parents. Several others will rely on their parents' means to carry them through, much as they did through their school years. But for a handful, this time can be a deeply crushing few weeks. For those kids, after sufficient gritting of teeth and cursing at photocopiers, a wish for the future is released into the world in the form of college essays stuffed into manila envelopes. All one can do then is hope for the best. And wait.

For now, my main concern is with Tarun M, who will soon park himself in my office to discuss his situation. I wish I had something new to say, but it is likely the conversation will play out as it has done in years before.

'Come in, Tarun,' I say, as he pokes his face into my office. 'Please, have a seat. Tell me – how's your semester going?'

'Very good, Mr G! Exams are good so far. So far, I'm doing well.'

'Yes, I finished grading your maths exam. A few small mistakes, from what I remember, but quite good!'

'Thanks, Mr G.' The conversation trails off awkwardly, and I realize it is my role to pick it back up again.

'So, Tarun. We are supposed to talk about your college plans, right? The application deadlines will be here soon, so have you given thought to what your plans will be? Or what you want to do?'

'No, Mr G. I'm not sure.'

'Well, what do you want to study? Or what do you want to do afterwards?'

'I don't know, Mr G. My grades are pretty good in all subjects. I really want to travel, but I don't think you can study that in college.'

'What do your parents say?'

'My father's business isn't doing well, Mr G.' Tarun looks down at his shoes. 'We have not talked about college applications. But I heard him telling my mother that there might not be much money left next year. So I don't know if I will be able to pay capitation fees.' Tarun's family runs a food export business, from what I remember. They live in town, and Tarun also gets some reduction in fees based on need.

'You're talking about capitation fees. Have you decided that you are staying in India?'

'I don't know, Mr G. I can't afford to go abroad . . .'

'Look, Tarun, your grades are good. Why don't you do some checking? You don't have to look only in India, because there are also scholarships that you could apply for to go abroad. And of course, you can still apply in India as well. But enough about this. Let's talk about what you want to study.'

'That's just it, Mr G. I don't know. My father wants me to take over the business eventually. He thinks I should study business. And go to a bigger place so that I can make some useful contacts to help grow the business.'

'Is that what you want to do?'

Tarun swallows before continuing. 'I don't know, Mr G. My parents work very hard in their business, and I don't want to say no to them. They've given up a lot to get me in here. I don't really want to work in the business, but I just can't tell them that.'

It occurs to me that the doors leading out of childhood should be emblazoned with the words: 'Close securely – Avoid contamination of childhood dreams.' I can tell that Tarun is staring at my face and waiting for clarity. Except I don't have any, so I look at the collar of his T-shirt and notice that the seam is fraying. The whole school seems to have gone quiet, as if waiting on my next words.

'Look, Tarun. You don't have to know what you want to study right now. First, go talk to Mrs H. She has a list of colleges and universities abroad that can provide scholarships and will let you apply on the Common Application. And we can fill in the financial aid paperwork together so you won't have to pay the application fees.' I had not intended the last few words to sting, but they do. Tarun's mouth contorts to one side, as if he's tasted something unpleasant.

'Do I have to tell my parents about the application fee being waived?'

'No, not if you don't want to ...'

'I don't want them to know ... I don't want to embarrass them.'

'Nobody but you, me and Mrs H need to know about this,' I reply. 'But you should definitely tell them that you are applying abroad! Otherwise, what will you say to them as you get closer to graduation?'

'I was thinking about taking a year off after school, Mr G. And maybe doing the IIT prep course and taking the exam. I have a cousin who did the course full-time for a year and then got in.'

'That's a good idea! Do you want to study engineering?'

'Not really. But IIT has much lower fees – if you can get in. And my parents would be very pleased!'

'Yes, of course, Tarun. But you also have to get out the other end, don't you? Why don't you take some time to think about this more? And talk to Mrs H soon, please, you don't want to miss the application deadlines!'

'Okay, Mr G.' He seems tired and put upon. I feel I have to press the point home a little bit more; teenagers can often agree to get away from the situation without any real intention of following up.

'So how about this time next week, Tarun? You'll come

and tell me what you found? I'll send Mrs H a note right now so that she will know it's urgent. Okay?'

'Yes, Mr G. Next week.' He still sounds non-committal and looks at me with an old man's gaze.

'I know it's scary, but we will find something, okay? You have many talents, Tarun!' I smile and nod to add some enthusiasm of my own to the words.

'Yes, Mr G.' He gets up to leave, and his movements are more purposeful than the tone of his voice would suggest. He leaves the door ajar for a moment, but then his face is back again. 'Mr G?'

'Yes?'

'Have you seen students like me get into college?' His eyes rest on me in a dilated gaze and he is swallowing hard. He doesn't realize how tragic the question sounds; teenagers don't know enough to separate their personal qualities from their immediate circumstances.

'Yes, Tarun. I have. Many times.' I lie.

'Okay.'

'Oh, and Tarun, there's one important thing you have to remember. You will have to believe in yourself, too. I believe you can do it, but this is not going to be Mr G pushing to get Tarun into college. Are we clear?'

'Yes, Mr G, we're clear.' And he gives me the first real grin I've seen in the entire conversation.

The walk home is a relaxing one. I hope Tarun does the thinking I ask him to do. He will be fine, but only if he applies himself. Sometimes, with children like him, you have to express faith in them before they have any faith in themselves. Somewhere between learning to walk and the end of middle school, children lose that faith. And the reflective ones – like Tarun – can't locate it again on their own. They become aware of the difficulties and limits of the world too early, so reasons for apathy come more readily than reasons to press on. Remedial optimism ought to be a school subject.

As I turn the last corner towards Penrose Cottage, I pass Koshy's place tucked away down the path on my left. There's a light shining from the windows on to the porch, and the ringing sounds of a piano carrying on the air. I don't recognize the piece, but I stop briefly to listen. Koshy must be practising something new, because there are stretches where the music stops abruptly and then starts again. Sometimes the phrase repeats, but at half speed, with clear, banging notes.

I think back to the last time I went there and my surprise at catching him during such an intimate moment. Maybe I should go over now and ask him over to dinner this weekend. Hopefully, there won't be anything untoward going on. Maybe he will introduce me to his girlfriend! I start down the path towards Craddock again. The progress this time is easier, as there is no fog and the air is clear. I take the turn to climb on to the lawn in front of the porch.

This time, I confess I am less surprised by what I see,

but I pause anyway. Koshy is not alone. He sits in an undershirt and pyjamas next to a woman, also in the same kind of undershirt, and wearing just her underwear. They are both facing away from the porch windows towards the sheet music at the piano. Her hands, not Koshy's, are on the keys. For some stretches they execute the melody perfectly, then at others, accentuate the notes slowly and in frustrated hammering. They both laugh occasionally, and Koshy wraps his arm around her, caressing the curve of her right hip before pinching her bottom. She slaps him away, attempting the phrase again. Then they turn towards each other and kiss, her arms drawing him into a warm embrace. Her loose hair obscures his face.

The kiss ends, and then they turn again to the music. Another phrase, at first melodious. And then the punctuated, difficult passage again. The difficulty of the music is compounded by the mounting distraction between them, and soon they both sit straddling the piano stool kissing each other. With the slightest turn of Koshy's head, he will see me standing below the porch, looking in. He reaches under the woman's shirt and starts to lift it. It is loose and comes off easily, exposing warm brown skin, taut as she raises her arms to remove the garment.

'Mr G!' A voice startles me, calling from behind. I turn quickly to look. Manish, my neighbours' son, is waving to me, about to walk up the path to Craddock. I don't want to be caught in the middle of this situation, so I decide to cut him off and walk quickly towards him.

'Oh, hi Manish!'

'What's going on, Mr G? Is everything okay at Mr Koshy's place?'

'Yes, I was walking home, and I stopped to listen to some music.'

'Oh, that's nice. He's supposed to be very good. Very popular with the high school girls, as well!' he adds with an impish grin.

I pretend not to notice the comment. 'Well, it must be quite tricky, because he's practising hard. I didn't want to distract him. Let's head home ...' I start to walk down the path towards my house and, thankfully, Manish follows.

'Are you in a rush, Mr G? You're walking very fast!' My desire to leave the area quickly has become too obvious.

'Yes, you know, lots of grading and corrections!'

'I've never seen my parents rush to do more corrections!' As I've noted before, Manish is an astute sort.

Reaching the steps to my front door, I turn and wave to him. 'Have a good night! Say hello to your parents.' Manish waves back and continues walking with that bounding, loping step typical of boys his age after a satisfying day at school. Once inside, I toss aside my bag and remove my shoes while staring out into the gathering dark. Sivakumari's dinner sits arranged neatly on the table. The encounter was a fraught one. Manish could easily have decided that he wanted to hear some music too, and then it would have been embarrassing for all concerned.

And I would have developed a reputation as a peeping tom that would have travelled quickly through the school. And I'm not sure how I could explain my presence to Koshy.

Come to think of it, it really is inconsiderate of Koshy not to mention his girlfriend or fiancé, or whoever that was. Typically, I wouldn't care, but if there are people coming and going, it's good to know about it; who they are, and why they're there. And it's not as if I have ever seen them together on campus, like most other teacher couples. Maybe they're not married or engaged, perhaps that's why I've never seen her on campus. After all, I imagine the administration might not look kindly at a teacher 'living in sin'. I should mention this to him, next time we talk. Of course, I'd have to bring it up in a gentle, offhanded way. Maybe as part of the invitation to dinner? I should probably just talk to him at school and invite him while he's there. That would save me from these now regular intrusions on his love life.

It's not that I resent the presence of Koshy's girlfriend, declared or otherwise. I have to admit, if only to myself, in a passing moment of clarity, it's the absence of my own that bothers me. This is the second time I've chanced on Koshy and his partner, and just like the first time, it leaves me feeling that I have mentally stubbed my toe on some stubborn rock. What appeared to be an innocuous stone to be kicked aside ends up causing me to stumble and fall. Thankfully, this is an internal stumble and I can restore my sense of equilibrium unobserved. Perhaps I should ask Ms Little-K for a walk, by way of restoring the balance? I don't even know how I would start to do that without becoming a bumbling mess. And when, exactly, should I do this? Ask her to my office under the pretence of having a meeting? That would be creepy and probably an abuse of my position as her boss. That's the other thing – so few eligible candidates!

I'm sure the handful of eligible women on this hilltop could say the same. After all, what makes me so uniquely eligible? That I'm a college-educated man in my mid-thirties? Started a teacher, still a teacher, likely a teacher for the foreseeable future? To whom would I seem eligible? Actually, I am a chimera – one of those fragile orchids inside glass bubbles, bred to occupy its unique ecological niche. I move between school and Penrose, partaking of the steady drumbeat of classes, meetings, concerts, assemblies, graduations, that mark the passage of time at a school. Leave the school, drive down from the hilltop, and all of a sudden, none of these rituals and rites carry any weight. Is a priest who has no temple or congregation even a priest? Or would he be considered self-important or delusional? What if I am an eligible bachelor, but only within the context of the school?

During the summers, while travelling to visit my parents outside Calcutta, I appreciate just how odd I must seem to others. The awareness came in stages. The drive down from the hilltop is the first stage. You are greeted with the combined slap of the heat and heavy air of the plains. People mill about, attending to their own business, and the cloak of authority and recognition that surrounds me in school and in town is gone.

At the train station, in the throng of bodies, all pushing to get on to the train, you realize you are but one of many. In this second stage, you are made atomistic – a particle in Brownian motion. You could push on to the carriage, just like the others, or you can stand aside and wait patiently while the first wave of eager passengers clambers on board. Nobody here knows that I am in charge of shaping future scions of the wealthy and famous in our country. And what if they did? A Brownian particle is, by definition, part of the same gas as the others, fated only to make apparently random movements. In the event that one particle felt it was special, and stood apart from the struggles of the others – well, it would still be a particle in a cloud of gas.

The third and final stage is the creation of that insulating bubble that I place around myself as I travel. Occasionally, I toy with the idea that there is another person, just like me, somewhere else on the train. They have also created their own bubble; they also stand aloof, avoiding small talk with fellow travellers. Perhaps we share a similar childhood, steeped in our insular world of books and travel, outside the bustle of bandhs and pujas and extended family wrangling, not even aware that something might be missing. Maybe they are a teacher like me. Perhaps they also spend their journey rereading favourite books in the sweltering upper berth, where the anaemic breeze from the train's ceiling fans does not quite reach. Then, if we come into close physical proximity, and are able to recognize each other, we can join our bubbles.

The danger with bubbles is that they have a tendency to burst when you least expect it. Over the summers, I realize that some of my closest childhood friends have fallen out of our bubbles. Except for our shared past, we can now no longer conceive of ever having occupied the same flimsy enclosure. Their lives are now preoccupied with spouses, children, careers, the mortgage. Or they have been transplanted into other bubbles – the right foursome at the right golf club, the ascendant committee at work. Things we never cared about when we were young. Only a select few have managed to preserve our shared bubble. Despite everyday cares of family, career, ageing parents, they carry in them the warm shared spark that helps us smile together, on the inside. With them, conversations continue as if the intervening two, or four, or eight years have not caused any interruption. At the end of each summer, as I leave the plains and climb back up to my niche in the hills, it is these people that I miss the most. That is how I think about that eligible someone: a person with whom I can join bubbles, without having either one burst. It's a delicate manoeuvre, and can only happen if the surface tensions match just right. And if Koshy has been lucky enough to find that matching bubble, and succeeded in drawing someone close without bursting, how can I begrudge him that?

I have spent more time than I realized contemplating bubbles. My knees are tired from standing and staring into the darkness. There must be a storm coming, as the wind is picking up and I can see faint outlines of trees swaying drunkenly in the distance. I turn my attention to dinner, which will definitely need reheating. Sivakumari must anticipate this, because the tawa to warm up the roti is clean and ready on the stove. And a clean saucepan waits on the other burner to heat up the vegetables she's prepared. In a few minutes, I am sitting down to a warm meal, and with each mouthful I feel my mood improve.

After dinner, I settle down at my desk to begin grading essays. But first I have to read the notes from Mrs Mani about meetings scheduled for tomorrow. The first is with Dr and Mrs Singh. They are making an impromptu visit to town, oh, in fact they are already here, and would like to meet with me about their daughter's college plans. Hmm . . . So that would be Payal again. Wonderful – another possibly tearful and awkward conversation about parents' unfounded aspirations for their daughter's future. Hopefully the young lady has not burnt her portfolio again!

The second is a note scribbled on Chapman's stationery.

It's typical Chapman – over-eager about things we should not concern ourselves with and comically formal:

Ghosh –

Stopped by your office – informed you are teaching a class now.

Do you have leads in the photograph investigation? I would like to forestall any discussions on the matter before we have children travelling home and informing their parents.

Ms Kalyani informs me that she has made no progress on this front. I would like to be informed of any progress you have made.

Sincerely,

Jason Chapman

Vice Principal

For a hand-written note, Chapman need not have added 'Vice Principal' – it's unlikely that I would forget the person who sits in the office next to mine. I mentally compose a suitably witty retort; the version I would want to send, but of course never will. It would have to arrive as a telegram that reads:

No further movement in breast issue STOP Photograph secure STOP

No abnormal chatter re nipples or areolae detected STOP
Parents still unaware STOP Await further instructions
STOP

Tickled by my own construction, I wonder what Chapman, humourless as he is, would do if he were to actually receive such a telegram. I imagine our school postman would hand-deliver it with that 'of course I have not read it' expression that he uses when delivering telegrams deemed too sensitive for the mailboxes. I'll just have to step into Chapman's office tomorrow.

I put aside the two notes and take a deep breath before starting on the first essay.

12

A School Begins

'A capital idea, Finley!' Rumson exclaimed. It was their first meeting after Finley's fateful walk to the place he now thought as the providential overlook. Despite his interaction with the guests at the hotel, Finley still felt an unspoken allegiance to his original host, so it seemed natural to broach the idea with George first. 'I wondered what plans you have been conjuring up on those long walks of yours – closer supervision and instruction of the older children would certainly not go amiss. You are just the person to do it!'

Haight and Cadbury also expressed encouragement, though Haight seemed more circumspect, a marked departure from his usual rambunctious manner. He seemed acutely aware that a Collector's authority could not automatically transfer to pedagogic matters. Perhaps memories of Reverend Norcross played on Haight's mind. The transformation in Haight's manner created an uneasy awareness in Finley. He had grown accustomed to Haight's jocular, ham-fisted charms, but now felt a burden of responsibility settle upon his own shoulders.

The reaction from Mrs Rumson the elder served only to strap that burden on more securely; she immediately took it upon herself to commend Finley's enterprise and suggested that she would soon back that up with generous financial support should the need arise. This made Finley even more uneasy; it was true he did not have an income, but the church made allowances for such things in the form of a stipend that Haight had helped him secure. Now Finley found himself once again unable to remonstrate against the matriarch's demands that hours of instruction should be in the morning and continue for a few hours past lunch, followed by some physical activity. Such an arrangement would, in her estimation, allow sufficient time for the children to rejoin their families and be presentable for dinner, while leaving little room for idleness and mischief. Finley chafed at the notion that his private and largely self-directed daily routine would now be reshaped so drastically by others. And yet, with a growing stillness inside, Finley accepted that perhaps for now this was to be his primary responsibility. As for the other men, they were accustomed to building and administering the infrastructure of empire, so providing instruction to a few young men and women could hardly be considered an undue burden. The person whose opinion he wished to learn the most had simply not proffered one. Eliza Rumson, despite overhearing multiple rounds of excited conversation on the topic, offered nothing more than her warm smile. And this only caused Finley to wonder more as to her true feelings on the subject.

Only Harrison expressed firm reservations about the plan. He made it clear that his primary duty was to run the hotel and he did not see how he could be expected to extend his already busy staff to accommodate the needs of a schoolroom as well. It took some convincing from both Haight and Mrs Rumson (the elder) to point out that this 'school' – Finley noted it was Harrison who had first made regular use of the word – would hardly entail much additional work, as the students were already resident at the hotel. If only he would be so kind as to spare some space and furniture, then the enterprise could begin without delay.

A school needs a location, one large room at least, and a few pieces of furniture at which students and teacher can apply themselves to their lessons. Apparently, there were few options for such a space. The guests did not want a schoolroom too close to their own suites. Haight and the other men were loath to give up their library and desks near the terrace. They made it clear that that particular line of thinking was tantamount to jeopardizing their professional commitment, and so would never do. In the end, it was Harrison who, having warmed to the idea over several days, suggested that the large storeroom above the boathouse could be cleared out. The room was used to store supplies for various activities: extra tables and chairs, miniature lanterns and carpets, and the poles and canvas required for pavilion tents. These would now be moved into the 'kitchens' and sheds near the natives' cottages, and the space would be prepared for the school.

The establishment of a location prompted the first positive twinge of excitement Finley had felt in quite some time. He had not savoured the calm of a classroom since he had left his own seminary, which now felt so very far away in both time and space. If he could pass on to the children just a moment of that peace and introspection that he had so enjoyed, in a classroom of his own, then he would surely be elevating the world in some small way. Finley's aspirations were buoyed even more when he went to look at the space with Harrison. The staff had done some of the moving and cleaning, and there was clearly more to do. Still, Harrison walked him up the stairs and beckoned him in with evident satisfaction.

Finley could see why. It was a large rectangular room, and the furniture and supplies that had yet to be cleared lay in piles along the edges. All along the far wall were a series of windows with slatted shutters that could be thrown wide open. The middle section of the room had been cleared out and one could walk to the centre of the far wall where full-length shuttered doors led on to the terrace beyond. And as they were thrown open now, Finley could see the shimmering green surface of the lake, below the terrace. Sunshine streamed through the slats, creating a pattern of strong, angled shadows across the rough floor. Though the elements were rustic, they spoke to the simple, quiet reflection that Finley held so dear, and he could not contain his excitement.

'You have outdone yourself, Harrison . . .' he whispered, as if speaking at normal volume might disturb the peace of the place. 'I would never have known that such a beautiful room lay hidden away above the boathouse.'

'Then I am very glad you approve!' Harrison replied. The smile on his face showed that he too was relishing the moment. 'The thought came to me suddenly, that we had left this space unused. Now, we can put it to a most edifying use. There is still much to be done, to prepare the space . . .'

'My heartfelt thanks to you and your staff!' Finley was gesturing to a set of four slates that had been rustled up from somewhere. They were obviously new and did not belong with the rest of the paraphernalia stored in the room.

'Yes, the flotsam and jetsam of running a hotel. It boggles the mind what manner of objects have made their way up to this hilltop!'

'Can we go out to the terrace?'

'Of course!' The two men made their way out into the

open space above where the boats and oars and netting were stored. A short wooden overhang protected the shutters from rain, and beyond that the surface of the terrace consisted of weathered wooden boards, some of which had grown warped and uneven. They could have used some planing and painting, but to Finley the whorls and knots in the warped wood made the scene even more charming. Facing back towards the hotel, he could see in one single sweep the fields, his own cabin to the right, and the wooden stairs that made their way upwards to the hotel. The main building of the hotel was draped along the ridge of the hill. If he turned to look the other way, he could see the lake laid out before him as a shimmering expanse, with the knotted trees on the opposite shore merging into thick, uninterrupted greenery.

There must have been several moments of quiet as Finley took it all in. 'I should be returning to my duties, Finley,' Harrison cut in. 'This is your classroom now, use it as you see fit!'

'You have my deepest gratitude, Harrison. I would not have imagined a place such as this existed.'

'I endeavour to please, Reverend!' Harrison replied, smiling and secure in the knowledge that his efforts had been recognized. 'You may wish to think of a name. If I may be so bold, "Lakeside School" seems fitting.'

Finley had not thought of a name and had assumed Highpoint School would have sufficed. Or perhaps

Rumson Academy, after its major benefactor. But Lakeside School could fit the bill, too! 'Perhaps we should leave such matters to our benefactors,' Finley grinned.

'Of course, of course.' Harrison waved and descended the boathouse stairs, making his way back to the hotel. Finley returned to the classroom and surveyed what was available in the area that had been cleared. A single desk and chair were set to one side of the room, and a carpet had been set up in the centre. A table had been placed on the longer edge of the carpet, and six chairs, the most that could fit along one side, had been provided, presumably for the students to sit in. The chairs seemed to be older versions of the rattan chairs used in the dining hall. These particular specimens were a little the worse for wear with several shims and joints to aid their integrity. But they were serviceable, and the overall effect was that of a credible if rustic, and uncommonly scenic, classroom.

Judging from the first day alone, the school did not have an auspicious start. The morning was unseasonably cold and the fog that had gathered during the night was not eager to depart. Mrs Rumson (the elder) was to give an inaugural speech, and a small crowd of hotel guests and staff had gathered for the occasion. Wetherby had set up his equipment, but the damp air was thwarting his efforts to preserve the moment as condensation accumulated on the glass plates. As the audience grew too large for the width of the path, several of them had to stand in the field, which began to turn muddy and slippery underfoot. Haight, rising to the occasion as the most senior official present, bounded up a few steps and called everyone to order before introducing Mrs Rumson in suitably flattering terms.

Mrs Rumson was in her element, and she executed with her best formal trill: 'My fellow guests, it has been my observation that while we here benefit from all that Mr Harrison and his excellent staff provide, these excellent services and entertainments are better suited to those who possess the grace and discipline to make worthy use of our time here. The same cannot be said of the children, who have not yet achieved sufficient maturity and must be shepherded towards more fitting pastimes.

'Now, here in our own beautiful corner of Her Majesty's empire, we shall have that too – the means to instruct our children through a correct and proper education. Today, I am privileged to dedicate the opening of this school, closely attached to our beloved Highpoint Hotel. I therefore dedicate this building, along with a sum of two hundred pounds from my husband's estate, to the Highpoint School.'

A collective gasp rose from the small crowd, followed soon after by polite applause. Finley noted that the native staff appeared perplexed by the applause, but Cherian began to clap loudly, and they soon followed suit. But the speech was not yet over.

'As such, I would expect that Highpoint School become the centrepiece of the day for the children who have grown beyond the minding of their ayahs and are now able to participate in the reading and writing of letters. The school will instruct its pupils on how to become worthy members of society and through their actions, deserving of the privileged place that they occupy among Her Majesty's subjects.'

The fog, showing no signs of lifting, had now transformed into misty droplets that sprinkled down on the restive, muttering audience. There was some audible coughing and shifting of feet. Finley noticed Cherian gesturing the native staff to not disperse and remain standing with the crowd. He felt sympathy for them, especially as they were unlikely to understand what was being said. Judging from young Evelyn Haight's expression, neither was she.

'Finally, I proclaim that we are fortunate and privileged to have with us Reverend James Erasmus Finley, who will guide and tutor our young charges. The Reverend has already demonstrated that he can provide ample spiritual sustenance through his Sunday sermons and has opened new vistas to us through the Reverend's Walk. It is fitting, then, that he guide our children more fully and impart to them the Christian knowledge and wisdom that is their birthright. And, God willing, they will leave this schoolroom wiser, more capable souls than when they entered. God save the Queen!'

Relieved applause rose from the audience. Finley had planned to say some additional words of welcome, but it was clear that the small crowd had achieved the limits of their patience. After some hastily mumbled thanks, Finley gestured to his students that they should come upstairs to the classroom.

As the students filed into their classroom, it was evident that they did not share their teacher's enthusiasm for the space. They observed the room cautiously from near the door and made no efforts to find their seats at the long table. Evelyn Haight, being both the eldest and the most forthright of the group, expressed herself first.

'Harrison has really extended himself . . .' she pouted. 'This may possibly be the furthest he could have placed us while still on the hotel grounds.'

'Not too shabby . . .' Oliver Cadbury commented next, contradicting the first comment. 'I always wondered what they did with this room before the autumn ball!'

Andrew Rumson had made his way over to the shutters overlooking the lake. They were closed on account of the weather, but he raised the slats to look outside. There was little to see except the fog and the green water of the lake below. It occurred to Finley that Andrew, being the youngest, may need cautioning.

'Please walk with care, Andrew, the parapet on the terrace outside is not tall and I wouldn't want you falling over it.' Finley warned.

'There's a terrace outside?!' he exclaimed with renewed curiosity.

'Yes, but perhaps we shall leave that for a clearer day.' Realizing that he should be the one issuing instructions, he added, 'Do come in, children, and find your seats.' There was some shuffling and negotiation, but eventually the children settled themselves. Evelyn took one of the centre seats, Alice Rumson the other one. Andrew elected to sit next to his sister, flanked on the outside by Jonathan Wetherby. Oliver Cadbury appeared to consider the seats that remained and upon realizing that he could either sit next to Evelyn Haight himself, or allow Harold Attlee to sit there, quickly took the position. Harold, a shy sixteen-year-old, perhaps only mirroring his parents' own patterns of interacting with others, assumed the last remaining seat closest to the door.

Once all were seated, Finley experienced a faint but growing feeling of panic, and that his recent memory of being sufficiently prepared was now withering away. Pedagogy did not come naturally to Finley. A willing and pliant pupil himself, he had not conceived of how to teach children with dispositions like the spirited Ms Haight. Six pairs of eyes fixed firmly on him awaited his next instruction, and Finley realized that this would be very different from speaking to a congregation. At church services, the order of the service, with each element in its appropriate place, usually had a calming effect on him. Every step, once complete, led to the next one. The congregation understood that. What was the first step here?

'Greetings, children!' Finley could hear his own voice, but it seemed to come from some other part of the room. A muffled sensation seemed to take over from his collar and extend up into his ears. 'In front of you, you will see a collection of Bibles that I have temporarily borrowed from the chapel. We will begin with a reading from the Bible. Please turn to ...' And so, by turning his first lesson into a religious lesson about the prodigal son, Finley was able to fall back on the training he had received at the seminary. Alice did the first reading, followed by Harold. It became clear that Master Andrew could not handle the difficulty of reading on account of being so young, so he was allowed to speak first once the group debated the meaning and moral of the story.

With the fog still dithering outside, Finley had little notion of the passage of time. Soon, it became clear that the children had had enough of this particular subject and their attentions began to wander. Alice Rumson had begun to look upwards and study the beams that held up the ceiling with more interest than was warranted. Her face tilted upwards, and her mouth grew lax and fell open. Around the same time, Jonathan Wetherby's eyes took on a glazed air, as if he had suppressed several yawns. As ever, it was Evelyn Haight whose closing commentary indicated that some change was in order.

'Reverend, if one were to find oneself in the position of the elder son, would it not be aggravating to endure the celebration in honour of the younger brother?'

'How so, Evelyn?'

'The younger brother might have rather enjoyed his merrymaking and debauchery. And all the while, his elder brother was dutifully serving the family. So why should we not have a feast for the older brother instead? Does he not deserve the greater reward?'

'The father calls for the feast as an expression of thanks and gratitude for repentance and a return to the fold, Evelyn. In the same way that Christ grants salvation to those who repent their sin. The celebration is in recognition of a wrong being made right.'

'Certainly, Reverend. However, what of the elder brother, who has done his duty and stood by his father and his family? Is he not also deserving of feasting and recognition?'

'But, Evelyn, the elder brother is already assured of salvation, and the satisfactions of doing one's duty ought not to require further worldly rewards. The privilege of doing one's duty is a reward in itself.'

'If you say so, Reverend . . .' Finley could see the entire group was now considering the possibility that they had all misunderstood the parable and that perhaps one should engage in sinning first and then repent, so as to be rewarded with a feast. He certainly saw the look of mischievous confusion playing across Andrew Rumson's little face; being younger, he was less capable of hiding the various speculations clouding his mind. Finley reckoned it was best to call an end to this inaugural school day before the confusion got worse.

Once the children had left, Finley was able to sit in the silence of his classroom and ponder the events of the day. It became clear that he would have to set forth a better plan for each day, if only for his own sake, and to avoid frantically searching for his next words. Tomorrow would be arithmetic; he could easily cobble together a set of grocer's sums and ask the children to calculate the monies required. The day after could be devoted to grammar and literature. And this, Finley realized, could be the basis of a repeating pattern for each week. Three days instruction from the Bible. One day of grammar. One day of arithmetic. And one day of poetry and literature. That seemed a firm foundation from which to begin.

A creak on the staircase alerted Finley to someone outside; and it was followed by a firm knock. 'Reverend?' It was a friendly woman's voice.

'Come in!'

The door opened, to reveal Eliza Rumson. 'Good morning, Reverend!' she said. Her eyes surveyed the expanse of the room. The candles were still lit, and Finley was seated at his desk at the far end of the room. 'Where are the children, Reverend?' she asked, as she stepped further into the room. She peered into the corners as if they could be hiding there. Some of the hotel supplies remained in the far corners, but most of the room had been cleared for the school's use.

'Ah, Mrs Rumson. I have only just dismissed them for the day. I thought we might begin with a gradual introduction to this new manner of filling their days.'

'This is certainly a schoolroom now! The last time I was here, I was making my way out to the terrace during the end-of-season gala.'

Finley felt a constriction beginning near the top of his stomach and rising gradually through his chest. 'W-would you like to see the terrace?' he stammered.

'I don't want to trouble you, if you are busy,' she replied.

'No trouble at all!' Finley sprang up from behind his desk, almost tripping over his own feet as he walked over to the shutter doors and clumsily threw them open.

'Well, then, Reverend, I don't mind if I do!' Eliza Rumson strode across the classroom and followed Finley on to the terrace. The fog had begun to clear and as happens at such times, glimpses of the scenery were starting to reveal themselves. After a brief pause to assess the state of the terrace, Eliza Rumson walked out to the corner closest to the water.

Finley followed her, but maintained a respectful distance. She was taking a very careful look around the vistas that had opened up, and Finley caught himself studying her lips and jawline, and the manner in which her waist tightened and then blossomed out in the silhouette of the travelling dresses she favoured. The travelling dress was simpler in design than the ornate bustles that many of the other women wore, but it allowed her to move more freely and go boating with her children.

'I have never been able to see from this vantage before.' The comment broke into Finley's thoughts. 'The gala is in the evening, and it is not possible to see as far into the distance then. You may have the most scenic schoolroom this side of the equator, Reverend Finley!'

'Yes, I count myself extremely fortunate.' And as if remembering that there could be more to add, 'I am indebted to you and Mr Rumson for the invitation to come with you here.'

'Oh no, you must not think of it that way, Reverend. It was our good fortune that you found your way to Madurai.' She paused before continuing. 'If I may be so bold, what was it that induced you to travel so far on your own?'

'I felt a purpose, Mrs Rumson. I believed the needs of Christ would be better served by spreading knowledge of his words and deeds among the heathens ...'

'Believed, Reverend?' she cut in. 'Or perhaps you consider us heathen? You should have mentioned your concerns sooner!' She turned sharply, but a teasing smile played on her face, and her eyes twinkled at her own joke.

'No, no, Mrs Rumson. That is not what I intended to convey at all . . .'

'Forgive my wicked sense of humour, Reverend. I could not resist.' She beamed a smile that made Finley want to find a chair and sit down. 'I hear similar words from my mother-in-law often enough that I am compelled to mock them, if only in private.'

Finley did not know how to reply to this. He could not speak ill of his benefactor, but he appreciated the humour. He continued on his original path. 'Quite. I had hoped to establish a congregation in some location where the church had not yet made its presence felt. I had not anticipated the warm reception you gave me in Madurai. Or that our travels here would lead to my teaching in such beautiful surroundings.' The gesture of his hand sweeping across the scenery ended up pointing at Eliza's figure.

'Oh, your flattery will take you far, Reverend!' She half curtsied, and the wrinkling at the corners of her eyes struck Finley as a warm ray of sunshine after days of rain. Then, realizing that she had probably embarrassed Finley, Eliza's smile vanished, and a bright flush of colour animated her cheeks. They both glanced quickly downwards at the warped boards underfoot. The silence seemed interminable.

'Pardon, saar!' a voice broke in.

'Yes, Cherian, what is it?' Finley looked up and turned

back towards the terrace door. His voice had resumed a stable timbre and the constriction in his chest was clearing itself away.

'Lunch service starting now.'

'Cherian, do you know where Alice and Andrew are?' Eliza asked.

'Already at lunch service, ma'am,' came the crisp reply. The statement surprised Finley a little, because Cherian did not use complete sentences in most of his interactions.

'Then I shall go and join them. Thank you for showing me your wonderful schoolroom, Reverend. May this mark the start of a long and happy voyage!' She strode quickly through the terrace door, causing Cherian to spring aside to make way.

Eliza moved briskly through the room, and Finley followed, observing closely as she lifted the bottom of her skirt to ease her nimble footsteps over the lintel. Her hair flounced with each step down the stairs, and the upper portion of her hips seemed to follow the same rhythm. Finley watched, entranced and then remembered that he was not alone. 'Come, Cherian. Let us lock up, and before luncheon.' They closed the shutter doors and made sure to blow out all the candles. Finley carefully stacked the Bibles on an empty bookshelf that Harrison had kindly made available. With one last look around the room, Finley stepped out of his new schoolroom and allowed Cherian to do the locking up. Across the field he could see the shape of Eliza's dress making its way up the stairs to the hotel.

Most of the hotel's guests were already seated for lunch. Finley was hoping for a quiet repast, but that hope was quickly discarded as he walked into the dining area. It was full, and Haight, upon seeing Finley enter, made a series of expansive gestures of welcome from the other side of the room. Clearly, he wished that Finley would join the Haights at their table.

'Evelyn informs me of a scintillating first day, Finley!' Haight began, just as Finley sat down and was rapidly served the onion soup.

Finley looked up, first at Haight, then at his daughter, and both seemed to take the comment earnestly.

'Prodigal son and all that. This hearkens back to a much earlier time for me, long before I met Mrs Haight, you know.'

'I see . . . ' Finley could not think of anything more appropriate to say. The brevity of his reply allowed him to return to his soup.

'Yes, Father. The parable tells us that even for the most wayward among us, there is a path back to righteousness. Does it not, Reverend?' Evelyn probed.

Perhaps because the soup was hotter than expected, or perhaps because the comment was made by Evelyn Haight, Finley almost spat out his first mouthful. He recovered his composure with the help of a napkin and a glass of water.

'Indeed it does, Miss Haight. I am pleased that you have grasped the meaning so rapidly,' Finley replied.

'However, there is a distinction between merely grasping the meaning of a parable and actually putting that lesson to work in one's own life. Is that not also true, Reverend?' Mrs Haight added.

Finley nodded rapidly. He had arrived late and the rest of the party were finishing their main course while he was still struggling through the first mouthfuls of soup. And the Haights seemed to have, for the moment, at least, a firm grasp on the lessons that the parable was supposed to impart.

'I agree, Bernadette. But we must all get there in our own time and manner,' Haight replied to his wife. Until now, Finley had not heard Haight speak to his wife using her full first name. Informally, he might refer to her as 'my Bernie', so the formality was probably for the benefit of the assembled company. The conversation was mercifully interrupted with the arrival of the main course – a kedgeree accompanied by a side of roast fowl.

After lunch, Finley quickly made his way down to this cabin before he could be buttonholed on the hotel terrace. He had reached the limit of what he could tolerate by way of interactions with people and was eager to shake off that sensation of being trapped in an unblinking public gaze. Alone at last in his cabin, Finley watched the afternoon sun streaming through the windows. But he could think only of the twinkling eyes and smile from the terrace. The happy floating wisps of hair and the faint smell – was it lavender? – that accompanied the flushed, glistening skin. Haight may be constantly preoccupied with worldly things, but at least he clearly understood his place in the world. Finley could not say the same for himself. When someone like Haight needed spiritual guidance, they knew they could come to Finley. But what about when someone like Finley felt the need for closer companionship? Finley knew of many parables to guide the wayward back to the righteous path. But he could think of no parables, anywhere, that showed the righteous how to be safely wayward.

13

In Search of a Crime

Today promises to be one of those days, the kind that need to be trudged through; the less reflection, the better. My alarm did not ring at the intended time, so any feelings of being well rested are immediately swept away. I know I am late for a meeting. A brisk pace on the walk to school can only make up part of the deficit, and I arrive at my office glistening with sweat. Mrs Mani looks up from her desk with surprise as I stomp breathlessly into the reception area.

'Good morning, Mr G. Dr and Mrs Singh are waiting in your office.' She blurts this out more as warning than greeting.

'Thank you, Mrs Mani.' I pause, since I now have to collect myself outside my own office. In trying to wipe off the sweat on my forehead and neck, it appears I have left my handkerchief at home too. Mrs Mani holds out a tissue, which I accept. 'Good morning to you, too!' I grimace.

Dr and Mrs Singh are seated quietly in the chairs that face my desk. I wish I had organized it before I left last night, as the multiple sets of papers strewn across the desk do not create the right impression. The Singhs stare quietly out of the window behind my chair. It looks out over the campus buildings, which fall away with the downward slope of the hill, ending at the lake. Dr Singh pats his wife reassuringly on the shoulder and leaves his hand there afterwards. I clear my throat purposefully before I enter, and his hand jumps away.

'Good morning, Dr and Mrs Singh! I am so sorry to have kept you waiting.'

'Good morning, Mr Ghosh,' the doctor replies, rising slightly from his chair. Mrs Singh offers a measured nod of greeting.

I assume my seat at the table. 'How was your journey up?' I ask, venturing to start with some niceties. I have been told by several people I need to do this and guard against my natural tendency to launch into 'why are you here and what do you want?'

'Very good, very nice. Our hotel is very comfortable also,' Mrs Singh replies.

'So, what would you like to discuss?' I decide to walk over to the filing cabinet pre-emptively and extract the file for Payal Singh, their daughter. The daughter is in class, so it's just the three of us today.

The father takes a deep breath, and the mother looks closely at his face. 'Mr Ghosh, we want what is best for our daughter. And Mrs Singh and I have lived in the Gulf for many years to make a good income for my family.' I nod. I had expected the man to begin with a tirade about how the school is not serving Payal's needs well. But I cannot guess the direction of this conversation anymore.

'We have had many phone calls with Payal,' Mrs Singh begins. 'And, Mr Ghosh, I do not like to see my daughter so unhappy.'

'So, we have come here to take your advice,' Dr Singh concludes.

'Has something happened to Payal? I am not sure what your question is . . .' A sense of alarm is beginning to rise inside me; perhaps something bad has happened and I am unaware of it.

'No, no, Mr Ghosh,' Dr Singh reassures me. 'Payal is very happy here. But she is only very happy when she is allowed to do her artwork. Any time we mention biology or chemistry she becomes very upset.'

'What my husband is saying is . . .' Mrs Singh begins, lilting into the conversation.

'What I am saying is, it makes Payal very unhappy to talk about studying medicine.' He pauses, struggling with the next part of what he's going to say. 'So . . . We are not going to tell her to follow in my footsteps.' Dr Singh is affected enough by this public declaration that he is forced to look around the room to compose himself.

'You must understand, Mr Ghosh,' Mrs Singh continues, filling the long pause in the conversation, 'Bhupinder's parents agreed to sell much of their farmland to put him through medical college. Even though his father did not want to at first.' Now it is Mrs Singh's turn to pat her husband on the arm. 'He is a successful doctor in the Gulf now, but at the beginning, Bhupinder's father made him promise that he would give his children the same gifts. Now Bhupinder feels he is not being a good father if he cannot help her get into medicine also.'

Dr Singh exhales heavily and begins to polish his glasses.

'So now we need your advice, Mr Ghosh,' Mrs Singh says, wiping her own quiet tears with her dupatta as her husband stares ahead in dejected silence. 'How can Payal have a career if she is only doing well in subjects like English and art?'

I feel relieved. First, nothing bad has happened to Payal. Only her poor dear parents are struggling mightily to confront the reality that their daughter will not follow the plan they had laid out for her.

'Of course, I understand.' I can now reassume my calm consigliere role; the balance of the day is restoring itself.

'There are excellent careers now for students who go on to art and English. Tell me, are you thinking that Payal would study here in India, or go abroad?'

'Foreign is okay, Mr Ghosh. We are outside India now . . .' Dr Singh has found himself again. '. . . And our friends tell us Ivy League would be best.'

'Yes, those colleges are very good. There is art history, studio art, architecture . . . many choices. There are many good choices. And, of course, journalism and law are also options.' I try to be cautious with aspirations. 'Also, if Payal studies abroad, she will not have to choose one area right now. She can go to graduate school or law school later. Of course, those can also be very expensive abroad.'

'No problem, Mr Ghosh, fees are not a problem.'

'Then that is wonderful, Dr Singh. Payal should start applying to some colleges right away!' I think of Tarun and wonder what it would be like if that same magic wand could be waved for him.

'It will be okay, Mr Ghosh? She can have a career if she studies in this line?' Mrs Singh asks this with residual scepticism.

'Yes, Mrs Singh, many people have had very good careers with an education in art and design,' I reassure her. 'And her grades are very good in those subjects.'

'Thank you, thank you.' Mrs Singh seems placated, but does not entirely believe me.

'But, Dr and Mrs Singh, I must ask you one favour.'

Dr Singh leans forward to listen more attentively. 'You must tell Payal all this yourself. And you must tell her to save her artwork. Remember she burnt it last time?'

Dr Singh straightens up, stung. 'We did not tell her to do that.'

'Dr Singh, I have seen many children and their parents come through this school,' I begin. 'And when the parents are like you, who support their children, it is always better if it comes from the parents themselves! And maybe you want to tell Payal what you told me? There is a reason you wanted her to study medicine so much! It would bring you close together.' I interleave my fingers to emphasize the point.

He pouts, looks down and nods a few times. 'You know, Mr Ghosh, you have a very nice, fancy school here. Payal joined when she was fourteen – ninth standard, no?'

'Yes, that's right.'

'Preeti and I thought we will send her to the best school in India we could find. And Payal has been very happy here. But in a way, you also took my daughter away from me.'

'Arre Bhupinder, what are you saying?' Mrs Singh is trying to ward of trouble.

'No, no, I'm not angry . . . I'm just saying . . .' Dr Singh continues. 'If I had told her that story about the family land at the time when she came to this school, it would have made no sense to her. Now she is old enough – I think she will understand. But there is no time in the holidays to tell her these things. She is always out with friends, or we are going somewhere or coming from somewhere. Or I am at the clinic or the hospital.' I let Dr Singh continue – he isn't really speaking to me or his wife. But she is nodding with the shared understanding of what he is trying to say. 'Chalo, it is time for us to talk properly to our daughter,' he says to his wife.

The conversation is at an end, and Dr Singh stands up and offers his hand. 'Thank you, Mr Ghosh.' His eyes look tired and relieved. Something in his gaze unsettles me; it's a quiet admonition that says, 'I hope you know what you're doing with my daughter's future.' Not having children myself, I realize I am not best placed to know how it feels to give up a long-held wish for a child's future. The good doctor has a medical speciality, and he can judge the value of his care by his patient's symptoms. How do I establish the value of my counsel? I find it hard to meet his gaze.

'Payal can stay with us tonight? In the hotel?' Mrs Singh asks.

Normally we don't allow students to be outside the dorms with out-of-town guests. But these are her parents, and they have come far, in every sense, for their daughter. 'I will talk to the dorm parent and get her the permission, Mrs Singh,' I reply. And I escort them out of the office.

I close the door to my office and sit quietly at my desk. There's the scattering of paperwork in front of me, but I don't want to touch it just yet. I'm not sure how to handle being accused of taking someone's child away. And I haven't had the quiet time in the office that I use to collect myself at the start of each day. Still, I am not too late for a run to the teachers' lounge for a restorative coffee and egg sandwich. Before that, I need to make a quick call to Mrs K, that Payal will be staying with her parents tonight. Since I don't remember the codes to any of the dorms, I will have to ask the switchboard to connect me. I am about to pick up the phone when the door opens again.

'Ah, Ghosh, there you are.' It's Chapman.

'Hello, Jason!' I muster up my best collegial tone. 'I saw your note.'

'Yes, I was wondering what to do about all of this. As I said, Ms Little-K hasn't found anything. Have you?'

'Well, to be honest, I have not spent any time chasing it down. I certainly haven't heard anything new on this front from students.'

'Or from parents?' he ventures.

'Certainly not from parents, either, Jason!' I am surprised at his concern on this front. 'Why, have you heard something?'

Chapman is a purposefully mysterious sort. During our brief exchange he has made himself comfortable in one of the chairs facing my desk and is smoothing the midriff of his shirt with splayed fingers. Something in his manner reminds me of those lizards that live in the desert. The ones that skitter along before resting on their stomachs, raising their hands and feet up in the air to cool off from the hot sand. Chapman's gesture is distractingly reptilian.

'Let's just say I am curious. After all, who would take a picture of breasts? From what I remember, it is hard to see how that could be a self-portrait.'

That was not the first thought that had come to my mind. I try to think back to the details of the image, but can only focus on the fact that Chapman's lizard-like presence is keeping me from my egg sandwich.

'I'm not sure what you mean, Jason,' I reply, but regret saying that immediately. I have ninety minutes till my next class, and I had hoped to use the time to eat and then prepare for class. Impromptu chats with Jason can often last longer than one might initially suppose.

'Well . . .' It's a drawn-out delivery for such a simple word. 'There must be an accomplice. A second person who knows about the picture. Someone behind the camera.' His eyes twinkle for a moment at the thought – it's actually more a chameleon-like twitch, and I wonder if he can also move his eyes independently of each other. 'Do you still have the picture?' he asks.

Of course, I still have the picture. But the question is, do I want to be dealing with this now? I pull out the yellow envelope after rummaging through the detritus in the bottom drawer of my desk and hand it over. Chapman opens it carefully, slides the photograph out and holds it up from the corner with the tips of his fingers. As if his own fingerprints might end up incriminating him. He stares at it for a while, but I can't tell what he's looking for.

'Jason, I have a class in an hour that I need to prepare for. Why don't you hold on to the photo?' I am trying to bring a close to this strangely unproductive meeting.

'No, no. Couldn't do that. You hold on to it.' And Chapman quickly shoves both the photograph and envelope back across my desk. I can see why he was staring. The breasts are beautiful, shapely; they invite you to reach out and fondle them. The sheet of music that hides the face is a tease – it makes you want to discover the face of the person with even greater urgency. I insert the photograph into its envelope and put it back in the bottom drawer.

'We must get to the bottom of this,' Chapman muses.

'I don't see how, Jason,' I reply. 'Unless something new shows up. I certainly don't want to draw attention to this one photograph in any way.'

'I understand, I understand. Just think about it.' He gets up to leave, and on his way out, just as he's about to close the door, he adds, 'I'm sure you can come up with something.'

Ah, that old administrator's gem. The sly shifting of the burden on the way out of the door, so he can come back to me in a few weeks and credibly claim that he had, in fact, asked me to attend to the matter. I have no desire to take care of it at all. Would it be important to know who the girl in the picture was? Absolutely! If only to tell her to stop embarrassing herself and stop taking naughty pictures. And as long as there was nothing more untoward going on, no blackmail or coercion or anything like that, I would just leave things be and trust that the students would stop their ill-advised attempts at avant garde art.

To be fair, the problem is hardly mine alone. Chapman is well aware that should discussions about the photo resurface, a roomful of teachers who have already seen the evidence will know that both he and Darling have failed to contain the problem. I wonder whether the school board knows. Perhaps Chapman should raise it at our next board meeting. That's the funny thing about this kind of secret. Unlike most other kinds of information, there's little to be gained by hoarding this. If you share the secret, you also share the burden. Maybe that's what Chapman was trying to do in the staff meeting? He's a clever sort, always thinking three steps ahead. I sometimes wish I could be the same way.

Speaking of planning ahead, I must get back to my lesson plan. And before that, I have to call Mrs K. I pick up the phone again and dial the operator, who connects me to the dorm parent's residence.

'Hello, Mrs K?'

'Yes, hello! Is this Suman?'

'Yes, Mrs K, how are you?'

'I'm very well, Suman. Is everything all right? I don't normally receive calls from you in the middle of the day!' Mrs K never betrays worry in her voice, but I can tell she's listening carefully at this point.

'Nothing to worry about, Mrs K. I just had a meeting with Payal's parents.'

'Payal? Payal Singh?'

'Yes, her parents are in town. And they wanted to know if she could spend the night in the hotel with them. I said I would get her the right permissions.'

'Oh, I see.' There's a pause. 'Okay, that's all right. I will tell Payal that her parents need to come here and pick her up from my residence. That way, I can be sure to meet them.' Mrs K has been a dorm parent for a long time, and so she understands that she is responsible for raising reasonable objections. She also knows every possible trick in the book that students use to get out of their dorms and be off-campus when they shouldn't be. And she takes special care to get to know the parents whenever she can. It's precisely that kind of care that makes our school the sort of place that students look back on with fondness. There's no way to put that in a handbook. If I had been a student here, I would have wanted Mrs K as my dorm parent.

'Of course, Mrs K. Could you let Payal know if you see her? And I will ask Mrs Mani to send a message to her in class as well,' I reply.

'I will. Thank you for calling, Suman.'

'Of course, Mrs K,' I say. I realize that talking to her always leaves me feeling reassured, so perhaps I should be the one doing the thanking. And then I remember the meeting with Chapman. 'One other thing, Mrs K . . .'

'Yes, Suman?'

'You remember the meeting about the photograph?' I ask.

'Of course, such an unseemly way to handle things!'

'You have not heard any more on the topic, have you?'

'No, Suman, I have not. And if I had, I would certainly let you know.' I can picture the tight-lipped manner in which she is delivering these words. 'Why? Has there been another photograph?'

'No, Mrs K. Nothing like that. Just that Chapman came to my office this morning asking for an update on the investigation.'

'Update? Investigation? Is this a criminal matter now?' she snorts. 'That fellow – hard to know why he cares so much about this. It's unnatural, really.'

'I think we just need to make sure it doesn't become a bigger problem, that's all.'

'You know, as long as there aren't more photographs that come out of the woodwork, I don't think it will be. This has happened before, you know.'

'I didn't know that!' The surprise must have been evident in my voice, because she went on.

'Yes, a few years before you joined the school, I suppose. Turns out one of the teachers was running a side business taking dirty pictures of the students and then selling them to someone at the luxury hotel right next to the school. Who would then sell them on for even more money, of course.'

'Oh no! That's terrible!'

'Yes, one of the parents discovered it when he was here. The hotel person was trying to sell him the pictures and did not know he was the father of a student. And the parent brought it straight to the school. There was a big hullabaloo, the police got involved, and the teacher was fired on the spot.'

'I have never heard of anything like that. It's shocking!'

'Yes, everyone forgets quickly. And, of course, with new people coming every year, most don't even know anymore. But I told Lila about that when she first thought of restarting the photography programme. And I also told her she must go to the administration when she found the photograph. That's how this all started, you know.' The line was quiet for a bit. 'Suman, are you still there?'

'Yes, Mrs K. I just hope that this is not a case like that one.'

'I don't think so, Suman. There were lots of pictures and a trail of money last time. So far, there seems to be only one. And Lila has a very tight grip on who handles that equipment.'

'So, then it could only be one of her students, right?'

'Yes, but there are twenty or so of them. And they could have taken a picture of someone else. Or someone could have taken the camera. We've already been down this road, Suman . . . what are you going to ask them? "Are these your breasts?" "Is this the chest of someone you know?" You can't do that . . . it makes no sense.'

'You're right, Mrs K, of course. I think Chapman expects me to do something about it, though.'

'Chapman can expect whatever he wants. To my mind, he is a little too interested in this photograph, and he should just focus on his own work. But who am I to say that? After all, I'm just a dorm parent.'

'Nobody thinks that. You're an institution within the school, Mrs K.'

'Thank you, Suman.' It's a curt but flattered reply. 'And by that I think you mean I'm gathering cobwebs because I've been around so long . . .'

'No, no, Mrs K!'

She's teasing me. 'Relax, Suman. When you get to my age, you realize that what appears new or difficult has already been encountered by someone in an earlier time. Maybe the specifics were different. But the hopes and fears, the plotting and scheming, the jealousies – these are human things that have always been around.'

'So then there's nothing to worry about, I suppose.'

'No, we all have to do our own share of worrying.

Chapman will be Chapman, but you can still decide for yourself how much you really want to do about this picture.'

'All right. Thanks, Mrs K.' I am about to hang up the phone, but she continues.

'And there is one last thing, though, Suman.'

'What's that?'

'I've realized now why I feel less worried about this photograph. I just never had to say it out loud before.'

'Really, why? I would be relieved to know . . .'

'In the earlier incident, the one before your time, the girls in the photographs looked sad and scared. I was still a dorm parent then, and the first time I saw those pictures, their expressions made me want to throw up. I have never felt so much like I failed them. I cried and screamed – mostly at Mr Kalyani who was still alive then. That was a real tragedy. But this photograph is different, I think. You can only see the mouth and chin, but it looked like she was smiling. Still, I wish I could see the eyes – just to make sure.'

'I'll keep that to myself, Mrs K.' I am not sure how Chapman would react; nor do I want to explain it to him.

'I think that's best.' Signalling that she was now done with our phone call, she added, 'Thank you for calling, Suman.' And the line clicked quiet.

A master teacher, one who has accumulated sufficient confidence through experience, has the ability to draw on knowledge and patterns of instruction that can be called up for use at short notice. Or rather, this is what I tell myself every time I have not prepared sufficiently for a class I am about to teach. So far, we have completed trigonometric identities and proofs and now we're moving on to vectors and matrices. Last class we had defined vectors and matrices, but now we need to move on to vector addition and transformations through matrices. I suppose I'll leave dot products and matrix inversion for next time, and that will require more careful planning.

So, let's think through today's session . . . First, a quick review of vector definition and matrix definition. Then show a vector mapped onto the x-y coordinate grid. I'll need to draw out the grid fairly quickly on the board since I have not printed out transparencies for this yet. And then, I'll define matrices and talk through matrix addition. That should probably be enough. But as I think through this in my mind, it already sounds terribly boring.

The other way to do this is to show a transformation of the vectors on the grid first. So, $(1, 0)$ goes to $(3, 2)$ let's say, and $(0, 1)$ goes to $(5, 7)$. And then I can group the ending vectors together in a 2x2 matrix and show how that matrix represents where the unit vectors will end up after matrix multiplication. Yes, that's good! And it also allows me to explain then why matrix multiplication is set up the way it is . . . That part is often confusing to students when they see it for the first time.

I leaf through the rest of the syllabus. Okay, next time is extension to 3-d vectors, linear transformation definitions and then cross products and definition of a plane. After that, it's determinants and matrix inversion. And then an in-class quiz on vectors and matrices. I should probably assign a problem set that's due before the in-class quiz. Which means that for next time, I really have to be ready to hand out the problem set. I'm sure I have one I can adapt from last year – I don't want to have to start one completely from scratch.

The bottom drawer of the desk has a set of hanging folders, and that's where all the old problem sets and exams are kept. I take a look, leafing through the various folders – maths eleventh grade, first semester; maths eleventh grade, second semester; maths twelfth grade, first semester – yes, that should be the one. I lift it out and realize that the stack is much larger than it should be. I have forgotten to throw out the problem sets and exam papers from last year. I'm going to hang on to them for now. Someday, I want to look back and check for myself if my secret hunch holds true – that each year the students I teach are getting progressively less intelligent. As an average, of course. There is always that handful each year that stands out above the rest. Here it is – the problem set I was looking for. Ten questions, going all the way from drawing out vectors on the x-y grid to calculating dot products and inverses. I set that aside so that I can modify it and ask Mrs Mani to make copies.

As I'm returning the folder to its usual spot, I notice
the yellow of the envelope staring back at me from the
bottom of the drawer. I wonder if what Mrs K said is true.
Is the girl in the picture really smiling? I put the maths
folder back and pick up the envelope, first making sure
that the door to my office is closed. The picture is the same
as before – soft grey hues against a darker background
that seems to fall away behind the body of the girl. And
the mouth is smiling – Mrs K was right! I want to look
at the picture longer and imagine what it must be like to
be part of such an intimate exchange; I want to become
part of the picture, the person behind the camera. What
happens next? Does she grab the camera from him? Do
they embrace and kiss? Do they go on to make love or
make breakfast? Is it morning or evening? I can't tell.

The sound of the first bell clamours loudly through
the halls. I quickly slide the picture back into its envelope
and stash it carefully below the rest of the files in the
drawer. I grab my notes as well as the old problem set
and put them into the folder that I carry in my bag. And
then it's off to class – quickly, before the next bell sounds.
Outside my office the corridors are full of children racing
to and from their various classes. Some are trying to get
things in and out of their lockers, while others are striding
purposefully past. A few are fooling around with their
friends in small groups, and every so often a group of
boys goes running through, faster than the others. I truly

enjoy this chaos. As long as I don't have to encounter other teachers, the thought of being placed in this river of young energy makes me feel like I get younger every time I am in it. I wonder if I was also like this as a boy – running around, making dirty jokes that caused my friends to laugh uproariously. I can't remember anymore. Anyway, better speed up and get to the classroom.

I fall in with some of my students as we make our way to the same room. 'Hello, Supriya. Hello, Tarun.'

'Hi, Mr G,' they reply, almost in chorus.

'Are you getting something ready for the concert, Supriya?' Supriya is an accomplished flautist, but struggles in maths class. I try to engage the kids on what they do best first. I want the students to know that I see them as whole people, not just as someone who sits in my maths class.

'Yes, Mr G.'

'What is it?'

'*Afternoon of a Faun*, by Debussy. It's quite hard, Mr G.' She grimaces a bit.

'I'm sure Mrs Cama thinks you're up to it, Supriya,' I smile. 'Okay, let's go in and get started.'

I drop my notes on the teacher's desk and start drawing the grid lines. Better to get it done now, rather than taking up class time and have the students staring pointlessly at my back for several minutes.

'Oh yes, Mr G. Finally we're studying noughts and crosses!' says Preetam G, the class wit.

'Ha ha, very funny, Preetam,' I reply, as the second bell rings. I turn to face the kids. Most of them have found their seats and opened their notebooks.

'All right, let's get started, everyone. Vectors and matrices – here we go!'

14

The Element of Fog

Finley had assumed the children would be eager to leave at the end of the school day – that way, he would be left alone to spend quiet, sunny afternoons reading above the boathouse. Instead, he was surprised to find that his pupils preferred to remain there, chatting or playing games. Occasionally, they might go downstairs and get on a boat – as long as the boathouse workers allowed them to – or play games in the field nearby.

He discovered this miscalculation early. The second day of school, unlike the first, was sunny and warm. After dismissing the students, Finley had propped all the doors and shutters open, and a refreshing breeze wafted through the room, ruffling the curtains. The boathouse terrace proved a welcome change from the din of the main hotel terrace. As Harrison and his staff had cleared out more of the room, there was now space for a few bookshelves and a separate seating area. The biggest treat of all, at least to

Finley, was the addition of a pair of reclining chairs placed on the terrace, under the overhang of the roof. These were the kind with the arms that extended out, allowing one to recline and raise one's feet. An ideal location for Finley's first reading of Thoreau's 'Walking'.

Over the years, departing guests had left behind a small bookstore's worth of assorted titles, many of which Haight considered unfit for the official library where he and his colleagues spent their working hours. Harrison was only too happy to move them out of the main building, and now Finley was the beneficiary of the miscellaneous volumes that had arrived along with the shelves. Many were of no interest – *Little Women*, *Mrs. Beeton's Book of Household Management*. But there were others – *Grimm's Fairy Tales*, a well-thumbed Goethe and several more – that could be of use at school. Finley tried to imagine whether it was foresight or ambition that might prompt a guest to pack Spinoza's *Ethics* for perusal on this hilltop. But now, having settled into the comfortable chair, Finley opened Thoreau's little volume and was soon dozing comfortably in his warm, sunny perch overlooking the lake.

He did not know how long he had napped before he was awakened by sounds in the room behind him. It may have been a substantial time, as the sun had changed position and the shadows grown longer. He peered through the open windows to see the children assembled in the seating area, most leafing through the books, while young Andrew Rumson sat at the table, drawing.

'I hope we have not disturbed you, Reverend,' Evelyn's voice rang out. 'Many of the parents have retired for the afternoon, so we decided to repair here.'

'No trouble at all, Ms Haight,' Finley replied. He struggled to raise himself out of the armchair with suitable decorum, deciding finally to heave himself forward with momentum from his arms.

It dawned on Finley that perhaps the children wanted a place of their own. The men had the terrace and the main library, the women had their own living rooms in the suites. And the younger children were accompanied wherever they went by their ayahs. The older children had nowhere to go, so the schoolroom had now become their de facto meeting place. Still, he chafed at the intrusion into what he had assumed would be his own private space.

'Children, it is fitting that you peruse the books in the schoolroom,' Finley began. 'But I must remind you, that this is a schoolroom first, and not a playroom. Please leave everything exactly as you found it. And do not forget to close the shutters and the door tight when you leave. We do not want the monkeys investigating our classroom!'

Perhaps the tone of his speech surprised them, because all six pairs of eyes looked up at him suddenly, but none replied. Alice Rumson broke the silence with a hushed 'Yes, Reverend'.

'And please do not come here if lanterns or candlelight are required. I do not wish to have any accidents befall any of you, or this schoolroom,' Finley continued. The students nodded. 'And I have one last requirement of you. The contents of that desk' – Finley pointed to his own desk – 'are not to be touched or disturbed.'

'Yes, Reverend,' they replied in unison.

'Very good, children. And remember, God sees all.' Finley felt a strange sensation that he had been taken over by the voice and tone of his instructors from the seminary; it was their speech emanating from his mouth. The children had gone back to their reading and drawing, so perhaps what he said did not sound so strange to them, after all. He shuffled out of the schoolroom, uttering a hurried 'Good afternoon, children!' as he left.

The quiet of the cabin felt reassuring and provided better air in which to reflect. He, Finley, was now a schoolmaster and a chaplain for this small community of Englishmen that had made their way up to the hilltop. He had conducted his first week of instruction with the assorted pupils at hand, and to be honest, he had found the experience rewarding. His own schoolmasters had trudged through their lessons as if they were being dragged through the pulp of their own lecture notes. There were a few exceptions, who revelled in their particular areas of instruction. The mathematics tutor, for example, whose eyes would glow with a violent enthusiasm when he lectured. He was always eager to explain how it could not have been anything but a benevolent God that left puzzles, strewn all over His creation, for man to discover and solve. How else could one explain the mathematical regularity of tides, of seasons? Or how one could use the heights of shadows to estimate distances?

But Finley felt less certain. Should he be satisfied with his life at Highpoint as it was? Had God not intended for him some greater purpose? The responsibility to bring Christ's teachings to those who did not yet benefit from His light still remained – the work not done. During the school's opening day, the native staff who watched the ceremony were eager to turn and leave after the applause. It was Cherian whose stern glance had brought them back. As if the native staff were there to be corralled – they were nothing more than well-trained animals. The servants' attempted departure was only because no one had taken the time to explain the significance of the occasion to them. What about the significance of the chapel and the events that took place there? Surely this was also his, Finley's, responsibility?

The chapel was not put to any use for most of the week. Perhaps he could use it in the afternoons for the instruction of the native staff? After all, if Mrs Rumson could summon the wherewithal to start a small school, perhaps she might also be the person to approve the use of the chapel for crucial pastoral care. Finley resolved to seek out Mrs Rumson (the elder) and gain her blessing in this regard.

Striding up the steps and into the main corridor of the hotel, he was able to locate the door to the Rumsons' suite without much difficulty. He knocked, tentatively at first, because he did not want to intrude. The second time he knocked with more resolve. After receiving no answer, Finley began to realize how ill-conceived his plan truly was. He had not made an appointment. Perhaps Mrs Rumson was resting or otherwise indisposed.

'A moment, if you please,' a young woman's voice trilled from behind the closed door. It was Eliza. Finley had assumed she would be busy with the children on the lake, just as when he had seen her last, but then remembered that the children were in the schoolroom. The clatter of the latch being undone was followed by the door sweeping open. Eliza – her hair done up perfectly, her lips parted in surprise – stood before him.

'Reverend?'

'Hello, Mrs Rumson.' Finley's voice had suddenly gone hoarse and lost much of its resolve. They stood for a moment, staring at each other from either side of the doorway.

Eliza broke the silence. 'Do come in, Reverend, I seem to have forgotten my manners.'

As Finley stepped into the parlour, he realized he had never seen the inside of any suite. Given that every single item either had to be transported up the hill, or fashioned on site, the décor was sumptuous. A large framed painting of a hunt hung on one wall, and amply upholstered furniture was arranged around a small fireplace.

'I do believe it is the first time I have visited one of the suites,' Finley observed, craning his neck as he looked around the room.

'Then, Reverend, you must let me to show you around.' And she commenced a quick tour of the suite. Most of the doors on the other side of the room led to private chambers, except one. That side door opened out on to a covered walkway which ended in a large, partially covered terrace. The view was breathtaking and revealed a large stretch of the lake as well as the hills beyond. It was here that the family clearly spent most of their time together, as the table under the awning was weighted down with needlework, books, ladies' magazines and writing supplies. On another table lay a tray with a tea service. Mrs Rumson, the elder, was sitting in one of the wicker chairs near the tea service, enjoying her afternoon refreshment, squinting out at something in the direction of the lake. Finley couldn't make out anything specific.

'Mother, look who I found knocking at our door!'

Mrs Rumson turned slowly. 'Reverend! What a pleasant surprise! Do join us, won't you?' She dispensed with the formality she carried in public. 'Pullur!' she raised her voice, which also made it quake slightly. 'Pullur!'

Pullur emerged quietly from the other side of the terrace, nodding at Finley as he drew closer. 'Pullur, can you get one more cup for Reverend Finley, please?'

'Do sit down,' Eliza added with a smile. Finley did so gladly, as his legs felt inexplicably feeble from hearing her voice so nearby. 'Come, Reverend, surely you did not visit us to have tea in silence?' Her twinkling eyes and gentle chiding were proving too much for Finley, and he could have reached over and clasped her hand so very easily. He studied the tiled floor of the terrace for a moment to collect himself.

'Thank you for welcoming me so warmly,' he announced to a potted plant in the corner of the terrace. And then, remembering the reason for his visit, he continued, 'I had a matter to discuss with you, Mrs Rumson.' Speaking directly to the elder Rumson was considerably easier.

'Why, certainly, Reverend. Do tell.' The elder Rumson was in a more agreeable mood than usual.

'It is a matter of pastoral duty, Mrs Rumson. We all ought to provide the greatest benefit to society based on our respective education and training,' Finley began. 'For myself, I believe there is a great need to share the word of God, especially with those who are not fortunate enough to see it in the normal course of their lives.'

'Who precisely do you mean, Reverend?' Mrs. Rumson had put down her teacup, and furrows of concern darkened her forehead.

'Mother,' Eliza cut in, 'you need not trouble yourself – the good Reverend is not referring to us. I believe he is referring to the natives around us.' Mrs Rumson, the elder, sat back, placated that Finley was not laying an accusation at her door. 'I knew you would happen upon this, Reverend!' Eliza continued. 'Yours is far too righteous a nature to be content with simply tending to those as fortunate as ourselves.' This compliment, along with Eliza's sincerity, brought a hot glow to Finley's face.

'Precisely,' added Finley, with some embarrassment.

'Very well, how do you propose to begin this work?' the elder Rumson asked. 'Do you now wish to start a school for the natives?'

'No, Mrs Rumson. My first concern is ensuring that knowledge of Christ is spread to those who have not yet benefited from it.' Finley was surprised by the firmness and coherence of his own answer. So he continued. 'As my pastoral duties do not extend to all parts of the day, I believe an hour, or two, of instruction every week in the Bible could suffice. For the benefit of our native staff, and their families.'

Mrs Rumson pondered this. 'Harrison's man Cherian is Christian. Can he not take on this charge?' she began. 'And should you, Reverend Finley, be teaching this message quite so freely? No reason to squander precious seed on barren soil, as it were.' To Finley, the reply seemed surprising and mean-spirited.

'Providence has already revealed to us what the natural order of the universe is. Teaching God's message can only help ensure that this order be understood and pervades to all who live around us.' Finley had already considered these objections. 'After all, Christ did not preach to his disciples that they keep the word of God secret. Indeed, His early disciples faced persecution for doing so!'

'I see you have considered this more carefully than I have, Reverend,' Mrs Rumson replied stiffly.

'But that is my calling, Mrs Rumson. It was also my ardent wish even before I set sail for India,' said Finley.

'I believe you wish to follow in that tradition of churchmen who create bulwarks at the very edges of Christendom,' Eliza interjected. 'Is that not true, Reverend Finley?'

Finley felt something jump in his chest. Eliza had expressed in plain words the very things he had dared not share until now.

'It is a worthwhile ambition for a young clergyman, no doubt,' said the elder Rumson. 'To what, then, do we owe this particular visit?'

Eliza quickly blunted the question. 'Let us not be testy, Mother. This is only the first time the Reverend has visited our rooms. And any man, or indeed any woman, should surely feel free to voice their aspirations among friends!'

'Eliza, dear, what are these unrealized aspirations of

yours?' Mrs Rumson enquired. 'Are you not gratified with
your life as it is?'

Eliza paused and stood up, thoughtfully refilling the
teacups. As asked, each moment of silence after the
question only increased the tension.

'I do not speak of *my* desire for something different,
Mother. I speak of the greater human need to pursue
aspirations that provide meaning to one's existence. Those
surely bear heeding!'

'My daughter here is a gem among her peers, Reverend,'
Mrs Rumson reflected, smiling.

Finley did not know how to respond, and nodded
gravely into his tea to hide the hot glow that was returning
to his face. The conversation had taken a turn he had not
expected. Relationships between mother-in-laws and
daughter-in-laws were something he knew little about,
and Finley could not make sense of the swings between
argument and endearment. He decided that the last sip
from this teacup – which he had been emptying in quick
gulps – would be the appropriate time to take his leave.

'It has been an illuminating conversation, Rumsons,'
he said as he stood up. 'Enjoy the remainder of your
afternoon!'

'I hope you are not disappointed at our company,
Reverend,' Mrs Rumson added. 'I think your goal is most
worthy, and I will be sure to pass that along to Haight
and Harrison. Unfortunately, in my position, I am often

entreated to underwrite various endeavours by men – and they are always men – far less forthright than yourself. You should not take my initial reticence to heart.'

'Let me walk you out,' Eliza added, standing up.

'Thank you, Mrs Rumson,' he addressed the elder, and followed Eliza out of the terrace.

Once inside the suite, Eliza began to say her goodbyes. 'Thank you for paying us a visit, Reverend . . .' She must have said more, but Finley was lost looking at her eyes and how the movement of her cheeks changed them from diamond to oval and back again, and throughout kept their lively twinkle but the star would change its position when she smiled. Their faces were close enough that he could smell the scent of lavender and warm skin wafting from her. And then the movement stopped, and her eyebrows rose in bemused enquiry. 'Reverend? Are you all right? About the walk?'

'I'm so sorry, Mrs Rumson,' Finley blurted, his eyes coming back into focus. They were standing by the door to the suite now.

'As I was saying, Reverend . . .' Her lips formed into a quivering smile. '. . . I will see you tomorrow at the Reverend's Walk.'

'Yes, yes, of course!'

'Good day, Reverend Finley.' The door was open.

Finley stumbled out of the door. 'Yes, good day, Mrs Rumson!' And he walked down the long hotel corridor, unsteadily at first, but gradually regaining confidence in his stride as he approached the dining room, the sunlit terrace, and the company of people not as beautiful as Eliza Rumson.

In the classroom the next day, Finley found himself distracted. As on the first morning of school, the fog dawdled and moped overhead. Throughout the slow hours, he made several nervous checks of the sky through the schoolroom shutters.

'Reverend Finley, are we delaying the Reverend's Walk?' Evelyn Haight asked. She had obviously noticed his repeated checks.

'I hope not, Evelyn. I have planned to take us to a special lookout that I discovered, one that I wish to share with all of you. And timing is of the essence.'

'Why is that, Reverend? Could we not simply go next week?' Andrew Rumson asked.

'Dear boy, that is precisely what I fear!' Finley grew animated. 'I have discovered a special kind of flower that does not bloom every year. But it is in bloom now, and I should like to present it to all of you before the season is over.'

Mention of the season being over naturally brought other topics to the fore. 'I am very much looking forward to the end-of-season gala. It may well be my last one!' Evelyn said, very self-assured. And then, looking at the crestfallen faces of a few of her compatriots, she hastened to add. 'Not for certain, of course. But Father did say I may be in England at this time next year.'

'All the more reason to make the most of what we have before us today, children!' Finley continued, redirecting the discussion to more productive topics.

Before long, the sun did emerge timidly from behind the great banks of fog and began to burn them off. By the time lunch was completed and the party had gathered near the flagpole for the Reverend's Walk, the sky contained only high clouds with a distant band of grey marring just one corner of the horizon. Finley was extremely pleased that he would share his private discovery, with its great bundles of purple flowers. He and Cherian had walked the path before to check that all would be well, despite the precipitous incline and narrow path, and he noted that his reminders to the party to wear sturdy boots had been heeded. Due to the narrowness of the path, and the relative proximity to the hotel, there was no need for additional catering, but satchels of sandwiches and flasks of lemonade had been packed instead.

'Tell me, Reverend, what is this place you are taking us to?' Eliza had asked as they crossed over the central green outside the hotel.

'Mrs Rumson, it is a location of my own discovery!' Finley had replied, with some pride. 'Although truly, God has provided the wonder that is to be seen there.'

'A mystery, then? Or do you care to describe this

destination at greater length?' The question sounded serious, but when Finley looked over at her, he could see Eliza's eyes twinkling, a smile below the brim of her pith helmet. Her cheeks were beginning to grow brighter, and Finley could again feel the tightening in his chest.

'We will be there soon enough, Mrs Rumson,' he chided. 'We should be mindful of the path ahead for now.'

They had arrived at the break in the forest cover where the steep downhill began. On account of the clear sky, the valley floor could be seen below. But as Finley looked further out, he could see that the dense bank of grey clouds had taken charge of more of the sky than when they started.

'Surely, Reverend, you must unfurrow your brow at such a wonderous vista!' Eliza exclaimed.

'Yes, of course, Mrs Rumson!'

Cherian had had the forethought to tie a rope to several of the larger trees above the incline, and this served as a hand-hold for each of the children as they clambered downwards. It wasn't as treacherous as Finley had first remembered, but he suspected that Cherian had scouted out a location with a more gradual descent to help the group. Once down, Cherian was doing a highly efficient job at marshalling the children and making sure they stayed in single file, as he led the way. Eliza held the rope and nimbly made her way down the slope, despite the length of her travelling dress. Finley suspected that ample practice climbing in and out of boats at the lake had prepared her to quickly crouch low and close to the ground when footing became unsteady. Finley followed after her. The path remained narrow, but intact. Occasionally, Cherian would halt to allow Eliza and the children to take in the expanse of the valley below and the plains beyond.

'It seems so strange that we must make our way down there again and find our place out in that distance,' Eliza commented. 'I have grown so accustomed to our aerie of green trees and fog and hills.' She said this with a sadness that attached itself to Finley. He could think of nothing to say in return. Luckily the group had started moving again.

When they turned the final corner and came to the tongue of rock, the children shouted in surprise. 'Mother, it is a meadow that stretches to the sky!' Alice shouted to Eliza. But her mother was not looking to the sky or the valley below. She was staring in open-mouthed wonder at the bushes of bright purple flowers that lay scattered across the meadow.

Finley felt he ought to say a few words. 'Children, please come close so that I do not have to raise my voice in these sublime surroundings. These beautiful blossoms that you see around you are a sign of God's bounty. And we should feel so very gratified to see them. They do not bloom every year, but this year, we have been granted this boon. Before we enjoy our food and drink, let us bow our heads in a moment of prayer for all that we have before us.' The children bowed their heads. After giving thanks for the wondrous surroundings, and the fact that the fog had held off for the day, Finley found himself also quietly giving thanks for Eliza Rumson's company. And when he lifted his eyes from his internal reflection, Finley caught himself looking directly into hers over the few bushes that stood in between them. Her eyes were open wide, and welling up. She looked quickly away, so he did the same.

While the children devoured their sandwiches and lemonade with glee, Finley sat quietly by himself on a tussock at one edge of the meadow, his back to the hillside. From this vantage, he could see the entirety of the meadow and admire Eliza's silhouette as she picked her way between the bushes of bright purple flowers, stooping occasionally to examine them closely. The dark green of her dress provided a stark contrast to both the flowers and the tresses of her hair which had loosened themselves from their moorings. For just a moment, a fleeting moment, Finley allowed himself to pretend what it might be like to be George Rumson. To imagine that the shapely green silhouette floating between the bushes, looking out into the steel-grey sky, was his companion in life. That she would be the one he would see every time he made his way through the cabin door. And for just that moment, Finley's heart was full, and he felt rooted to the spot where he sat.

'Saar,' Cherian cut in. 'Go back to hotel, saar.' He was gesturing towards the same sky that Eliza had been staring at. And Finley realized that the bank of clouds that had seemed so far away was now nearly upon them.

'Gather the children, Cherian!' Finley exclaimed. 'Get them back on the path!'

Cherian sprang into action, shouting 'Master' and 'Miss' and waving his arms, entreating the children to come away from the edge and back to where he stood, in the middle of the meadow. Finley began to move towards Eliza. She was standing with her palms gently brushing the bushes of flowers on either side of her, and staring straight out over the valley into the rapidly approaching wall of steel-grey fog.

'Mrs Rumson!' Finley was shouting. 'Mrs Rumson!' Perhaps his sounds were getting lost. 'Eliza!' he shouted, feeling impetuous and flustered at the same time. She turned suddenly, with a puzzled look on her face, but immediately realized the situation. Most of the meadow was enclosed in light, but thickening cloud. She could still see Finley clearly, gesturing frantically towards her. Finley and Eliza rapidly closed the distance between them, but by the time they stood close to one another, the rest of the meadow was blanketed in soft grey mist.

'The children!' Eliza looked frantic.

'Cherian!!' Finley shouted into the fog. He knew the general orientation of the meadow.

'Saar, yes, saar!' came a muffled reply.

'Have you found the children?!' he shouted again.

'All children, yes, saar!' The reply sounded further away. 'I take back to hotel, saar.'

'Cherian's got this in hand, Mrs Rumson. He knows this area well. We should make our way back.'

'Very well, Reverend. You found the route here, so I will trust that you can navigate us back.' Eliza sounded severe, and Finley glanced at her, looking closely at her face in the fog. She looked back expectantly, so Finley began walking. First, gingerly through the bushes towards where he knew the side of the hill would be. And then, turning right, he followed the curve of the hillside until he could see where the narrow portion of the path started. Every so often he would turn to look, making sure Eliza was still behind him.

They moved slowly, and the fog grew thicker. At the point where Finley knew the path was at its most treacherous, he held out his left hand, and Eliza looked at it for a moment, before taking it with a shy smile. If Finley could have stood stock-still in the fog, holding Eliza's hand, he would have done so. But he walked slowly on with careful, awkward steps until he came to the incline where the rope hung down. The only sounds were the muffled hush that accompanies heavy, creeping fog and the sound of their breathing as they stepped carefully along the narrow path. He let go of her hand, and pulled hard on the rope, testing to see if it would bear his weight.

'Mrs Rumson,' he whispered. 'I believe you should ascend first.'

Eliza's eyes flashed, but it was neither anger, nor her teasing wit. 'With your assistance, Reverend.' And she put out both her hands to grab his. Instead, Finley placed both arms around her and lifted her up and around himself, so that she was now closest to the rope. The constricting bands around his chest felt stronger than ever, and he held her body for a moment longer. The embrace was awkward; Finley realized he did not know how to hold a woman. He felt the warmth of her palms, pressed firmly on his back, and she held on in return. Finley searched her eyes with longing and fear, before Eliza turned her gaze away. Her head sank slowly down on his chest, the pith helmet cutting off her eyes from view.

'Saar! Rumson madam!' came a voice from above. Cherian had found his way to the upper path.

'James, my dear, we ought to return to the party,' she said, in a disembodied, warm voice that could easily have been the fog speaking. Finley released his embrace and Eliza's hands fell slowly away.

'We are here Cherian! Where are the children?!' Finley shouted.

'All children here, saar!'

'Excellent! Please assist Mrs Rumson in climbing up, Cherian!'

Soon, Cherian's face appeared part-way along the rope.

Eliza grabbed hold of it, and with Cherian's assistance she was able to follow the rope up the incline. Finley followed a few yards behind, and the party was soon reunited at the top of the incline.

'Alice! Andrew!' Eliza shouted as she neared the top.

'Yes, Mother!' Andrew replied. 'This was quite an adventure! Cherian knew of another route, so we did not have to take the scary path on the way back! We came through the forest.'

'Are you all right, Alice?' Eliza enquired.

'Yes, Mother. We simply followed Cherian.'

'Excellent, excellent. The path we took is considerably more dangerous, especially when one adds the element of fog!' Eliza replied, looking around to make sure all the children had returned. 'All here, then? Come, Reverend, let us make our way back to the hotel.' And she gave Finley a wistful smile that came almost entirely from her eyes.

15

Evidence Goes Missing

Pandian does not like meetings. In fact, the man is fundamentally incapable of sitting still for longer than fifteen minutes. The end-of-year planning meetings, which often drag on well past the usual half-hour, are especially difficult for him. This was as true in college as it is now, but since we had very few overlapping classes, I did not have to endure his constant fidgeting or huffing and puffing then. I sometimes forget this and sit next to him. At present, we are both enduring Chapman's monotone updates regarding the end of term, and I can feel the fidgeting and shifting starting up next to me. The semi-annual concert is to take place tomorrow evening, Chapman reminds us. For me, the concert is a rare treat, as many of the students who perform are impressive musical talents. The part of themselves that they pour into music does not always show up in the classes I teach. One has to recognize this in children, so that if they grow despondent over their maths homework, they should still see themselves as capable in music or art or something completely different. Because I know Pandian's tendencies, I initially ignore his nudging. But it becomes more insistent, so I turn to him.

'Look at him, what confidence, eh?' Pandian whispers, tilting his head to indicate someone else across the room. Pandian's notion of a whisper is actually more like a stage whisper and several teachers turn to look at us. Pandian pretends to focus straight ahead with rapt attention as Chapman drones on. After the turned heads resume their normal positions, Pandian pokes my thigh and points to Koshy. Koshy is two rows ahead of us, sitting next to Ms Little-K.

'And last, but not least, Ghosh will walk us through the plans for the end-of-year examination schedule,' Chapman intones.

I must have looked startled. For several moments my mind has been weighing the possibility that Koshy and Ms Little-K are in a relationship, unbeknownst to the rest of us. With the distractions of rain and fog, and the angle at which I was standing, it could easily have been Ms Little-K on the porch! What a sly fellow Koshy must be to come in and steal Ms Little-K's affections out from right under our noses. I shoot Pandian an irritated glare as I stand up to talk. It is a difficult frame of mind in which to present examination arrangements for the end of the term, but I do my best.

As the meeting disperses, I make an effort to watch Koshy closely. He gives a nod and smile to Ms Little-K before quickly grabbing two sandwiches and making his way towards the door, smiling and excusing himself along the way. She smiles back and gives him a little wave. It's actually a half-wave, performed at medium height and close to the body. I suppose it could be nothing, but it could also be meant as a discreet gesture, so as not to attract attention. Then Ms Little-K gracefully makes her way over to a group of science teachers that has gathered to coordinate examination logistics with each other – as I have recommended in my presentation. If I were in their shoes – Ms Little-K and Koshy, that is – I would leave a meeting separately as well, if I didn't want to create gossip. I want to get away from campus as soon as possible now. On the way to pick up my bag and papers from the office, I see Tarun in the corridor.

'Hello, Mr G!' he calls out.

'Yes, Tarun, was there something you wanted?' I am not in the mood to make small talk anymore.

'No, nothing, Mr G,' he replies. 'Just that you had asked me to talk to Mrs H about application fees, and I did.'

'And?'

'We've got the waiver paperwork together, that's all . . .'

I am about to blurt out something to the effect of '. . . and is that why you stopped me?' when I realize that he's cowering, as if expecting a harsh retort. I have to collect myself.

'That's excellent, Tarun. This means that your applications can all go out on time, right?' I hope he can't tell how hard I'm trying to maintain an even tone.

'Exactly, Mr G!' he replies. 'That's why I thought you would want to know!'

'Good job, Tarun. Now – fingers crossed!' And I give him a smile and nod before I walk on towards my office. Poor Tarun shouldn't have to bear the brunt of Koshy's wily behaviour.

I gather my corrections for the evening, stuff them into my bag and leave the office. Mrs Mani has left some time ago, and her table is as organized as ever. Chapman is still at the meeting, still leeching energy from the fawning of the junior teachers, I'm sure. I leave the campus through a side gate that most people don't use or know about. I don't want to be seen and I don't want to have to talk to anyone. Most of the ground is easy to cover in brisk strides, because there's still enough light. In my annoyance, I don't pay enough attention to one of the roots sticking out and end up stumbling on the mud and gravel. It's a lesson to slow down; this never happens when I take my time. As a child, whenever I grew angry, my mother would remind me that such accidents were the world's way of telling you to calm down and get a grip. The lesson apparently also applies when you stub your toe on a piece of furniture, or bang your head on an open cabinet door you forgot to close in haste. Very well – I walk the rest of the way home more deliberately, but I'm still seething. Sivakumari's dinner is cold. But that's how I will eat it. The first of many self-flagellations for waiting too long to tell Lila Kalyani how I felt, before this Koshy fellow rode off with her. Corrections are my next penance – my punishment for not having the intestinal fortitude to approach Ms Little-K first!

The next day, Friday, passes in the usual flurry of activity. Normally, I would enjoy staying on campus for dinner because Friday evenings are light with the promise of weekend events and leisure. And today is the concert, so I try to not let yesterday's discovery mar my experience. But it's difficult, especially as I review the advance copy of the concert programme over dinner. Koshy's name shows up in seven different places. Out of the thirty or so pieces being played, this fellow has so ingratiated himself, that there are seven – yes, I have counted and rechecked – entries which indicate 'Instructor: D. Koshy'. One would think that the rest of the music and drama departments almost didn't exist!

After the dinner of hot curry and delicious chocolate ice cream, I begin to feel better. The best thing I can do is be gallant in loss, I suppose. And enjoy the concert as if

I know nothing about the whole Koshy and Ms Little-K debacle. At the very least, I can enjoy the music. As I am not chaperoning, I take a seat early near the front of the auditorium. The students and audience members trickle in over the next several minutes. I am close enough to the stage to see the first few performers setting up with their teachers. Koshy is also backstage, and as if to taunt me, his narrow form in the too-crisp white shift, flitting between the angled stage curtains. Soon, more teachers join me near the front of the room, and that two-seat margin the students use to avoid sitting too close to teachers begins to fill up. Mrs K and Ms Little-K are here too. Mrs K waves, and out of instinctive politeness I indicate that there are some empty seats near me. As they get seated, Mrs K next to me, Ms Little-K one seat beyond, I can't help but reflect on the irony of the situation.

'Your Mr Koshy has been a very busy man!' Mrs K comments to me.

'Pardon?' I don't understand what she means. Is she trying to wilfully goad me?

'I mean, look here, Suman, he has so many of his students performing in the concert. And only one semester in!' She is pointing to the programme.

'Oh, I see . . .' I pretend to not have realized this. 'Yes, very impressive indeed.'

'His students really seem to like him!' Ms Little-K offers. She seems to have dressed up a bit for the concert: the dark red lipstick contrasts deliciously with the rest of her face and her smile picks up the dimple on the left cheek.

'That's very good, glad to hear it!' I do my best to stay calm. If this is what is required to maintain a surreptitious relationship, perhaps it is better that I did not have the chance to throw in my lot with Ms Little-K after all. She seems far too adept at maintaining the sly deception. I decide that I should go on the offensive in the few moments before the concert starts. 'Have you got to know him well?' I venture.

'No, actually,' Ms Little-K replies. 'I've only seen him at staff meetings. Our paths don't cross very much at all.' She says this nonchalantly, a natural prevaricator, it seems. Perhaps years of living under an all-seeing maternal eye forces one to hone that skill.

'What about you, Suman? Don't you live near him?' Mrs K asks.

'Yes, just the next cottage over.' The question has caught me off guard. 'I keep meaning to invite him over for dinner – maybe once the semester ends.'

'Yes, you should!' she exclaims. 'You know, you young people have to socialize more. I keep telling Lila this.'

'Please, Amma,' Ms Little-K cuts in with an apologetic smile.

'What? I am not saying anything unusual. You shouldn't be spending all your time sitting by yourselves in your own houses.'

'Enough, Amma . . .' Ms Little-K is getting annoyed – clearly not the first time she is hearing such advice from her mother. 'I have not exchanged two words with the man,' she says, gesturing towards Koshy. 'He's basically a kid that just finished college. What would I say to him?'

'Fine, fine. All I am saying is that it would do you all good to be around people at your own stage in life.'

Ms Little-K doesn't reply, but she is visibly annoyed. I find I don't have to reply – the first few bars of *Für Elise* have started up, so we really shouldn't be talking anyway. The exchange has left me confused – Ms Little-K's annoyance at her mother, and her implication that Koshy was simply too young for her, both seemed genuine. And she is still sitting there in an endearing huff, her lips pursed and arced downwards at the corners of her mouth. Her face relaxes with the progress of the performance. Shalini Kochchar, ninth grade. Instructor: Mrs Momen.

The ordering of performances in school concerts is something of an art, and the preparer of this programme knows it well: younger performers are interspersed between older, more accomplished ones. For the next piece, as expected, titters and giggles rise from the audience when the dancers – a group of boys from tenth and eleventh grade – emerge shirtless in their ornate, brocaded dhotis. It is usually at this time that I cast a baleful eye over those students sitting near me. The children, much as they hate to admit it, will take their cues from how the adults in the room are behaving. I try to cut off any Perkins-esque tendencies to treat performance of Western classical music as more desirable than Indian classical dance. It is in the Bharatanatyam style, and is carefully choreographed and instrumented. The music for the piece would have been worth listening to in its own right, as the live flute and mridangam accompaniment was far better than the usual backing tracks played from a cassette.

Several pieces later, I was able to take special pleasure in Supriya's performance of *Afternoon of a Faun*. Mrs Cama, her instructor, performed the accompaniment on the piano, and for once I was relieved not to have to see Koshy's involvement. It makes me smile to think of Supriya as a twelfth grader. When she joined the school in tenth grade, she was a shy husk of a personality. But after making friends, and finding a mentor in Mrs Cama, she has become someone much more self-assured. Of course, she still struggles in maths, but I have learned not to take such things personally. I wish I could tell each of my students – perhaps whisper it into their dreams at night – that they will each have to find the thing they most want to work hard for. For now, Supriya's is the flute – and it shows. It is a confident performance, and I clap loudly to show my appreciation. She gives the three of us seated together a big smile after she's done with her piece. The relief on her face is obvious. Next are a few performances of songs from *The Little Mermaid*. This group of kids appears to have mastered the delivery of Disney musical numbers that require multiple characters. Their timing is impeccable, generating much laughter and earning a hearty applause from the audience.

This is followed by hushed silence as WonSik Choi comes on stage. He's a timid, slightly built tenth grader who would not normally attract any special attention. But at the piano on stage, he definitely does. He is known to be among the most accomplished students in the school, and is preparing for the highest examination level that the Royal School of Music board offers. It's a crucial step before a performer can gain professional licensure. Tonight he's performing an original composition, titled *Dueling Tahr,* a composition for two pianos. Of course, Koshy is playing the second part. It starts off with heavy brooding bass notes from WonSik's piano, and a melody motif that imitates the steady, sure steps that a Nilgiri tahr (a local species of mountain goat) would take. The second piano adopts a different melody, at a much higher register – the second tahr is standing high above, distant for now. The timing and syncopation of the music indicate when the two tahr start to notice one another. And then comes the fight – the register of the melodies grows closer, there's a run-up, and then a clash of chords. At first, the chords are evenly matched; it's a fair fight to begin with. But soon, the clashes become lopsided – the second piano is playing dissonant, broken chords that feel off balance. Eventually the second piano slinks away while WonSik's piano, presumably the victor in this fight, maintains a strong rhythm, and holds on to the consonant notes. It's a clever piece and WonSik has succeeded in expressing the idea. Koshy springs quickly up from his piano once the last chord has rung out and claps in WonSik's direction with a small bow. WonSik returns the appreciative gesture, and soon the entire audience is clapping and hollering their admiration.

The next performance is a sixth-grade skit, comedic and cute at the same time. It brings some levity and audience participation, a welcome contrast to the rapt attention demanded by WonSik's piece. We are nearing the end of the concert, which is a good thing, as the audience is getting restive. Another piano piece, and by one of Koshy's students again. This one is by Maya Chatterjee – the visiting student whom I had to warn about not going off-campus by herself. *Spanish Dances – No 2. Oriental* by Enrique Granados. I fear I am also losing interest and start to look around the room. The only thing that attracts my attention is that Maya is one of the few students who has taken the trouble to dress up for the performance, and she wears a full-length dress – much like a proper concert pianist. This is different, and the audience also notices. I look at the programme to see how many pieces are left – three after this one. Thank goodness.

The piece starts with moody arpeggios on the left hand, and only later does the melody in the right hand become clear. There is an entire section in the middle that is ponderous and disjointed from the initial melody. It is only once the reprise begins that I realize I have encountered this undulating pattern of music somewhere before. I just can't remember where. And they are not normal arpeggios in the 1-3-5 sense, or chromatic scales. They carry more of a sadness with them – perhaps a lot of second intervals. Where have I heard this repeating pattern before? I can't remember. I mentally list out the music I have listened to recently, but I don't recall choosing anything by Granados. Maybe it's the snatched sounds of melodies emanating from the piano practice rooms that I can sometimes hear from my office? There's a round of applause from the audience, and Maya stands up and gives the audience a bow. Still, the pattern sticks in my mind. For some reason, I can't seem to set it aside.

The next two pieces are mercifully brief, and the last one, while longer, is a rousing choral performance. As the lights come on, students have already begun to stream out of the doors at the back of the auditorium. Everyone appears to have had their fill of culture for now – perhaps we should break these up into two smaller concerts next term? I stand up and wish Mrs K and Ms Little-K goodnight. Outside, students are dawdling and chatting with each other, avoiding returning to their dorms. I see a few couples striding purposefully off to more private corners of the campus, but I feel suddenly tired, and don't have any inclination to enquire after their plans.

Before going back to my office to get my bag and papers, I decide to make a quick stop at the staff washrooms. I have a fifteen-minute walk ahead of me, and in this dark, it's unwise to try to cover the ground in a rush. I am about to open the door to leave, as I see, of all people, Koshy coming in. I know it would be churlish not to, so I congratulate him on the wonderful pieces his students have played. He seems genuinely moved and puts down the stack of music books he is carrying in order to shake my outstretched hand.

'That was fantastic, Koshy! Your students did some amazing performances!'

'Thank you so much, Mr G!' he replies, almost as a student might. 'It's easy to look good when I have such talented students.' He straightens his glasses and pushes back the flap of hair that is meandering down his forehead.

'Please, call me Suman. Anyway, fantastic work, Koshy. You should be very pleased.'

'I am, Mr G!' And after a brief pause, 'I mean, Suman. I really didn't know that this is how it would be to teach here.'

'What do you mean?'

'Well, you know. Many of the kids I work with take this very seriously.' Suddenly the air seemed to go out of him. 'I will miss them.'

'Why do you say that? Are you leaving us, Koshy?' I joke.

'No, no, nothing like that!' He seems alarmed at the misunderstanding. 'But you know, they graduate and all that.'

'Oh, of course. But don't worry, Koshy, we have a long tradition of good students here.'

'Yes, of course. I'm just new . . .'

'Well, from what I can see, Koshy, you are a naturally talented instructor!'

'Thanks. Thanks again! I should . . .' He gestures nervously towards the bathroom door. 'Have a good night.'

And he proceeded into the bathroom. I wondered if I should offer to wait for him. We could, after all, walk back together since we live next door to each other. This is one of those situations I detest, and usually avoid. Waiting outside the restroom for a colleague is awkward at the best of times. But to do so without prior agreement would seem downright strange. I look down at the pile of sheet music Koshy has left on the table outside. *Spanish Dances – No. 2 Oriental* sits on top of the stack. Maya's piece. I take a closer look at the arpeggios that so entranced me when I heard them. And that's when it occurs to me that that, even though I have never heard them played before tonight, I have seen them somewhere. I grab the score from Koshy's pile of music and leave the corridor quickly before he comes out. He can walk home alone tonight – I have to get to my office.

Most of the school lights are turned off, and I don't want to attract the attention of the few straggling students returning to their dorms. And I especially don't want to see any teachers. I keep Koshy's music tucked under my arm and fumble with the keys for the administrative offices. It's dark inside, which means that Darling and Chapman are not here. I navigate around Mrs Mani's desk, and go through the door to my own office. Now I can turn on the lights and take a good hard look at the music I have temporarily borrowed from Koshy. Once at my desk, I open the drawer and pull out the envelope with the picture inside. Lots of piano pieces have up-and-down, arpeggio-like runs for the left hand. Maybe I am feeling more pressure from Chapman than I realized. Perhaps I'm deluding myself.

But it turns out I am not delusional, after all. Every yearning I felt as a child, of wanting to draw level with Sherlock Holmes's outsized sleuthing abilities, now feels rewarded. The link lies clearly in front of me. The music on the photograph is indeed the first page of Granados's *Oriental*.

My first impulse is to rush outside and tell someone, anyone, that I've found a clue about the picture. But there is no one to tell right now. And besides, what would I say? That I've found the matching piece of music? How many copies of this music are floating around the school in any case? Perhaps not so many. In which case, who would have a copy? Well, Koshy certainly did. I look more closely at the score. It's not just the notes on the staff, but there are also handwritten scribbles – the word 'slow' in pencil and a circle around the first trill. That is not part of the printed score. I look closely at the picture. The image of the breasts is distracting, but the picture also shows some blur of writing, and the same hand-drawn circle around the trill.

And then it occurs to me. Maya played the piece this evening. Cover the breasts in the photograph – pretend, for an instant, that the girl in the photo was wearing a loose sweatshirt instead, and all of a sudden, the lower half of Maya's face is staring back at me from behind the music. After all that, it is a photo of Maya Chatterjee that we have been staring at for so long. The realization makes the photo suddenly more alluring and attractive. So that is what was under that concert dress tonight!

I catch myself. I am the only person who knows the origins of the photograph, even though many are aware of its existence. What I still don't know, I now realize, is how the photograph was taken. She couldn't have done it herself – both hands are holding the piece of music in front of her. I look around the picture for any clues in the background. The problem with these sorts of enquiries is that, left in the hands of amateur sleuths such as myself, the attractiveness of the breasts is distracting enough to preclude clear observation of everything else in plain view. Maya's hair in the picture is undone, falling loosely over her shoulders. Today, it was held back during the concert, but as she bowed much of it tumbled forward. And I have seen that same tumbling movement before. Yes – that drape, that movement, that same hair. I had seen it at Koshy's house. On both occasions when I thought to pay him a neighbourly visit, it was Maya who was with him! She must be the woman on the porch, and then again sitting at the piano.

Of course it was Maya! The same Maya who used her camera from photography class to take pictures of the kurinji flowers. Did she already know Koshy then? Were they already seeing each other? It would not have been hard for her to walk the hundred yards down to his house. She could easily have taken a route from the scenic overlook point on Finley's Walk, cut through the thicker growth and got to the field where I found her taking pictures. Maybe she was on her way back from Koshy's place when she first noticed the blooms?

The other implication of all this made me smile. I had been a fool; Koshy had nothing to do with Ms Little-K at all. I had spent the better part of a day conjuring up the image of Lila Kalyani as the woman on the porch, when all along it was Maya. There was nothing to hold against Koshy – no grudge I could bear him on that front. Pandian should be the one to blame for putting the thought in my head; but then again, I was the one who embellished it brilliantly. And now, what was there to do? Report my findings to Chapman and initiate disciplinary proceedings against Koshy. And Maya, of course, because it clearly states in the school handbook that students should not fraternize with members of staff. Chapman would be pleased to put this to rest. Perhaps I would enter his good graces as well. Yes, that was the way forward. I carefully restored the photograph to the envelope and placed the envelope inside the sheet music. All of which went carefully into my bag. I had been sitting in my office for over an hour now – it was definitely time to walk home.

At eleven in the night, when the moon has had a chance to climb high, the same paths that seem treacherous and forbidding at dusk can appear well lit in silvery, erratic light. I make sure to walk through the larger corridors and leave by the main gate – the guards do not take kindly to surreptitious movements around campus late at night. The night has cleared, and I feel grateful that I am wearing a jacket in the cool air. The shops on the main roads are boarded up, and the normally vocal stray dogs are curled into repose. When it's dark, sounds seem to become clearer, and for a while it is only my footsteps and breathing accompanying me down the road as I head away from the campus.

Maya will be leaving soon. She is only here for the semester, as Mrs K had told me. A week or two left, and then the kids all head home. Perhaps that's why Koshy seemed suddenly deflated when he talked about missing his students. He is a teacher, though, and he should really know better than to have a relationship with a student. This cannot be allowed at school. At this stage, it's the principle of it, really. What would we do with Maya? Tell her future college that she behaved inappropriately? Wasn't she in some sort of special accelerated programme? What would that achieve? It didn't seem that she was an unwilling participant either. Koshy and Maya could scarcely be five years apart in age – if that.

The cattle trap at the gate to Lake Compound requires careful negotiation. Even though the shiny metal bars glint in the moonlight, you wouldn't want to twist your ankle here. My thoughts return to Maya and Koshy's circumstances. What if it had been I who had found someone? And our bubbles had joined together, even for just a short while? And then, after a happy interlude, what if the arms that embraced me, the hands that tousled my hair, the warm skin that held me close, were to disappear forever? What purpose would further sanction serve? Would it make me repentant? Convince me that I would have chosen differently had the opportunity arisen? No. I would choose as Koshy and Maya had done. I can be honest with myself, at least in this small measure.

I am passing Koshy's cottage now and turn right for the last few steps towards Penrose. Will Chapman think more highly of me now that I have 'cracked the case' and presented him a complete accounting of what has transpired under our noses? And what will I do with this increased regard from Chapman? Bottle it? Put it on a shelf to dust off and admire from time to time? Will darkening Koshy's world serve to brighten mine? Will the strict execution of my administrator's obligations make Koshy's music lesson any more effective or enjoyable for his students?

Opening the door, I turn on the lights in the living room and see Sivakumari's dinner, waiting and gone cold. I quickly turn off the lights and get under the covers. What if Lila were here with me now and I could put my arm around her hips and stomach – would I feel differently? Would the walk home feel easier? Would we talk about the concert we had seen and how talented the kids were? Or would we talk about how scandalous it was that a young teacher was having a relationship with a student? Would we wonder aloud about how justified we were in our relationship, while at the same time hacking away at Koshy and Maya's bond? Or, would we kiss and agree how lucky we were to have found each other?

There is nobody here with me, of course. The absence I feel now is of my own conjuring. There has never been anybody here with me. Soon Koshy will feel a great absence too, except his will not be conjured but real. I start to drift off and I am looking at the field of flowers through Koshy's eyes. I see Maya and she is pleased to see me. She runs up to me and we walk hand in hand to the spot on the other side of the forested bit, where you can look over the paved footpath of Finley's Walk. Over the heads of the tourists snapping pictures on the big rock that sticks out over the deep green valley below, I look down to see our hands together and I see the fingers are different now, stained with silver. They are Lila's hands, and my hands are my own; Lila stands next to me where Maya stood, and it is Lila's face and jawline that form into a look of contentment. If Lila is here with me someday, would I be more pleased to tell her that I kept Koshy and Maya's little secret, in our little corner of the world? Or would I be proud to say I did my duty and turned the two of them in? No – I want no hand in creating such law-abiding misery.

16

Tea and Fog

Harrison flashed an angry stare at Finley. 'I cannot grasp why hotel buildings should be used for the natives!' he spat. 'Surely the word of God can also be taught outside the compound?'

'Come, Harrison, where would you suggest the Reverend preach?' cajoled Haight. 'There will be consternation if we use any of the natives' own gathering places. I believe you mentioned using the chapel once a week, Finley? Then those who wish to attend may do so – it will not be seen as a requirement or an imposition of those outside. And they will not actually enter the hotel building.'

'Indeed. And we need not extend the invitation beyond the native staff, if that is an acceptable compromise,' Finley replied.

'This will become the thin end of the wedge, mark my words. First, they are taught the word of Christ. And then, they will ask to worship together with us on Sundays! And before long, they will be sitting at our tables asking to sup with us!' Harrison thundered.

'Preposterous. Do collect yourself, man!' Haight was losing patience. 'Reverend, if Harrison cannot be convinced of this arrangement, then I am afraid, for the time being, you may have to preach from some other location.'

'Forgive my intemperance,' Harrison cut in. His tone was apologetic. 'The arrangements for the end-of-season ball, while also ensuring that guests are prepared for departure ... It is all proving quite challenging.'

'May I be of assistance?' offered Finley.

'Thank you, Reverend. For now, if you would instruct Cherian to pay greater mind to his responsibilities at the hotel, that would be most helpful.'

'All's well, then?' Haight asked. 'Finley can hold his meeting?' And, pausing awkwardly, 'Pardon me, Reverend, I am sure a more appropriate word must exist for sermons delivered specifically for the benefit of heathen souls.'

'Very well ...' Harrison turned and marched purposefully off towards the kitchens.

Finley nodded, relieved to see the end of this tense conversation. On the terrace outside, Chapman was serving coffee to guests nearby, and his company provided a welcome distraction. Finley was acutely aware that he had not set eyes upon Eliza in the two days since the Reverend's Walk. The absence caused him to fret when alone. It was not imagined – she had returned his embrace.

He could still remember the weight of her head on his chest, the felt of her green dress and her body pressed against his. How he wished he had had a few more moments to speak with her before Cherian's call had cut in. He would tell her how he had conjured her smiling face and wind-swept hair over and over in his mind. How much he yearned for her company, her touch, the smell of lavender and warm skin. Perhaps she had informed her husband of Finley's inappropriate behaviour. Were his days in arcadia soon to come to an end?

Lunch was a nerve-racking affair. He entered the dining area and looked around. The room was less crowded than usual, and Finley did not know why. At a table on the far end of the room, a few of the Rumsons sat together, but there was no Eliza. George was seated facing away from the door, but someone must have alerted him to Finley's entrance because he turned to look. Finley wondered whether he should leave the dining room now, before anything untoward occurred.

'James!' George called. 'Reverend Finley!' There was no rancour in his voice.

Finley looked over – something he had tried to avoid. George was motioning for him to come over and join them. Making his way over between the tables, he noticed that the room had never seemed so interminably large before.

'Do join us, Reverend!' George's voice was cheerful.

'Mother told me of your plans to begin ministry here.' No hint of animosity. 'We shall not have the pleasure of your company for much longer, Finley – we should dine together whilst we still can! We depart for Madurai day after tomorrow.'

Surely George knew. Finley's face must have betrayed his growing sense of alarm.

'Nothing to fear, Reverend! We can still enjoy ourselves at the end-of-season ball!' George laughed. 'Surely even a man of God is allowed to celebrate the passing of the seasons!'

The wave of initial relief was tempered by a gulp of sadness that lodged itself halfway down Finley's chest. 'Ah, I was not aware of your departure,' he replied, his voice suddenly hoarse.

'Is something the matter, Reverend?' Andrew enquired.

Finley nodded. He could not find a direction in which to look, and it was growing misty and confused. 'Possibly a head cold, dear boy,' he heard himself say.

'Mother, Eliza and Alice are engrossed in preparations for the ball,' George added. 'They send their greetings.' With that offhand revelation, Finley's heart grew just a little lighter, and he found himself able to summon a smile for George and pick at his food.

As soon as it was polite, he made his excuses and left, drawing as little attention as possible. Finley needed quiet. He needed to conceive of the world around him with no Eliza Rumson in it, and reassure himself that he could exist in such a world; that the departure of her glowing smile after boating or tromping through the hills would not render him inert – like leaves that hang on past autumn and persist limply into winter's snow. He needed to remind himself that in choosing to sail for India, he had not made the arduous journey with the mere intention of growing fond of a beautiful creature, let alone another man's wife. Was Christ not also tempted in the desert? Perhaps it was only fitting that before embarking on serving Him, that he, Finley, should also be tested. Perhaps the lush emerald surroundings that he had mistaken for Eden were actually the grounds of Gethsemane instead?

It was in this brooding frame of mind that Cherian located Finley in the cabin – curtains drawn, his head resting on hands and staring blankly at the dining table. 'Saar, Rumson family leaving in two days,' he remarked.

'Thank you, Cherian, I know,' Finley mumbled. The man's pattern of inopportune intrusions was starting to grate on Finley.

Cherian inhaled the atmosphere of the cabin, and his customary energy seemed to wane. He stood there gazing at a point in the floor midway between the two of them. Finley did not want to be drawn away from his own thoughts, but Cherian's upright stance in the doorway had become a distraction.

'Was there something else?' Finley asked, trying to temper the irritation in his voice.

After a brief pause, 'Will saar also be leaving?'

It had not occurred to Finley. Just as he had been preoccupied with the prospect of Eliza's leaving, others too were thinking of their own futures. He glanced over at Cherian with some surprise, and with a dawning awareness, noticed that he was being closely watched; that he had, in fact, been closely watched for some time now. Cherian's weather-beaten face and baleful eyes, accustomed to compromise and bending to the desires of so many masters, were now making a demand of their own. They held out no judgement or expectation, just a measure of certainty about whether the happy distractions of the last few weeks might continue. If they would not, then it was incumbent on Finley to declare their end had come.

'Why do you ask?'

'Eliza madam also going . . . ' he replied, expressing the remainder of the implication with a wave of his hand, much as a bird would take flight.

'How dare you?' Finley roared. He could feel his temper rise and a ringing in his ears. Where had this ingrate found the temerity to speak of such things? Cherian's eyes grew wide, and he took a quick step backwards. Finley stood up and stepped forward, fists clenched, ready to strike a blow and teach this upstart servant a lesson. He raised his fist, ready to bring it crashing down on Cherian's face. Cherian turned his face to one side to receive the blow, but never once averted his gaze. His body did not cower and his shoulders stayed squared. He had taken beatings before, from cruel masters and overwrought relatives, but Finley was neither. And the blow never came. Finley opened his hand and placed it on Cherian's left shoulder. It was an awkward gesture – neither apology nor blessing – and Finley stepped back and sat down.

'Pardon me, Cherian,' he mumbled. And with a stronger, clearer voice, Finley continued, 'You already know that Christ is the Saviour. I want to stay and teach all those people who live in those huts there. And in the villages. Their souls can also be saved, just as yours will be.' Once he stopped talking, Finley was not sure if he had said all that for Cherian's benefit or his own.

'I go now, saar.' With a backward glance, as if to check that Finley had sufficiently regained his composure, Cherian left the cabin.

Finley no longer wanted to sit alone, wallowing in the dregs of recent events. If he were truly to teach the word of God to the natives who worked at the hotel, then it would require more preparation than teaching the children of guests. He would need to marshal his materials and prepare a plan for ministry. The seminary had not prepared him for this. A pastoral role in a congregation already well versed in the Bible and the story of Christ is very different from one in which there is no shared understanding. How should he even start? With the transformation of Saul on the road to Damascus? That could be easily confused with the stories of ghosts and dacoits that the natives often shared with each other. The story of Adam and Eve in the Garden of Eden? That could be a plausible starting scene. But why were these two people heeding the words of a snake? Surely, they should know to run away from this creature, already known to be dangerous? At the centre of it all, how should one talk about a God who was entirely set apart from the deities carved in stone? Was this a powerful god-king, or was this a godling, subservient to the gods that were already known? What part of their pantheon did this particular god occupy? And the idea of a father willingly leaving his son to suffer at the hands of unjust people – well, that simply would not accord with the stories of gods and kings Finley had been told about. Further reflection was required. Finley resolved to collect the Bibles from the schoolroom; perhaps the illustrated plates in those Bibles would spark his imagination.

Retrieving the Bibles would not be the simple matter that Finley had envisioned. On approaching the boathouse, he realized that the normally serene structure had become a hive of frenetic activity. The boats had been moved from their moorings and tied to stakes away from the boathouse. The jetties were now the location for several small wood fires, with spits over them for roasting meats. The carpenters were busy hanging bunting and decorations along the terrace, while the oil bearers were pouring mustard oil into lamps that had been placed at regular intervals along the edge of the terrace and stairs.

The lack of people on the stairs up to the schoolroom was misleading. Inside, the room had been transformed, and further preparations were in full swing. Should it happen to rain, the room needed to accommodate the majority of guests – certainly the women and children. The central portion, which was normally devoted to the classroom, had been turned into an improvised ballroom, while chairs, schoolroom furniture and tables had been moved to the edges. Harrison stood nervously in the centre of it all, clutching a small ledger and chanting over its contents with great attention. Occasionally, he would bark out an instruction, and Cherian or one of his other employees would translate, relaying the instruction to the appropriate group of workers. It emerged that the carpets stored in a corner of the classroom had mildewed since the last season and Harrison was trying to find a solution that revealed as little of the unsightly stains as possible, while still covering up the uneven boards of the terrace.

'Good afternoon, Reverend,' he called out, still studying his ledger. 'May I be of assistance? As you can see, we are preoccupied.'

'No, thank you, Harrison. I simply wish to collect the Bibles and take them to the chapel in advance of the first sermon to the native staff, tomorrow.'

'Bottom shelf, to the right, behind your table,' came the brisk reply. 'I made sure they would not be damaged by any of this commotion.'

'Much obliged,' Finley nodded. 'I will leave you to your preparations.' And he gathered the six Bibles from the corner of the room.

'Oh, and Reverend . . .' Harrison continued, 'whatever it is you mentioned to Cherian, it appears to have considerably improved his diligence. I presume you shared the missive that he should pay greater mind to his primary responsibilities?'

'Yes . . .' Finley reflected. 'Yes, precisely.'

'Thank you, Reverend!'

Finley decided he would walk along the lake to the chapel, avoiding the central portion of the hotel compound. Afternoon was turning to evening, and the shadows of the trees on the other side of the lake were just starting to spill out and touch the water.

If there was ever a place where one could be content to be lonely, then surely Highpoint was just such a place. For Finley, Highpoint would be full of reminders, though the sacrifices the Lord demanded would be just one necessary piece of his experience. Is a sacrifice made more worthy if it is remembered and brought repeatedly to mind? Or is it best if performed and quickly forgotten? Should he blot Eliza's image from his mind? If Eliza were soon to leave, should there be something to remember her by? Surely, a sacrifice is made more potent in the remembering and not in the forgetting? If so, should he not make arrangements to remember his sacrifice, rather than forget the presence of those dancing eyes and smiling lips? A decision to let go of a memory can be made later; the actions to remember would have to be taken now.

His footsteps soon led him to the chapel, and he placed five of the six Bibles on the table that served as the altar. By then, Finley's attentions had shifted to an entirely different task. He strode briskly out of the compound and across the green at the centre of town. He covered the ground with remarkable vigour, moving swiftly through the forest and out to the incline. Cherian's rope was still secured and he scrambled down, half walking and half running the distance along the narrow path to the meadow. At the meadow, he surveyed the bushes of purple flowers, picking out one with the brightest purple hues that were closest to the edge, looking over the valley below. He marked the larger branches of the bush with a sharp piece of stone – mishappen, urgent gashes, that could not have been created by any animal. This is where he would come to remember her. And from the topmost twigs of the bush, he plucked several of the healthiest flowers and placed them carefully inside the Bible.

Having achieved his goal, Finley turned back from the overlook to make his way home, when an unnaturally large object caught his attention from the far end of the meadow. He walked down the centre of the meadow, up to the point where the ground started to incline upward into the forest. There, planted in the ground was a large piece of canvas. And further beyond, smaller pieces of canvas, planted as flags to mark a path – the kind Cherian would use to mark trails for the Reverend's Walk. Finley launched into a sad chuckle at the realization. This had been Cherian's plan all along; he had marked two paths – one for the walk to the meadow, and a different one for the way back to the hotel. Cherian had conspired to provide Finley a moment of privacy with Eliza. It was no accident that the children had been so efficiently evacuated from the meadow and found their way safely back to the top of the incline. Finley felt a swelling of gratitude in his chest – the man he had nearly struck earlier this afternoon had found a way to satisfy something that Finley had not admitted even to himself.

With Cherian's markings already in place, the path back to the hotel was an easy ascent through the forest, past the green at the centre of town, and back to the cabin. The location of Finley's cabin, close to the path that led from the main hotel building to the boathouse, allowed him to observe the guests as they arrived. The early ones were the children and their ayahs. Finley removed the flowers from the Bible and placed them carefully between sheets of blotting paper, which were then placed in an envelope. The envelope was addressed in Finley's best copperplate:

'To Mrs Eliza Rumson', and sealed. Cherian, who had been occupied with arrangements at the boathouse until very recently, watched this unusual activity with great interest. After rapid ablutions and a change of shirt and collar, Finley was ready for his dinner jacket. Once the cummerbund was tied and Cherian had placed the dinner jacket around his shoulders, Finley felt he needed to explain himself.

'Thank you for your additional flags on the Reverend's Walk,' Finley began. A glint of recognition suggested Cherian understood Finley, but there was no verbal response, just a nod.

'I must ask your help one more time. Can you please see to it that this envelope is given directly to Eliza madam,' he said. 'Only to Eliza madam, please!'

'Yes, saar,' came the reply, delivered in the same tone as if Finley had asked for some sandwiches or tea. 'Saar, tomorrow, for chapel time . . .'

'Yes, Cherian?'

'I can come to chapel?' he enquired.

'Certainly, Cherian!' Finley replied, surprised by the question. It occurred to him that Cherian could help translate the parables. 'That would be wonderful! You can help me teach the other staff.'

Cherian gave a broad grin.

'Reverend will please ask Mr Harrison?'

Finley recognized the concern. 'Yes, Cherian, I will

have a word with him later this evening. If that is what you would like.'

'Thank you, saar,' Cherian replied.

Despite his concerns that he would be late to the boathouse, Finley need not have worried. He arrived before the Rumsons and Haights, who, given their larger families and the finery with which the women had adorned themselves, arrived at a more leisurely pace. As the entourage drew closer, he could see that some of the smaller palanquins, normally used for transporting families up the hill, had been put into use for the evening. Bedecked women were alighting from them, although Eliza, much to Finley's delight, deemed herself spry enough to walk alongside George and the children. Finley stood discreetly on the terrace, away from the top of the stairs, as the Rumsons made their way up the staircase, George supporting Eliza's arm.

Once they were announced in the main hall, husband and wife made their way out to the terrace where Finley had positioned himself. As Eliza passed him, Finley was struck by the familiar constriction in his chest and a quivering sensation. She was resplendent in her light purple-and-white ball gown. Its design laid bare the expanse of her chest underneath a string of pearls, usually hidden under her travelling dresses. Her face was flushed from the exertion of the walk to the boathouse, and Finley looked down at the carpet, silently hoping that they would pass him by and pay mind instead to Harrison's excellent decoration of the terrace. That was not to be.

'Reverend Finley . . .'

The warm, unmistakable tone commanded Finley to look up. 'Mrs Rumson.' He could summon a weak smile, but he floundered for words. He thought of that painting he had once seen of Diana and Cupid; Diana has taken Cupid's bow and the child-god makes futile attempts to grasp it back from her.

'I am most pleased to see you, Reverend. We are to travel down to Madurai the day after tomorrow, and George informs me we will do so without the pleasure of your company.' Her tone is soothing, measured, and it reminds Finley that he must reciprocate.

'Thank you, Mrs Rumson. Most kind. I intend to stay and teach the natives here.'

'So, then, you will fulfil your ambition of founding a church among the heathens?' Her lips formed into a smile, and her eyes twinkled in the lamplight.

'The physical arrangements will be in Mr Harrison's capable hands. But yes, the spiritual aspects will be my responsibility,' Finley replied.

'Then yours is surely the greater burden. The saving of souls is an ambitious task, especially as there are so many of them, and only one of yourself!'

'You are too kind, Mrs Rumson. God will reveal the path if He deems it worthwhile.'

'And some paths, while arduous, reveal greater truths than those that are well trodden,' Eliza continued. 'We must thank Providence that you visited our home in Madurai.'

'It is I who should express that gratitude, Mrs Rumson . . .' Finley replied. 'Without your hospitality, I very much doubt I would have made my way to this corner of God's earth.'

'Perhaps. Should we sit in Westminster Cathedral, many years from now, it is we who will wax eloquent about how we knew Archbishop Finley when he first began his ministry in those hills of endless tea and fog.' The twinkling has returned.

'You flatter me, Mrs Rumson.' Finley is finding it difficult to continue this conversation. 'I do hope we will not wait quite so long for our next meeting!'

'Sorry to intrude, your conversation casts an unnecessary pall!' George cuts in. 'Let us enjoy the evening! The opportunity may not arise again for some time!' And with that, he placed a friendly hand on Finley's shoulder and steered him towards Chapman, who was handing out libations at one corner of the terrace. Soon enough, Finley was drawn into the procession of food and drink and toasts that mark the end of the summer season. Haight made a speech, but few could recall its contents afterwards. A level of inebriation and exhaustion had overtaken most of the revellers, and the women and children made their way

back to their respective suites. By then, just a handful of
the men remained on the terrace, their banter hearkening
back to Finley's first evening at the hotel. He decided to
repair to his cabin, stopping to congratulate Harrison on
the evening's success.

'Much obliged, Reverend!' Harrison replied. 'Much
obliged indeed, sir!' The liquor had made him loquacious,
but he knew he must still hit his marks. 'By the way,
Reverend. It's all very well if you wish that Cherian help
you with the ministry, but perhaps we might begin those
duties after the guests have departed?'

Finley is in no mood to negotiate with Harrison. 'Why,
of course, Harrison. Let us leave the first ministry until
after the Rumsons have left.'

'Is the Rumsons' leaving of particular interest,
Reverend?' Harrison may have enjoyed his drink, but
little escaped his notice.

'I merely wish to spend the morning with them before
they depart. After all, I arrived here at your fine hotel as
their guest!' Which was only part of the truth. Finley
could not begin ministry in good faith until Eliza had
left the hilltop.

For most of the next day, while Cherian, Pullur and
the other staff arranged for a caravan of people and
possessions to be transported down the hill, Finley was
content to lie inert in his cabin. The festivities of the
evening before, and Harrison's fortuitous request to cancel

any ministry until the guests' departure, had left Finley mercifully uncommitted. That evening, Cherian arrived in his cabin with a curious lemon-based concoction, presumably to rouse Finley back to health. He also informed Finley that the Rumsons would be leaving the next morning, after an early breakfast.

'Have you delivered the envelope to Eliza madam?' Finley asked.

'Yes saar. Only to Eliza madam,' Cherian confirmed.

'What time is breakfast tomorrow?'

'Eight o'clock, saar.'

'Please wake me before that time, Cherian.' With that instruction, Finley drifted off into a fitful sleep, where he dreamt of being summoned to perform the final services for Eliza's funeral. The casket was closed, and he could not look inside. George, bent and wrinkled with age, looked on. Alice and Andrew cast suspicious glances at Finley for re-entering their lives at such an inauspicious time. By the time Cherian roused him from sleep, Finley's pillow was completely damp and toast and coffee were waiting on the table.

'Have the Rumsons left yet?' Finley asked, startled.

'No, saar, Rumsons at flag with Mr Wetherby.'

Finley ate and dressed at the same time and then made his way rapidly up the steps to the main hotel building, only slowing his pace once he could see the flagpole. Wetherby had set up a large selection of equipment, and he had just completed portraits of the Haights. The Rumsons were next.

'James! James!' George was calling to him. 'A good thing we sent Cherian to rouse you! It would all feel terribly amiss if we had left without a proper farewell.'

'Come, Reverend, you must join the sitting for our portrait!' It was the elder Mrs Rumson. She grasped Finley's hand. 'Our season at Highpoint has been enriched by your presence, Reverend. You must know that.'

'You are most kind, Mrs Rumson,' he replied. 'I would be honoured to join this sitting.'

With much rearranging of chairs and skirts, Mr Wetherby ensured that the group was in frame and holding still for a sufficient time, and the portraits were finally complete. Eliza said nothing to Finley, and only during the exposures of Wetherby's plates did she look over in his direction. Her expression was drawn and tired. Each time Finley attempted to attract her gaze, her eyes did not look at his, but instead wandered chaotically over the surface of his face. She was studying his visage in a way that Finley had not noticed before, as if studying a map. Trying to memorize the contours as an artist might.

'Reverend, do hold still for the exposure!' Wetherby called out. Finley tried to comply.

Once the Rumsons completed their portraits, the group made their way over to the waiting horses and palanquins. George and Finley stood while the bearers helped the elder Mrs Rumson, and then Alice and Andrew, into the palanquin.

'Goodbye, Reverend.' The same warm, calm voice from evening celebrations.

'Goodbye, Mrs Rumson, and Godspeed,' Finley replied, addressing the horses' hooves. He could not look up to meet her eyes.

'Very well, then, James!' George bid his farewell. 'Do make your way down to Madurai if you grow tired of this hilltop.' And they shook hands and embraced before George mounted the horse and rode to the head of the Rumsons' section of the caravan.

Finley could not stand and watch any longer. He returned to the flag area where Wetherby was taking portraits.

'Would you care to join the Cadburys for their portrait, Reverend?' Wetherby offered.

'No, thank you, Mr Wetherby. I'm afraid one sitting is quite enough for me.' And he was about to return to his cabin when another thought occurred to Finley. 'Mr Wetherby, may I ask a favour?'

'Why, certainly . . .'

'May I receive some of the portraits you have made today? Perhaps one of the portraits I was part of? This has been a most illuminating season for me, and I should like to preserve the memory in a more enduring form.'

'It would be my pleasure, Reverend!' Wetherby replied,

beaming. 'I shall have them sent to you before we depart tomorrow. You may rely on it.'

'Thank you, Mr Wetherby.'

Finley could not remember how he returned to his cabin – perhaps by walking along the lake, or perhaps by taking the shorter route by the stairs. The cabin door was now closed and the Reverend James Erasmus Finley sat by the windows, curtains open, staring out onto the field with nothing left to think or say.

17

Tea and Fog, Redux

The frenzy of the closing weeks of term are laughably predictable in retrospect, but always seem to arrive unforeseen and ahead of schedule. The days fill with the administrative work of ensuring that fees are paid and that several hundred students can make their way safely off the hilltop to their respective destinations. For students, papers and exam preparations loom large. For teachers, the interval between the time that exams must be set and final grades submitted feels frighteningly brief.

And then there are always the larger forces of circumstance to create darkly humorous situations at our collective expense. This time last year, soaking monsoon rains loosened up so much soil that landslides blocked the road down from the hill, and there was a real risk that no one would make it to their flights or trains on time. Pandian – putting his energies to good use, for once – arranged a work party of cooks, gardeners and assorted staff to clear a route across the swathe of mud and rocks. The school bus took students down the hill as far as possible. Then, they hiked the fifty yards or so across the muddy swathe of the resting landslide, following which they boarded buses on the other side to complete their journeys. Everyone hopes there is no repeat performance of that this year.

As for me, many of those normal concerns have become background noise – the hiss and crackle of LP records that one learns to ignore. Instead, a dissonant back-and-forth argument rages in my mind. Was the photograph symptomatic of a larger problem? Did Maya know that the photograph had been seen? Could someone else have intended it to be found by Ms Little-K? Could someone other than Maya have developed it? Perhaps Maya had intended to give it to Koshy? It hardly seemed the sort of image one would keep for oneself.

Perhaps Maya had never meant to develop it at all. On the other hand, it's difficult to develop a photograph by mistake. Could it have slipped into the enlarger and simply appeared on the developing paper? No, all that could not have happened by accident. Maya would have to develop the film, inspect the negatives, choose which ones to cut out and print, and only then place them in the enlarger. And if that were all true, then the print was surely intentional.

In the last exam I invigilate for Maya's class – why is she

even bothering to take the exam? – I can't help but wonder if she is aware of the turmoil she has caused. I study her face, taut with concentration on the paper in front of her, her left hand holding her hair out of her face. Has she spent the better part of her term frantically searching for the photograph? Does she know that the photograph was found by a teacher? She would be mortified if she knew so many teachers had seen it. The thought turns rancid even as I think it. Few things disgust me as much as teachers who wantonly make their students squirm, either out of cruelty or to cause insult. I know such teachers exist, but I never expected to become one. As I collect the papers, I can see the relief on the students' faces.

'So happy, Mr G, that was my last exam,' Akshay smiles.

'Good, good, when do you leave?' I ask.

'Early tomorrow morning, Mr G,' he replies. 'Really looking forward to the hols!'

'Me too, Mr G. Thank you!' Supriya adds, dropping her paper onto the pile.

'Mr Ghosh?' I look up, because few students use my full name. It's Maya's turn to submit her paper.

'Yes?'

'That was my last exam, too.' She breathes a sigh of relief. 'I'm leaving tomorrow morning as well, so I wanted to say goodbye.'

I stand up – I know she was just here for the term

– and extend my hand. 'I hope you enjoyed your time here, Maya.'

'Yes, very much. I will really miss being here.' Her eyes begin to tear up.

'What are your plans after this?' I ask, hoping to move the conversation to something more cheerful.

'I don't know. A few months at home, and then I'm off to college.' She seems non-committal. 'I might have to do some studying to brush up on things.'

'No school, then?' I ask. 'Once you're home with your parents?'

'No, I finished the credits I need for my programme. This was a year off – my parents wanted me to spend some time in India.'

'Was it worth it? Are you glad you joined us here?'

'Oh yes! I wish I could finish the year here.'

'Why don't you?'

'I promised my parents I'd spend the next six months with them, before I leave for college. It's a long, intense programme on the other side of the country, so they won't see much of me once I leave home.'

'I understand.' I am not sure what else to say. 'You're always welcome to visit . . .'

'Thank you!' She smiles. 'It's a very long way, though . . . And sometimes it is harder to come back to a place than it is to leave.' She adds, 'And stay left,' as if she's already said too many goodbyes.

I smile at her play on words. 'I know what you mean. Good luck!'

'You too, Mr G.' And she waves goodbye with a sad smile and a hand open-and-close gesture that small children normally use.

As with every term, I resolve to turn all my corrections and grading in on time. After all, if the high school coordinator cannot deliver, then how can I expect my teachers to do the same? But it is, as ever, a thankless task. With no students to explain the solutions to – they have all left for home over the last few days – I feel a particular pointlessness to this effort. No student has ever, in my memory, come back from the holidays and asked a teacher for a copy of their exam sheet. Not once. I toy with the idea of simply assigning final grades based on my assessments so far, but it wouldn't be fair. Maybe there's that one student, perhaps Supriya, who has worked hard to improve her performance for the exam. I couldn't deny her the recognition of her efforts. I wish I could give them all As and send the lot of papers packing. That wouldn't really work either. And I shudder to think if all the other teachers are sitting at their desks similarly plotting ways to be rid of this onerous task.

Happily, there is also an outlet for temporary distraction when I find my attention has drifted. It is early November and cold enough that it is better to have the stove on, especially when sitting in my office for long stretches.

When I need a break, I collect a suitably unworthy-looking pile of old papers and throw them by the fistful into the barrel stove. Mrs Mani said she could take care of it for me, but I have declined her offer. There's a certain satisfaction to getting rid of one's own detritus – after making sure that it actually is worth destroying. I enjoy the organized room more afterwards if I do the destroying myself.

'Eerm . . . Ghosh?' a voice says from behind the door. Guaranteed to be Darling. Chapman would have barged right in.

'Yes, come in!'

Darling enters tentatively, followed by Chapman. 'We've been thinking . . .' he begins. 'This whole problem that came up with the photograph . . .'

'Yes?'

'Well, perhaps it's best if Chapman takes over the matter,' Darling continues. 'There hasn't been much progress, you see, and, well, you're obviously very busy with the day-to-day work of teaching and being the high school coordinator.'

'Exactly,' Chapman cuts in. 'And now that I've got some more time on my hands, I thought perhaps I could do some sleuthing of my own . . .'

'I see . . .' Even though I decidedly do not see. I wonder if he has made the same discovery I have. 'Is there a particular line of enquiry you are pursuing?' I add – and, putting on my best detective dialogue line and picking up the magnifying glass out of my credenza – 'A clue I may have overlooked?'

Darling smiles nervously. Chapman does not. 'Unfortunately, no. But I was thinking if I could examine the photograph more carefully, I might unearth something,' Chapman remarks.

'To get all this behind us, once and for all, of course,' Darling adds. The mental image of Chapman closely examining a photograph of a student's breasts seem to make him uncomfortable too.

'So, if I could have the photograph, please?' Chapman chimes in, briskly efficient when it suits him.

I instinctively reach over to my desk drawer and realize the horror of my situation. The photograph is in my bag, inside the booklet of piano music that I borrowed from Koshy. I took it with me the evening of the concert and had not returned it to my desk. The shocking implication hits me – I can imagine what the headlines might say. 'Bachelor administrator found with dirty pictures of students.' Okay – perhaps too lengthy for a headline. 'Porn found in teacher's bag.' That's probably more like it. I stare blankly at the drawer, struggling for words.

A window suddenly opens. 'I'm sorry, I think I have burnt it!' I blurt out.

'What?' Chapman snaps. Darling's eyes are wide. I have never seen eyebrows scramble so far up a man's forehead.

I have to develop this story quickly. 'Well, gents . . . look around! I am trying to restore some order to my office files, so I have been burning the old exams and so on. And that's the same drawer where I kept the photograph. So I must have burnt it too – it's not there anymore.'

Chapman surveys the room. 'Yes, yes, I also saw it in that drawer,' he adds, mightily put out.

'Well, now,' Darling's voice is suddenly calm. 'It seems we have no explanation and no evidence.'

'Ghosh – really!' Chapman's face is beginning to glow red with frustration.

'I'm sorry,' I say. 'It's not where I usually keep it, and I've been grabbing papers from there, and all around here, and throwing them in the stove. You know I kept it there – you saw me get it from there last time.'

'I know I did, Ghosh!' he admits. 'But really, how will we make progress if you destroy the evidence?'

'It's not as if I did it wilfully.' I decide to play this out in full. Rarely, if ever, do I get to make Chapman squirm, so I want to enjoy this while I can. 'Remember, I even told you to keep it, just to be safe?'

'Did you, really?' Darling asks, surprised by my admission.

'Yes, sadly, that is true.' Chapman glowers.

'Sadly? What is sad about this?' Darling demands of Chapman. It's an uncharacteristic show of irritation.

'Well, Ghosh's organization skills, I suppose . . .' Chapman replies, after some fumbling.

'And we know of no more such photographs, do we?' Darling continues.

'No, Andrew, I haven't heard any more on this,' I reply.

'Well, then, for God's sake, let's just put it behind us. No photograph, no explanation – let's just move on.' Darling is unusually emphatic. He has seen a light at the end of the tunnel, and he clearly intends to reach it.

'Well, that's fine with me,' I say, trying to not betray the hilarity of the situation in my tone. Chapman mumbles something. I don't know what he feels he has been deprived of. The ability to ogle a student's breasts? Or the need to keep an administrative puzzle on the boil, just to keep feeling relevant?

'Thank goodness that is over,' Darling concludes, and the two of them turn to leave my office. 'Honestly, if I had known this is how it would all end, I would have burnt the damned photo myself!' Darling says to Chapman as they walk out. Chapman harumphs.

I close my door after them, and lean against it. I am not one to think quickly on my feet. Usually, the witty response comes to me a day or two after the initiating jibe. But on this occasion, I congratulate myself. This time, I really have come up with a cracker. And nobody knows – not a soul. I am not sure what I am supposed to be celebrating, but a bubbling elation is taking over, scattering whatever meagre willpower I have left to finish grading the exams. The fire in the stove is burning low, and

I have the choice of putting on another log or letting it go out. I don't want to stay much longer, so I let it peter out while I sit at my desk. I turn to stare out of the window behind me. Of the few committed tourists who come up in this weather, only the most intrepid have rented boats and taken them out on to the lake. They fumble with the oars, unable to match the cadence and depth of one with the other. It can't help that the staff at the boat club take a gleeful relish in sending tourists out – the rude ones, especially – with mismatched oars. They stand at the dock and giggle together as the brash alpha males begin to show off, and end up struggling mightily to move in pointless circles. It's an amusing show for those in the know.

I gather my jacket, bag and an optimistically large set of papers to grade. The grey drizzle of the morning has let up momentarily and I am in no mood to get unnecessarily wet, so I head out of the office. 'Have a good afternoon, Mrs Mani. See you Monday!' If I were in a theatrical production, this is the moment when I jump up and click my heels.

'Tomorrow is Friday, Mr G,' she replies. But she can sense my mood, so she smiles. 'See you tomorrow?'

'Exactly, Mrs Mani, exactly what I meant!'

On the walk home, I admire the still, shimmering greenery that contrasts with the grey of the sky, and the occasional gashes of brown where the ground has suffered the monsoon torrents. I was already pleased that I had found the origins of the photograph, but the burden of authority – that I was somehow responsible for bringing some dastardly perpetrator to account – was proving a bit much. I cannot think of a single student for whom I do not wish a happy future after they leave school. A tough lesson or two may be in order, delivered by life itself, but nothing by way of suffering. And Maya was far from any of them. Hence the elation. In one deft move I have slammed shut any further deliberation on this matter and even dealt a glancing blow to Chapman's ego. The greens appear brighter. A drop from the leaves overhead lands directly on my neck, aimed perfectly into the gap between hairline and collar. But it's refreshing, not irksome. Ghosh ascendant! And that is my last thought before the world suddenly turns sideways, and I feel a shooting pain in my right ankle.

The cattle trap, slick from rain and mud, has caused my ankle to twist, and I find myself sitting in the gate that marks the entrance to Lake Compound. One of those reminders from the universe, I suppose, to not get too big for one's boots. I pick myself up carefully and look around. Thankfully, nobody has observed this ungainly pirouette, so I walk on, but the ankle hurts. With the ground still slippery, this is one of those times to take the longer, more gradual route home. I move slowly, still pleased with myself, but more humbly so. As I turn to face the gentle downhill stretch that takes me past the open greenery to my left, I think of Maya again, and how I had seen her there, crouched low, photographing the kurinji flowers. My ankle hurts, so I pause to look over to the opening. The blossoms are no more and the bushes have regained their unremarkable brown. Had it not been for Maya, the drab clumps would not warrant another glance. I continue walking, but the bend in the road – and the pain in my ankle – prompt me to stop. Perhaps this would be a good time to invite Koshy over for dinner. After all, unless my deductions are completely wrong, he would likely be on his own. And perhaps he may even want some company.

I tamp down any buoyant expressions on my face as I approach the porch. There are no lights on, so perhaps Koshy is not home. As I draw closer, I can hear notes being banged out on the piano – not from any composition I have heard before. They are frustrated, hammered, rhythmic notes of a solitary animal pacing in a cage. Perhaps this is not the time for neighbourly invitations. Still, I walk up the path that leads to the front lawn and then to the stairs up to the porch. The music stops – he has seen me coming. The glass panes of the door shudder as the door is unlocked and it opens.

'Hello, Mr G!' I have never seen Koshy without his glasses. They usually dominate much of his face, in concert with the unruly straight flop of hair and the bushy eyebrows. The usual crisp white shirt has been replaced with a dark grey one, but I must have surprised him, because the buttons are in the wrong buttonhole. The lopsidedness of the shirt has taken over now that the glasses are missing. And now I can see the large eyes that are usually hidden behind the frames.

'Hello, Koshy!' I take a few steps forward, but the pain in my ankle draws my attention, and I have not thought through what I should say next.

'Would you like to come in?' Koshy says. 'Have you hurt your ankle?' My hobble must be noticeable.

'Well, yes. I suppose,' I admit. 'Originally, I was planning to invite you over dinner. Nothing too ambitious, mind you! Now that the term is over . . .'

'That's very kind of you!' he replies, and opens the door wider. It appears that I will be the one doing the visiting for now.

'Come in, come in. Make yourself comfortable.' He gestures to one of the armchairs. 'I'll go put on some tea.'

I look around the living room. It's a simple set-up with the usual furniture the school provides. The piano takes pride of place in the room – a choice carried over from the previous occupant – and against the far wall is a bookshelf creaking with just a few books, but mostly stacks of printed scores. There's a work table set against the windows facing the porch, and a couch and two armchairs arranged between the piano and the barrel stove. I am glad the fire is on, as it holds off the clammy dampness outside. A lone frame stands on the table, holding a picture of an older couple. Parents presumably, as the straight flop of hair on the man's head is similar to Koshy's.

'Yes, there isn't much here . . .' he apologizes, noticing my visual survey. 'Have been busy with school and all that since I arrived.'

'Oh, don't be sorry! My place is not much better.' I sit down in one of the armchairs. It faces the porch and the lawn beyond. It's starting to grow darker again, another cloud nestling down upon us. 'That's just what happens when you live by yourself.' I made the comment to put him at ease, but Koshy winces slightly before sitting down on the couch diagonally opposite. 'So, what did you think of your first term?' I ask.

'It was an education . . .' he replies. 'Talented students – not all of them, of course. But the good ones are really good!'

'Some of the performances at the concert were really impressive!' I agree. I don't want to turn this into a conversation about work. It's the last thing I would want – for Chapman to sit down in my living room and start talking about my performance! We sit in silence for a time. The tea kettle is rumbling but no whistle yet. 'Have you made any friends? Friendly acquaintances, maybe?' I ask. I realize it's an odd question, but the silence was becoming rather too long for my comfort.

He thinks for a bit before replying. 'No, not really. The others in my department are very nice, but they're older. Mrs Cama is almost my mother's age, although she behaves like an older sister. There are a few others. We're very cordial, but I wouldn't say friends.' He isn't much of a talker, but since I am not either, we appear fated to suffer through more awkward gaps in conversation. The whistle from the tea kettle breaks the silence.

While Koshy is getting the tea things ready, I walk over to his bookshelf. I like looking at bookshelves – especially smaller ones. A big bookshelf can be stuffed full of pretentious, aspirational volumes that are never read. A small bookshelf, especially for a younger person who has moved, reveals what they hold to be important. Multiple composition books, presumably diaries, without any clear markings. Several R.K. Narayan. A couple of Kundera books. Conan Doyle, omnibus edition, which makes me smile as it is clearly well thumbed. And a copy of Achebe's *Things Fall Apart*, a strange addition in this lot. It's one of the required textbooks for English literature. Oh, of course, I know why it's here. I pick it up to check, and on the first inside page I find what I suspected: 'Maya C. August 1994'.

Koshy has come in with the tea things. 'You've noticed my limited reading!'

'Just browsing – no judgement, really . . .' I smile, and quickly return the book to its spot, hoping Koshy has not noticed.

If he has noticed, he does not let on. Instead, he sits

pensively, staring into middle distance, clutching his cup of tea with interlaced fingers. I am sure he is in some form of mourning. But is it mourning if one cannot share the reason for grieving?

'Of course, some things about the school, about this term, I really never expected,' he says, out of nowhere. I wonder if he wants me to respond to this non sequitur. Is he confessing? Does he want to talk about Maya? Is that why I came here? Because somehow, unknown even to myself, I want to know the full story? I decide a polite, puzzled look might be best, so I deliver it. 'Yes, I suppose unexpected things will happen. Best to move on,' he continues.

'I don't understand. What do you mean, Koshy?' I reply. I want him to elaborate.

'One of my favourite pieces of music went missing. Granados – we used it a lot this term, and I wanted to give it as a gift. But I can't find it anywhere. That has never happened to me before.' And he paused, as if there was a longer list waiting to be itemized.

'Who did you want to give it to?' A lump is forming in my chest.

'You know how sometimes someone can become very important to you? They light up your life all of a sudden?' Koshy is not answering directly.

'And then what happens?' The lump has grown and is applying some pressure. I sip the hot, sweet tea to calm myself.

'Then it's over, I suppose. Some things burn bright and fast. You have to let them go, though. You're not supposed to follow.' All of this would be cryptic if I didn't know better.

'The light has gone out of our lives?' I say, quoting the famous speech.

'Ha! Indeed,' Koshy replies. His laugh is suddenly harsher and older than I have heard before. He clears his throat.

'Was this someone here? At school?' I fix my gaze on his face. I can sense the sadness, but I can't commiserate without knowing why and as far as Koshy is aware, I know nothing.

'Yes,' he replies in a whisper, and nods at the floor. 'But that time is past now.'

'Why do you say that?' I ask.

'It doesn't matter,' he replies. 'I have plenty of work to do with my other students.'

'Your other students?' I emphasize the word 'other'. He looks up from the floor, and into my face. His expression carries both fear and resignation. And the sadness is welling up in his eyes. I am in a position I never wanted to be in. 'Okay, enough!' I exclaim loudly, which startles Koshy, and he spills some of his tea on the couch. 'I know, I know, you miss Maya, don't you?'

Koshy's eyes grow wide with surprise. 'How do you know?' And then, as the realization dawns further, he continues. 'I will resign today. I don't want to cause any trouble for Maya. Or for the school.'

'No, that's not why . . .'

'I never saw it coming, you know,' he interrupts. 'One moment we were sitting and practising, instructor and student, and the next moment, well . . . it was clear that we weren't practising anymore.' He shrugs with a wan smile, runs a hand through his own hair, stopping when he has a fistful and stares into the distance. It's an animated gesture, even more now that it has got stuck halfway through. Koshy is still coming to terms with something that he hasn't managed to put into words.

'Why didn't you ask her to stay? She could have stayed and finished the year.'

'I suggested it once. She has a plan for her life – and I am not part of it. I was not part of that plan before she came here, and I didn't want to force my way in.'

'You could have gone with her,' I offer. 'There's nothing holding you here.'

'No . . . I thought about it for a while.' He pauses and fixes me with a steady gaze, but that's undermined by the tinkling of his cup against the saucer. 'You know how everything has a niche? The same plant flourishes in one place, dies in another?'

'Yes.'

'I think whatever we had was the same way,' he sighs. 'I like it here – my music, teaching students, the rhythm of concerts and exams. If I follow her, without all of that, I would spend my days clinging too tightly to Maya.'

'So you'd rather sit here by yourself?'

He doesn't answer, and takes a loud slurp of tea and sniffs. 'I will resign. I won't be any trouble.' He casts his eyes around the room. 'There isn't much to move.' He stands up and walks to the piano, toying with the keys. 'I understand if you don't want to have dinner.' He smiles, distractedly. And then he turns to face me fully, and his tone is not distracted anymore. 'But how did you know?' he demands. 'We were so careful. We didn't tell anyone!'

'It started with the photograph.'

'What photograph?'

'You know, the one we all looked at during the staff meeting. Don't you remember?'

'I was never at any staff meeting where we looked at a photograph!' He looks astonished. 'A photograph of Maya and me?'

'Not exactly.' It is my turn on unsteady ground. Koshy is glaring at me with what seems like rising annoyance. I need to explain myself.

'Well, I don't know why you were not at the staff meeting. You probably didn't know it was happening. It was called at short notice. But a picture was found in the photography lab . . .'

'Oh no . . .' he starts.

'You know about the picture?'

'No, but Maya told me she had found some naughty pictures I had taken of her on the camera. I do remember us laughing together after taking them, but I thought it was her own camera, not a school camera!' He continues. 'Maya said she would print them for me, but then I assumed she had forgotten about it or changed her mind. In any case, I didn't want to ask after such things.'

'I don't think she forgot at all. Lila – Ms Little-K – found a print on the floor of the dark room. And she brought it to Chapman.'

'But Maya never told me she was in any trouble at all!' Koshy is very surprised. 'And you say everyone saw it!?'

'Well, that's because your Maya is a very thoughtful young woman. There was nothing in the photograph that could prove it was her. So she never got into any trouble. Darling and Chapman told me to "investigate" – so I did.'

'So now they know . . .' Koshy looked crestfallen. 'Okay, I will send in a resignation letter. Thank you for coming to tell me, Mr G.'

'Koshy, I need you to listen carefully to what I say next.' He is obviously preoccupied with all the dreadful possibilities racing through his mind.

'Okay.'

'No one else knows the photograph is of Maya,' I continue.

'How?'

'I didn't tell them.'

'Why?'

I don't answer his question, because I'm not sure about the answer myself. 'I owe you an apology.' Reaching down to my bag, I push back the leather flap and extract the score for *Oriental* and hand it to him. 'For this. Look inside the envelope. It should be in the middle of the score.'

Koshy looks dumbfounded. He turns the score over and looks at it carefully to make sure it's the same one that was missing. Of course it is. He then walks over to the table and removes the envelope from the score. Unwinding the tie thread, he extracts the photograph. Even from across the room I can hear a sharp intake of breath. He replaces the photograph in the envelope, but keeps it in his hand before coming back towards me.

'Didn't you say there were several photos?' he asks.

'Ms Little-K only turned in one.'

'I should probably burn it. I wouldn't want to embarrass Maya this way.'

'I don't think you should,' I reply quickly. 'She went to some trouble to develop it, enlarge it and print it. And it probably wasn't for herself. She most likely meant to give it to you.'

'But what if someone comes looking for it?' he whispers.

'Nobody will. Darling and Chapman think I burnt it.'

'Why do they think that?'

'Because that's what I told them!!' I retort. The feeling of elation has returned. 'In my office. Today – just a few

hours ago. I was cleaning up and burning old papers in the
stove, and I told them I burnt it. As far as anybody else
knows, it simply doesn't exist!'

'And nobody knows this is Maya?'

'Nobody except you and me. And Maya, I suppose,' I
reassure him. 'And now, I promise you, nobody ever will.'

Koshy breathes an enormous sigh and runs his hand
front to back through his hair, which now stands almost
upright. 'We should have something stronger,' he says,
looking at our teacups. 'To mark the occasion. Have you
ever had black tea with Old Monk?'

'No, I have not.'

'Then let me be the first to make you some!' And he
gathers up the teacups, retiring to the kitchen to prepare
the concoction.

From the room where we sit, I observe the fog on the
porch has thickened and assumed a luminous quality.
Perhaps our bubbles match; in which case, I believe I have
found a friend.

Epilogue

At the end of each academic year, most students head down the mountain to their respective homes and families. A week or so later, after the pomp and bacchanalia of graduation is complete, the newly minted graduates leave as well. There's a lull, and for a few months the teachers' kids and the few children whose families live in town have the school to themselves.

So it happened, on an unusually hot day during this quiet period, that a group of kids were playing basketball and decided to take a break from the noonday heat. As a diversion, they explored the cool stone interior of the now deserted Rumson Chapel. They went up to the balcony, behind the stained-glass window that overlooks the nave. One of kids – we won't say who – dropped the basketball, which began to roll down the spiral staircase. The ball gained momentum, eventually bouncing and crashing into some framed photographs, knocking them off the wall.

The only frame that ended up broken was a group photograph of the school's founder, Mrs Adeline Rumson, surrounded by her family – her son, daughter-in-law, their children – and the Reverand J.E. Finley, the school's first headmaster. The photograph must have been taken when the school was still the Highpoint Hotel. The stamp on the back reads 'Wetherby & Sons., Fort St George, 1874'. Most of the faces in the photograph look sternly forward, directly at the camera in the manner of portraits from that time. Only the younger Mrs Rumson has her head tilted slightly upward and her gaze across the path of the camera. We can't see the Reverend's eyes clearly – the print has grown patchy – but from his position on the far right of the frame, his head is turned as if intercepting the path of Mrs Rumson's gaze.

The frame might have remained intact like the others, had it not been so full of writing paper stuffed behind the picture. In trying to mend the frame, the school authorities unpacked the contents, which included a carefully folded letter.

Windermere, Lake District
May 3, 1875

My dearest James,

I hope you are in good health and that your church and its many souls thrive under your tutelage. If I were to write here all that I wanted to say to you when we last saw each other, this letter might never reach you. The post office would refuse to deliver it with normal postage, I'm sure. And my husband might receive questions about whether his wife was turning her hand to becoming an authoress.

Your earnest purposefulness in our small corner of India would move me from irritation to admiration and then to outright longing. When we were in the hills together, I watched you work, maintaining always the necessary distance that I thought probity required, but tried to do no more than that. If I were not married, if there had been no family to which to give account, our times wandering in the hills together would have passed very differently. As it is, I keep the pressed flowers sprinkled through several volumes in the library here, and it would not require a very astute botanist to see that they did not grow on these British Isles. But what no eye can see – and no mind could conceive of – is how carefully they must have been gathered and how gratefully accepted.

Perhaps age or distance dulls the sensibilities. Or perhaps the banalities of our daily routines have inured me to the sadness I felt when we made our transfer down the hill. What I have not lost, and cannot forget, is that singular feeling of knowing, at least once, that desperate, yearning, scrambling love that comes with meeting a soul with whom one could truly spend the rest of one's days. I no longer think of you or feel the heaviness of your absence in the course of my daily tasks. But in the pauses in the day, the moments before sleep takes over, and if I rise too early, I can feel the dearness and weight of what I knowingly forsook.

One of the ayahs told the children a story before we left, about a boatman who was rowing a distraught mother across a river. The mother was wailing and bemoaning the loss of her young son who she could not find. She thought the boy had been kidnapped by bandits from the nearby forests. The woman asked for the boatman's help to find her child, but he refused to help her. Instead, he told her that if he ever saw a boy of the right age near the water, or trying to make his way across, he would tell the child which way his mother had gone and send him on his way with hope. After all, the boatman's place in life was to row people across the river. Nothing could be demanded of him that took the boatman away from that sole, sacred duty. I was distraught at the ayah for telling my children such disturbing tales.

Maybe the story holds a lesson for us. We did not arrive at the dock together, but we did undertake some form of crossing. Once back on dry land, we simply returned to travelling our own, separate paths. Since we happened to cross that water together, the boatman must have assumed that we knew all about each other; for my own sake I would have wanted to learn more. I don't know why I remember this story so vividly, and keep returning to it. Perhaps it is because I wish our boatman had said more to us.

Do not allow this letter to arouse sadness or anger in your heart. I mean only to recognize something that was too long

*unsaid. Perhaps in some future time, persons like you or I will
be allowed to bend the map of our lives to move more easily
towards each other. To move in to each other, and to hold each
other close as I have so much wanted to do.*

　　With firm fondness and adoration,
　　Eliza

The letter remains in the school archives, filed under
'Unpublished Correspondence'. It is not likely to be
widely shared.

Acknowledgements

The storylines in this novel are entirely fictional. That said, a few people have had a disproportionate influence in finally writing down the narrative.

My grandmother, Anasuya Sen (nee Gupta), passed away on 30 December 2019. I feel fortunate that I was able to go and see her one last time while she was still with us. She may well have been the earliest narrative influence, after my parents. While best known for her singing, she also had a knack for memorable storytelling and capturing the hilarity of life's circumstances. She preserved a sense of humour and humanity, perhaps in response to the dire situations she stared down at several points in her life. I am not sure she would have approved of this particular story, but I hope she would have enjoyed it.

Sheila Menon passed away in February, 2020. Sheila – who I will always think of as Sheila akka – and Pramod, her husband, really knew how to 'move the air around the classroom.' For those who cared to listen, they would address aspects of life well beyond the classroom walls, while cleverly restricting commentary to the literature at hand. As a child, without the benefit of their particular brand of witty observation, I might not have taken as much notice of how the adults – particularly the teachers and administrators – around me were behaving.

Of course, there are a multitude of people best left anonymous, even as their impressions on me form the basis of several characters in this story. I hereby indemnify them all from any liability for the final product; the responsibility for its quirks and errors is mine alone.

Finally, I am so grateful to be able to quarantine with Mary, Shonali and Shonkor. Thank you, Mary, for reading the first draft and for putting up with so much more!

Newton, MA
15 May 2020

juggernaut

THE APP
FOR INDIAN
READERS

Fresh, original books tailored for
mobile and for India. Starting at ₹10.

juggernaut.in

1

CRAFTED FOR MOBILE READING

Thought you would never read a book on mobile? Let us prove you wrong.

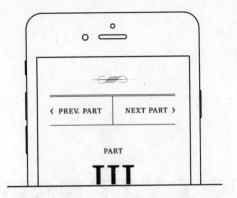

Beautiful Typography

The quality of print transferred
to your mobile. Forget ugly PDFs.

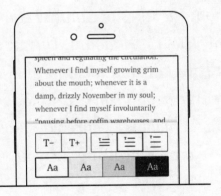

Customizable Reading

Read in the font size, spacing
and background of your liking.

AN EXTENSIVE LIBRARY

Including fresh, new, original Juggernaut books from the likes of Sunny Leone, Praveen Swami, Husain Haqqani, Umera Ahmed, Rujuta Diwekar and lots more. Plus, books from partner publishers and loads of free classics. Whichever genre you like, there's a book waiting for you.

DON'T JUST READ; INTERACT

We're changing the reading experience from passive to active.

Ask authors questions

Get all your answers from the horse's mouth.
Juggernaut authors actually reply to every
question they can.

Rate and review

Let everyone know of your favourite reads or
critique the finer points of a book – you will be
heard in a community of like-minded readers.

Gift books to friends

For a book-lover, there's no nicer gift than
a book personally picked. You can even
do it anonymously if you like.

Enjoy new book formats

Discover serials released in parts over
time, picture books including comics,
and story-bundles at discounted rates.
And coming soon, audiobooks.

4

LOWEST PRICES & ONE-TAP BUYING

Books start at ₹10 with regular discounts and free previews.

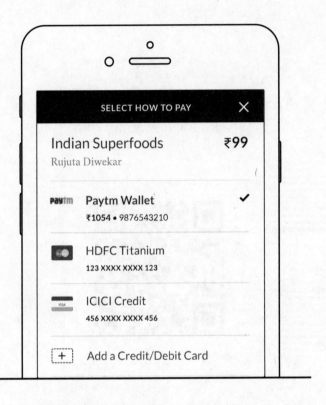

Paytm Wallet, Cards & Apple Payments

On Android, just add a Paytm Wallet once and buy any book with one tap. On iOS, pay with one tap with your iTunes-linked debit/credit card.

To download the app scan the QR Code
with a QR scanner app

For our complete catalogue, visit www.juggernaut.in
To submit your book, send a synopsis and two
sample chapters to books@juggernaut.in
For all other queries, write to contact@juggernaut.in